Enchanted Dulcinea

Jewish Women in the Americas

Editors

Rebecca Marquis and Elizabeth Goldstein, Gonzaga University

Founding Editor

Catherine Caufield

Jews have been present in the Americas since the fifteenth century; there is a growing body of scholarship examining this presence from multiple perspectives. The Lexington Books series Jewish Women in the Americas expands our knowledge of Jews in this geographical area through its particular focus on the diverse experiences and perspectives of women. These experiences and perspectives are often communicated creatively—through literature, plastic arts, dance, and other modalities. Reflecting on these expressions of lived experience through a range of interdisciplinary approaches enriches our understanding of what it means to be Jewish in the Americas.

Titles in the Series

Enchanted Dulcinea, by Angelina Muñiz-Huberman, translated and annotated by Rebecca Marquis

Enchanted Dulcinea

Angelina Muñiz-Huberman
Translated and Annotated by Rebecca Marquis
Introduction by Rebecca Marquis

LEXINGTON BOOKS
Lanham • Boulder • New York • London

Published by Lexington Books
An imprint of The Rowman & Littlefield Publishing Group, Inc.
4501 Forbes Boulevard, Suite 200, Lanham, Maryland 20706
www.rowman.com

86-90 Paul Street, London EC2A 4NE

British Library Cataloguing in Publication Information Available

Library of Congress Cataloging-in-Publication Data

Names: Muñiz-Huberman, Angelina, 1936- author. | Marquis, Rebecca,
    translator, editor, writer of introduction.
Title: Enchanted Dulcinea / Angelina Muñiz-Huberman ; edited and
    translated, and introduction, by Rebecca Marquis.
Other titles: Dulcinea encantada. English
Description: Lanham : Lexington Books, [2022] | Series: Jewish women in the
    Americas | Includes bibliographical references.
Identifiers: LCCN 2021062515 (print) | LCCN 2021062516 (ebook) | ISBN
    9781793634832 (cloth) | ISBN 9781793634856 (paperback) |
    ISBN 9781793634849 (epub)
Subjects: LCGFT: Novels.
Classification: LCC PQ7298.23.U49 D8513 2022 (print) | LCC PQ7298.23.U49
    (ebook) | DDC 863/.64—dc23/eng/20211228
LC record available at https://lccn.loc.gov/2021062515
LC ebook record available at https://lccn.loc.gov/2021062516

To Justin, Gabriela, Aubrey, Angelina, and Alberto—
for the precious gift of time and company, sharing stories
and the intricacies of language together,
surrounded by books in an apartment in Mexico.

And to the memory of Lydia Rodríguez-Hahn,
to whom the original novel in Spanish was dedicated.

Contents

~

Acknowledgments

My deepest gratitude goes first to Angelina Muñiz-Huberman. It was a decade ago that I first met Angelina at a LAJSA (Latin American Jewish Studies Association) conference and timidly asked her about spinning wheels and the possibility of reading *Dulcinea* through the Jewish mystical tradition of Merkavah. A few years later, we jumped into this translation project together and after a few trips to Mexico and Zooming during the pandemic, we have brought Dulcinea to the English-speaking world. I am so honored to have been in dialogue with her over the years and hopefully for many more to come.

I am extremely grateful to Miriam Huberman, who generously agreed to read and edit the first full version of the translation and whose insightful suggestions made the book so much better. I will always cherish the times that Alberto Huberman and Justin Marquis were with us to suggest a word, listen to a phrase, or opine if something "just sounded right." As I listened to Angelina and Alberto discuss these questions, I couldn't help but think I was witnessing Dulcinea with her Amadis. And I am so grateful to have had mine supporting me through this project as well; thank you for reading so many drafts. And thanks to Gabriela, whose poetic instincts and love of language also helped me in key moments.

I could not have embarked on this journey without generous support from Gonzaga University's Research Council and the College of Arts and Sciences. When I first proposed the project, Dean Elisabeth Mermann-Jozwiak readily helped to fund my work both in Mexico and at the Middlebury Bread Loaf Translator's Conference. I appreciate the scholarship I received and all the colleagues I met at Bread Loaf, including our fabulous leader, Suzanne Jill Levine. And born out of that transformational experience, I must thank my copy editor, Joyce Zonana whose quick turnaround and careful reading were so valuable. I would like to thank Dean Annmarie Caño, who graciously supported me with resources to complete the book manuscript. Thank you to my friends and colleagues who are always willing to discuss Jewish content: Tamar Malino, Lana J. Neufeld, and Elizabeth Goldstein. Also to Luciana Zilberman Izón, who spent hours with me as I worked through the first chapters. And I am grateful to my colleagues in Spanish: Alec Schumacher for his insights on translation and Rebecca Stephanis for her enduring support and friendship. I am especially grateful to my friend Christopher Lemelin, with whom I can talk about language and translation at all hours, and whose advice is especially useful when working on something tricky during sleepless nights.

Finally, I would like to thank my parents, Gene and Christina Darter. Although one of them is not here to see the fruition of my work, she will always a part of it. It is because of both of them that I have been able to do what I love in life.

~

Introduction

Who is Dulcinea? Named after Don Quixote's famous damsel, Angelina Muñiz-Huberman's Dulcinea is not who she seems to be. Spanish exile, lady-in-waiting, or even a medieval princess, Dulcinea defies definition, existing simultaneously in reality and in fiction, constantly in motion, (re)creating and (re)membering the world around and within her, wandering the world through language, searching for answers. At first glance, Muñiz-Huberman's *Enchanted Dulcinea* (*Dulcinea encantada*, 1992) would not strike the reader as a "Jewish" novel. There are no explicit references to Judaism, nor does the protagonist ever identify as Jewish.[1] Yet, it is fitting that this translation form part of a book series on Jewish women in the Americas whose goal is to bring to light their great diversity of experiences for an English-reading audience who may not be aware of Latin American Jewish authors and their cultural traditions. As a crypto-Jew herself, Muñiz-Huberman's Sephardic inheritance was hidden from her until her mother revealed her lineage and the stories that linked her to her Jewish past. It is no wonder that her novel, like other literature written by Spanish *conversos* or crypto-Jews, can pass as secular, or even Christian, steeped in the art and writings of Western intellectual history, but whose layers, when probed through its coded language, symbols, and philosophies, reveal a text deeply rooted in Jewish thought.[2]

1. Aside from references to Song of Songs, Naomi Lindstrom points to one usage of Yiddish and an extended reference to Jerusalem. Lindstrom, "Las narrativas visionarias," 7.

2. The word *converso* ("convert"), or New Christian, was a common way to refer to people of Jewish heritage who elected to or were forced to convert to Christianity or face expulsion from Spain in 1492 and, later, from Portugal, in 1496. All remaining Jews in Portugal in 1497 were declared to have

1

Much like its author, *Enchanted Dulcinea* is a text that is not rooted in any one country and defies easy categorization. Autobiography, biography, history, and fiction combine to create a unique text that embodies both the Jewish diasporic experience and the upheavals of Europe in the mid-twentieth century that forced so many people, like Muñiz-Huberman herself, into exile. Muñiz-Huberman's work is highly reflective of the historical context in which she lived, which fostered her unique writing style and themes. In order to best understand the novel before us, let us first consider Muñiz-Huberman's biography.

Angelina Muñiz-Huberman was born in Hyères, France in 1936 as a direct result of the Spanish Civil War. Her father was a Republican journalist. Fearing that his family would be in danger, Muñiz-Huberman's pregnant mother fled with her young son to France, where she had relatives and where Angelina would be born. Muñiz-Huberman's father arrived later. The family was safe in France for some years until Muñiz-Huberman's brother suffered a tragic accident that took his life. When the Muñiz family later fled France and the imminent World War in 1939, they were now a family of three. Muñiz-Huberman would never forget the loss of her older brother, who accompanied her in her imagination as a child and who often appears in her writing. Landing in Cuba, the family lived in the rural village of Caimito del Guayabal, where the young Muñiz-Huberman played freely in the countryside. Just three years later, in 1942, the family moved, once again, to Mexico City, where Muñiz-Huberman continues to make her home. When she was just six years old, now established in Mexico, her mother took her out on their balcony and informed her that she came from a long line of Spanish crypto-Jews—something that profoundly moved Muñiz-Huberman. Over the course of her life, through her professional work as both author and professor of Spanish Medieval and Comparative Literature, Muñiz-Huberman has explored her roots as a Spaniard and a Sephardic Jew. A prolific writer, she has published dozens of works of poetry, essays, fiction, and academic literature. Her work has received several prestigious awards and distinctions, from the Xavier Villarrutia award in 1985 for her book of short stories *Huerto cerrado, huerto sellado* (*Enclosed Garden*) to the first Sor Juana Inés de la Cruz award in

converted by the king. While some *conversos* continued Jewish practices secretly, others adopted Christianity as their religion of choice. *Conversos* were not fully integrated into Spanish society, as they were always suspected of secretly practicing Judaism (Judaizers). Due to such suspicions, the Holy Office of the Inquisition targeted *conversos*, often through violent and even lethal means. Consequently, *conversos* continuously had to prove that they were no longer Jews, and in cases when they were secret Jews, or crypto-Jews, their public face and interactions had to pass within normative Christian society. Many well-known writers of the medieval and early modern period were *conversos*, several of whom Muñiz-Huberman references in this novel.

1993 for *Dulcinea encantada* (*Enchanted Dulcinea*) to Mexico's National Prize in Arts and Literature in 2018. Recently, in January 2021, Muñiz-Huberman was named as the newest member of the Mexican Academy of Language.

Some of Muñiz-Huberman's works directly address and reference Jewish history and themes. For example, *Tierra adentro* (1977) narrates the adventures of a young Jew during the Spanish Inquisition and *El mercador de Tudela* (1998) is based on the medieval Jewish historical figure Benjamin of Tudela, who wrote about his travels across Europe, Asia, and Africa. Her book of short narratives *En el jardín de la Cábala* (2008) recounts stories from Jewish Kabbalistic traditions. She has compiled two anthologies and a book of essays about Sephardic culture, language, and writings, including Kabbalah, in her books *La lengua florida: antología sefardí* (1989), *Las raíces y las ramas: fuentes y derivaciones de la Cábala hispanohebrea* (1993), and *El atanor encendido: Antología de Cábala, alquimia, gnosticismo* (2019). Her work about Saint Teresa of Ávila, *Morada interior* (1972), explores the nun's identity as a *conversa*. Muñiz-Huberman has also penned poetry with Jewish themes and images. However, much of her work also explores the themes of exile, identity, language, and memory. She has created the term "pseudomemories" to refer to texts with a mixture of autobiography and fiction where memories come from within the author's experiences, from others (especially people from childhood), and from the author's imagination. Indeed, Muñiz-Huberman's literary corpus offers its readers a wide variety of themes and genres.

In fact, Muñiz-Huberman writes that for many years, publishers were not interested in her books and she was "set aside." Judith Payne writes that Muñiz-Huberman's experiences as a Jew and a Spanish exile shaped her books—often imbued with medieval and mystical imagery—in a unique way that didn't conform to the typical novel set in Mexico.[3] Her writing has not been easily categorized within a movement or a generation of writers. However, over time, Muñiz-Huberman's unique writing has been recognized, studied, and published in both Spain and Mexico. Her election to the Mexican Academy of Language shows that the skills, knowledge, and perspective that come from a language and identity constructed in exile are a valuable and even necessary aspect of Mexico's national heritage.

This translation brings a Sephardic perspective to an even wider audience. *Sepharad*, the medieval Judeo-Spanish word for Spain, became the memory of a people in exile (after the Jewish expulsion in 1492), yet the connection was maintained through language and literature.[4] Despite the imposition

---

3. Payne, "Writing," 435.

4. Ladino, or Judeo-Spanish, are different ways of speaking about the Jewish-Spanish language that originated in medieval Spain. Often written with Hebrew letters, Sephardic Jews living in exile

of a national identity based on Christianity, other Jews remained in Spain where they conserved certain practices, knowledge, and traditions. Muñiz-Huberman's work, and this novel, help to uncover layers of knowledge that have traditionally been hidden, prohibited, or haven't entered into mainstream culture. This translation symbolically represents a peeling back of layers so characteristic of *converso* or crypto-Jewish writing. Besides incorporating Jewish philosophical and mystical thinking, the translation reveals themes and ideas drawn from Spanish and Mexican cultural and literary traditions, which do not often permeate works in English. Much like Muñiz-Huberman herself, who occupies a space in between cultures, religions, and worldviews, *Enchanted Dulcinea* brings readers into a space of exile where they are free to explore the explicit and hidden meanings that are so characteristic of Muñiz-Huberman's work.

Structure and Style of the Novel

Enchanted Dulcinea is written in a lyrical, postmodern style, moving between and among time, space, and narrative voices. The main character, Dulcinea, is in conversation with herself. The fragmented narrative voice both reveals and reflects on Dulcinea's inner thoughts. Whenever the narrative voice uses second person, she is addressing Dulcinea the author, who speaks in first person. Although the novel never makes explicit what part of Dulcinea her inner interlocutor represents—her conscience, her public voice, her rational voice?—this fragmented voice inspires her to write her mental books, develop her thoughts, and examine her life. The overall framework of the novel thus takes on the feeling of a kind of confessional discourse, one that was common among nuns who related their spiritual or mystical life stories and that appears in other works by Muñiz-Huberman; for example, Saint Teresa pens her own confession in the form of a diary in the novel *Morada interior*. In her book of vignettes *Las confidentes* (1997; *The Confidantes*), two women take turns telling stories to each other, creating a larger narrative based on their (confessional) dialogue. One could say that for Muniz-Huberman, (literary) creativity comes from the interaction of a multiplicity of voices, even if they stem from the same person. Muñiz Huberman refers to Dulcinea's as an internal confession, later referring to her own "confession-confusions,"

---

maintained their language for more than five hundred years. Depending on where Jewish exiles settled, the language received influence from the local majority languages, but not so much that Sephardic Jews from diverse communities can't understand each other. During and after World War II, there was a steep decline in native speakers, but currently there are initiatives to keep the language alive. Muñiz-Huberman writes about Ladino and provides an anthology of Sephardic texts in *La lengua florida*.

playing with the similar words, to express that there are no limits when one dialogues in her own mind.[5]

Amid Dulcinea's dialogue with herself, she narrates the stories of three Dulcineas. These stories are written in Dulcinea's "mental books" because she does not want to be confined to the limits of pen and paper. She is free to narrate her stories whenever and however she would like. Consequently, as we read the dialogue between Dulcinea and herself, she also narrates the stories of her Dulcineas in third person. The first story, we assume, is the story of Dulcinea's own past: a young girl is sent, along with her brother, to Russia to escape Spain's Civil War. When World War II encroaches into the Soviet Union, Dulcinea's brother is shot and dies. After spending years in Russia with other exiled children, Dulcinea is sent to Mexico to be reunited with parents she has not seen in years. This event is traumatic, first because she cannot be sure they are her parents and second because she must face their grief about the death of her brother. Dulcinea must make sense of who she is in a new country with unfamiliar people around her. The second story takes place in the nineteenth century. Dulcinea travels to Mexico from Toboso (in Spain) to be a lady's companion to the historical figure, the Marquise Frances "Fanny" Calderón de la Barca. Together they travel around Mexico City and its outskirts. While the historical Calderón de la Barca kept a travel diary that described her experiences as a Spanish diplomat's wife in Mexico (*Life in Mexico* [1843]), in the novel Dulcinea keeps her own diary of observations as a Spaniard in Mexico. Finally, the third story takes place in medieval Europe. Dulcinea is a princess who yearns to travel and sets out on a quest to understand her life, or better yet her own story. Searching for hermits and sages, Dulcinea seeks deeper understanding through her constant journeys.

The three stories, combined with the narrators' dialogue, can be disconcerting at first. The text is set up to guide the reader through the use of spacing, italics, and changes in narrative voice. Every time Dulcinea begins to narrate part of one of her stories or moves from the stories to her dialogue, there are two spaces between paragraphs. When Dulcinea is in dialogue with herself, there may be a space between paragraphs as she moves to new ideas or associations. The novel also contains many intertextual references, from medieval to contemporary literature, art, and philosophy. When Dulcinea quotes from another source directly, it is in italics. Most importantly, the reader can follow who is speaking by paying close attention to narrative voice: Dulcinea the author/narrator (first person), Dulcinea the interlocutor (addresses Dulcinea in second person), and the three other protagonists in

---

5. Muñiz-Huberman, *Canto*, 184, 189.

her stories named Dulcinea from twentieth-century Mexico, nineteenth-century Mexico, and medieval Europe (referred to in third person).

Muñiz-Huberman's literary style is lyrical, evocative, and often humorous. She has written several books of poems, and her novels reflect a profound attention to word choice, sound, and rhythm. Some paragraphs appear in verse. Other phrases play with sound or meaning; for example, in one sentence she pairs "frases y fresas," playing with the inversion of the two vowels in the words to mark a tender moment between Dulcinea and her brother. The soft sounds and alliteration highlight the pleasure of the two children picking strawberries ("fresas") and talking together ("frases"). In another example, she uses polysemy with the verb "contar" twice in a sentence where its multiple meanings, both as "unimportant" ("no contaban") and "having counted" ("habían contado"), emphasize Dulcinea's ambivalent feelings about her years in exile in Russia, not to mention that "contar" can also mean to tell a story, so it could also refer to the fact that few people knew the stories of Spanish children exiled in Russia. Every word Muñiz-Huberman writes is intentional, selected precisely for what it can convey, and the novel often challenges the reader to decode and play with its language and its many possible meanings.

There are many humorous moments in the novel, despite Dulcinea's weighty contemplations about exile, identity, life, and even death. For example, when Dulcinea thinks about writing her book, she playfully contemplates using Snoopy's famous opening line, which, being silly in itself, when translated from Spanish is, "It was night and nevertheless it was raining," which is humorous due to its non sequitur. Much of Muñiz-Huberman's humor comes from wordplay or modifying well-known sayings or quotes. For example, when protecting her little friend Leninito, Dulcinea affirms she will "right wrongs and pursue scoundrels," a direct reference to the vocabulary and language Miguel de Cervantes used for Don Quixote.

Other humorous moments are clearly satirical, such as when Dulcinea jokes, "For you are plastic and to plastic you shall return," recalling God's words to Adam as a way to criticize humanity's buildup of garbage. As a narrator-author, Dulcinea is quick witted and ironic, using humor to play with the reader.

Finally, Muñiz-Huberman's style is not direct, but more evocative, rarely telling readers what to think, but asking them to interpret the many (inter)-textual references or combinations of words and images. She is known for her nontraditional usage of commas and colons and her predilection for combining different ideas in short sentences. Most notably, her overuse of colons highlights important moments where the reader should pause and consider the associations between the clauses connected by the colons. Though many of her phrases are short and concise, using as few words as possible to evoke an idea or image, other phrases—usually describing a landscape—can twist and turn, creating a detailed look at a scene, much like the mountainous paths that Dulcinea and Amadis walk. This combination of styles keeps the reader on her toes, both bringing her into the story and then, with a few more strokes of a pen, inviting her back into her own mind to ponder the mysteries of philosophy, religion and literature. For this reason, it is helpful to consider the analysis of this book at different levels, allowing the reader to move among different levels of approaching and understanding the text.

Analysis: PaRDeS

Returning to the idea that *Enchanted Dulcinea* is itself a crypto-Jewish text, instead of a standard literary approach to introducing its content, I will turn to Jewish traditions to propose a way of understanding and interpreting *Enchanted Dulcinea* that addresses its outward, secular layers as well as its more hidden Jewish themes.

There is a famous Talmudic Jewish story that explains the difficulty of entering Pardes, which means "the orchard," but is also associated with paradise. Muñiz-Huberman notes that exile began when Adam and Eve were expelled from paradise. When paradise was sealed off from humans, they lost access to both space and knowledge, thus initiating the long-standing desire to return to paradise.[6] Pardes can be interpreted in many ways, but often represents a space of knowledge as well as a mystical ascension that brings one closer to God. Not just anyone can enter Pardes; in fact, when you enter Pardes, as the legend goes, even the most learned do not know what will happen to them. In Rashi's (one of the most important commentators of the Talmud) explanation of the legend, four sages all enter Pardes, but each one has a difference experience. Ben Azzai dies at the sight of God. Ben Zoma gazes at the Divine Presence and goes insane while Acher becomes a heretic. Finally, Rabbi Akiva is able to enter and leave Pardes in peace, without harm.[7] The legend serves as a warning to those who would seek mystical experiences without proper knowledge and training. But it can also be a lesson in reading texts: sometimes, although you may think you are ready, you are not ready to gaze upon God or, in the case of reading, understand

---

6. Muñiz-Huberman, *Canto*, 67, 71.

7. Found in the Babylonian Talmud, Tractate Hagigah 14a, this story has been the basis of much commentary and interpretations. Muñiz-Huberman writes about it in her story "Cuatro Sabios en el Paraíso" ("Four Sages in Paradise") in her collection of stories, *En el jardín de la Cábala*.

what you read. Some people give up; some people are driven insane by the process; and some people resist what they read, choosing to embrace other ideas. Certainly, as the four different men experienced God in four different ways, this story teaches us that revelation exists at multiple levels and with multiple results. Dulcinea, like the sages of the story, seeks revelation with multiple results, depending on how the reader interprets the text. Aside from Dulcinea's metafictional storytelling, the novel also invites its readers to contemplate the process of reading—how do we enter into the novel to understand its revelations?

Over time, the lesson of Pardes developed into an important tool for Jewish scriptural exegesis. Instead of four men who teach us about the dangers and rewards of mystical practices, PaRDeS teaches us four ways of reading texts. Muñiz-Huberman writes "These are the four steps Moses de León recommends for any reading, above all, a Kabbalistic reading, if you want to understand the true hidden meaning of the words."[8] The acronym stands for Peshat (the plain meaning of the text), Remez (allegorical, hidden or symbolic meaning), Derash (explication) and Sod (mystical meaning). This approach to understanding Torah encourages its readers to move more deeply into the text, to peel the layers back and gaze upon God through the careful study of God's words. In this way, I propose to modify the system of PaRDeS to apply it to this literary text that functions at so many layers. My peshat will focus on the historical events that take place in the novel. Remez will examine the most important intertexts that help us understand the protagonist and her journeys. Derash will explicate the many ways in which others have read and interpreted the larger (secular) themes of the text. Finally, the section entitled Sod will explore the underlying Jewish mystical thread that ties the novel together and reveals its deepest meanings at a spiritual level.

Peshat

Enchanted Dulcinea is rooted in the twentieth century during two major upheavals, the Spanish Civil War and World War II. The author/narrator Dulcinea is a child when Spain's Civil War forces her family to send her brother and her to Russia for safekeeping while her parents flee to another country to later call for them to reunite. This story line is based on historical facts and is, in fact, partially drawn from the life experiences of Lydia Hahn Rodríguez, to whom the novel was originally dedicated and who spent time in the Soviet

---

8. Muñiz-Huberman, *En el jardín*, 17, translation mine. For more information on the origins of PaRDeS as Jewish exegesis, see A. Van der Heide, "PARDES," 148–50.

Union as a child refugee from Spain, and also from Muñiz-Huberman's own life experiences.

The Spanish Civil War exploded in 1936 between two major political factions. The Republicans were leftists who supported the liberal Second Spanish Republic (1931–1939). Republicans had rejected monarchal rule and advocated for progressive reforms, such as the separation of church and state, voting rights for women, and agrarian reform, to name just a few. They were in opposition to the conservative, right-leaning Nationalists, who were supported by Nazi and fascist countries, led by General Francisco Franco. After winning the war in 1939, Franco's government used fascist tactics to form a dictatorship that he headed until his death in 1975. Afraid of retaliation, violence, purges, and other forms of repression, many Republicans were forced into exile. According to Karl Qualls, in 1937–1938, amid horrific conditions, including violence and hunger, parents sent about three thousand children from Spain to the Soviet Union to be fed and sheltered, some ultimately being reunited with parents and others orphaned. The Soviets opened boardinghouses where the children were schooled and cared for as best as possible.[9] Later, as Nazis moved into Moscow, the children were quickly moved to other makeshift houses in the countryside, where conditions were poor and children could experience hunger, disease, and fewer resources for education and stability. Despite these hardships, notes Qualls, the children's memories of this time were "quite positive."[10] The children's return to Spain or other countries was complicated, as Moscow resisted their repatriation until after Stalin's death in 1953, for many, more than a decade after arrival. Some children whose parents were living in exile in Latin America left earlier, from 1945 to 1947.[11]

In the novel, Dulcinea and her brother spend several years in Russia (she never calls it the Soviet Union) where they form tender memories together. However, her brother is tragically shot to death before they leave, and Dulcinea endures the trauma of reliving her brother's death at the same time she is reunited with parents she doesn't remember (because she was so young when she was sent to Russia) in a new country, Mexico. As she travels in the

---

9. There was a specific international school, called the International House, that was for international students from various countries. It is unclear whether Dulcinea is referring to that school, which would not have been run specifically for Spanish children, or whether she is referring to the boardinghouses that were specifically for Spanish children in exile. What is certain is that Muñiz-Huberman developed this story based on information from her friend who was sent to Russia as child during the Spanish Civil War.

10. Qualls, "Niños," 3.

11. Qualls, Stalin's Niños, 160.

car with Amadis and "the strangers" (these parents who she doesn't remember), she tries to understand her place in a new country.

During the Spanish Civil War, Mexico created a unique and welcoming destination for Spanish exiles. The Mexican president, Lázaro Cárdenas, made the decision to remain loyal to the Spanish Republic due to a common political and social ideology based on progressive goals. When the Spanish Republic fell to Franco in 1939, half a million people, mainly Republicans, had fled Spain. Europe was in the clutch of fascist regimes and the beginning of World War II, so Spanish refugees found few options for safety, especially with France's destitute refugee camps and often closed borders.[12] With its common language and support for the arts, Mexico became an attractive destination for the community of Spanish Republican exiles, comprised of many intellectuals, artists, and writers. Literary journals and schools, such as the Luis Vives Institute, the Colegio Madrid, and the Hispano-Mexican Academy, were dedicated to providing opportunities for them to continue their work as writers and to provide their children with opportunities to stay engaged with their cultural heritage. Overall, it is estimated that twenty to thirty thousand Spanish exiles went to Mexico.[13]

This historical backdrop forms the twentieth-century context within which Dulcinea raises questions of identity and belonging. Additionally, the stories of the two other Dulcineas are also rooted in historical events related to Spain and Mexico. The nineteenth-century Dulcinea accompanies Frances "Fanny" Calderón de la Barca as a lady's companion. Fanny Erksine Inglis, born into a prominent Scottish family, was an independent woman whose family traveled and lived around Europe, eventually settling in the United States after the death of her father. While in the United States, Fanny met Ángel Calderón de la Barca, a Spanish diplomat. Soon after they were married in 1839, her husband became the first Spanish envoy sent to independent Mexico. While there, Fanny traveled around the country and recorded her observations and interpretations of Mexican life in journals and letters, which later would be published as her book *Life in Mexico*, a text that was well received and successful in Europe and the United States, but more controversial in Mexico due to some critical observations about Mexican society.[14] Her book would inform countless readers who were not able to visit Mexico what the country looked like to an outsider. Eventually the couple returned to Spain and, after Ángel's untimely death, Fanny Calderón de la Barca spent much of the rest of her life in Spain in the royal palace, tutoring

12. Hadzelek, "Places," 70–71. See also Payne, "A World," 47.
13. Hadzelek, 81.
14. Costeloe, "Prescott's *History of the Conquest*."

and later serving as companion to Princess Isabel, eventually receiving the title of Marquise. Much like Fanny Calderón de la Barca, nineteenth-century Dulcinea is a stranger in Mexico, taking in its landscapes, observing its people, and thinking about her own life as she writes about her observations in a diary. While Muñiz-Huberman only cites one selection of the original text, many of the scenes where Dulcinea is with the Marquise mirror scenes that Calderón de la Barca included in her text. Luz Elena Zamudio notes that because of these similarities, Dulcinea, like an omniscient narrator, must be aware of Calderón de la Barca's text before she publishes it, a playful take on the reluctant diary writer.[15] In sum, like the Marquise, Dulcinea is an outsider in Mexico and, similar to the twentieth-century Dulcinea, searches for meaning in a new land. It is in these sections that the novel shows Muñiz-Huberman's close ties to her adoptive home and what anchors this novel in Mexico, despite its many links and references to Europe and European thought.

Although the section about the medieval Dulcinea never gives any definite dates, based on a few historical references we can deduce that she is in the twelfth or early thirteenth century in Southern France. In the beginning of the novel, Dulcinea lives in a palace in unnamed lands, though through her travels, we know she arrives in Hyères, in southern France. The great mountains she crosses would most likely be the Alps or the Pyrenees. At that time, this region of southern France was a center of non-Catholic spiritual and mystical religious movements, tied to teachings among Gnostic groups such as the Cathars and Albigenses and other Christian movements, such as the Waldensians; it was also a site of Jewish Kabbalistic thinking. The religious environment was one of openness and tolerance. After the Albigensian Crusade in the early thirteenth century, during which many people including Cathar women and children were killed, these religious movements were suppressed, although some ideas spread to nearby countries and were adapted into later Protestant movements.[16] Medieval Jewish Kabbalistic thinking would be further developed in the following centuries in Spain. In the novel, this rich environment of spiritual ideas and mystical exploration undergird Dulcinea's own journey or quest for (spiritual) knowledge.

Remez

One could argue that *Enchanted Dulcinea* is woven from its intertextual threads. The novel uses many intertextual references to give deeper meaning

---

15. Zamudio, *Exilio*, 127–31.
16. Mark, "Cathars;" Weber, "Albigenses."

to Dulcinea's thoughts. Muñiz-Huberman provides readers with a wealth of sources from Western artistic, literary, and philosophical traditions, expanding on themes such as memory, love, silence, and apocalypse. Zamudio likens Muñiz-Huberman's use of intertexts to Jorge Luis Borges and Italo Calvino, and references Gerard Genette's concept of the palimpsest and Julia Kristeva's concept of a novel as "the sum of all other books" as key to understanding the novel.[17] It is true that in order to fully understand the novel, it is necessary to explore the intertexts.[18] At its root, the main characters, Dulcinea and Amadis, are themselves based on well-known Spanish literary figures.

The title of the novel is the first intertextual reference and introduces the protagonist, Dulcinea. In perhaps Spain's most celebrated novel, *Don Quixote* (1605, 1615), by Miguel de Cervantes Saavedra, Dulcinea is the great love and inspiration of the title character. Some readers claim that Dulcinea never appears in flesh and blood in the novel and is only known as the beautiful, refined lady who Don Quixote invents so that he may serve as her devoted knight. Others interpret Dulcinea as an idealization of the crass, unrefined peasant Aldonza Lorenzo:

> Her name was Aldonza Lorenzo, and upon her he thought fit to confer the title of Lady of his Thoughts; and after some search for a name which should not be out of harmony with her own, and should suggest and indicate that of a princess and great lady, he decided upon calling her Dulcinea del Toboso—she being of El Toboso—a name, to his mind, musical, uncommon, and significant, like all those he had already bestowed upon himself and the things belonging to him.[19]

Dulcinea is a captivating figure, both imagined and real, a woman enchanted in order to become an idealized figure, a woman worthy of a knight. Later in the book, Sancho tricks Don Quixote by proclaiming that the crass peasant woman whom Don Quixote sees in that moment is his Dulcinea. Is she merely Sancho's manipulation of reality in order to appease his master? Was Dulcinea only ever an imagined ideal? Or is there a piece of Dulcinea in every woman and Don Quixote sees this within the crude reality around him? Without a doubt, in *Don Quixote*, Dulcinea is never only one woman. She is a symbol of the inability of language to define a person, the multiplicity of

---

17. Zamudio, *Exilio*, 101–3.

18. I have chosen to explain the three major intertexts here. Other intertextual references in the novel will have footnotes to give a basic explanation of the source and its main idea. Zamudio closely examines how each intertextual reference to Fanny Calderón de la Barca and the Book of Revelation mirrors Dulcinea's thoughts and actions. Additionally, she has an extensive list of other intertexts in her Appendix (in Spanish).

19. Cervantes, *Don Quixote*, part 1, chapter 1.

perspectives that shape our conceptions of the world, the question of who or what defines reality, and the possibility of seeing in a new way.[20] Dulcinea is the concept to which we attach our greatest hopes and dreams, or to which we turn in moments of desperation. In Muñiz-Huberman's novel about Dulcinea, she remains a figure with many stories and interpretations, except this time, she is in control of her narrative. She is not a passive figure, but rather an active author who imagines her own muse, her version of the knight who accompanies her on her journeys.

It's also worth noting that "enchanted" ("encantado") in Spanish has several possible meanings. It can refer to someone under a spell, someone who is not herself while under the enchantment. In this way, Dulcinea can be seen as under someone else's spell. Perhaps under that of her parents who insist that she define herself through their Spanish eyes. Perhaps under that of a society who cannot see her for who she is. "Los Encantados" can also refer to a popular Spanish game, like freeze tag, where individuals are frozen by a wizard who enchants them until they can break the enchantment. Similarly, it implies that Dulcinea is trapped. But in Spanish, the verb can also be used to express delight or love, thus "Dulcinea encantada" can refer to a Dulcinea who is delighted, who is loved or loves. Instead of being trapped, this version of "enchanted" can refer to her search for unconditional love, for herself, for and from Amadis, or for and from God.

Amadis is the silent man who loves Dulcinea and whom Dulcinea loves in all her stories. He represents unconditional and transgressive love: a brother, a knight, a lover, and a (spiritual) companion. Amadis drives the car in the main narrative, and Dulcinea is free to write her mental novels while he is at the wheel. This strong and enigmatic figure also derives from a Spanish oral and written tradition. The novel *Amadis of Gaul* (*Amadís de Gaula*) was based on chivalric romances that circulated in Europe. Although it seems there was a written version as early as the mid-fourteenth century, the first known copy was published in 1508 in Zaragoza by Garci Rodríguez de Montalvo.[21] The stories of Amadis were so popular that he dominated Europe as the quintessential knight.[22] In fact, he was so popular that Don Quixote himself esteems to be a knight like Amadis (though Cervantes's novel satirizes the figure of

---

20. For an in-depth study of Cervantes's Dulcinea, see Erich Auerbach's "The Enchanted Dulcinea," an article that Muñiz-Huberman credits with contributing to her own invention of an "Enchanted Dulcinea" (pers. comm.).

21. Place, "Preface," 9–11.

22. In his analysis of courtly clove, Otis Green writes that *Amadis* is "a masterpiece. It was widely read and imitated throughout Europe, influencing deeply the ideals and the manners of gentlemen and ladies during the Renaissance." Green, *Spain and the Western Tradition*, 108. For his full analysis of *Amadis*, 104–8.

Amadis). In the multiple novels about him, Amadis proves to be the model of the chivalric knight: honorable, courteous, valiant, sensitive, and handsome, bravely fighting the manifestations of deadly sins.[23] The love story between Amadis and Oriana develops across the various books in which their love survives several challenges, including jealousy, Amadis's madness and his stint as Beltenebros, exile, sex and a child out of wedlock, but ultimately results in the marriage between Amadis and Oriana. Muñiz-Huberman deftly weaves an intertextual thread when Amadis inhabits Dulcinea's mind (the inversion of what happens the *Quixote*) and Amadis is there to witness her madness, her exile, and her search for love. Just as *Amadis of Gaul* laid part of the foundation from which early modern Spanish literature would emerge, Amadis serves as Dulcinea's rock, the heart of her stories. But in this version, the woman is the knight, the adventurer, and the one who controls the narrative, while Amadis is the idealized man she carries in her head, the faithful servant who accompanies her everywhere, whether in reality or only in her fantasies.

Apart from the two major intertexts that shape the protagonists of the novel, Muñiz-Huberman includes a multitude of direct quotes or allusions to other literary, philosophical, and artistic works. These references often serve as literary hyperlinks to help expand her development of a theme. Much like the Internet, or even Talmudic commentary, her intertextual references invite us to look further than the pages in front of us, to engage in the work that elucidates a reading. For example, when pondering the role of silence, Dulcinea takes us on a philosophical journey from Greek to Italian philosophers—Harpocrates, Hermes Trismegistus, and Giordano Bruno— perhaps a detour from the novel, but a path that locates her novel within the discourses of Western intellectual history. In this translation, many of these references have been noted, although common references from literature in English, such as Robinson Crusoe, have not. As an avid reader, Dulcinea suggests that people are profoundly influenced by the literature they read. Through examining the rich array of intertextual references in the novel, we learn that an individual's life story is intricately connected to the ideas and stories that have shaped her cultural inheritance(s).

It would be remiss not to mention one other important intertext for the novel: the Book of Revelation. Each chapter is titled one of the seven seals of the Apocalypse and each contains at least one quote from the Book of Revelation: two references to the image of God on a throne; a questioning of who can open the seven seals of the book; the release of the four horsemen;

---

23. Place, "Preface," 14.

another reference to a throne, its guardians, and the Lamb; an angel who gives the book to the first-person narrator to swallow; two witnesses who tell their stories over many days and then die; and finally a grand voice in the temple that tells seven angels to pour seven cups of God's wrath over the earth. There are several reasons why the novel is framed through the Book of Revelation. The structure suggests that Dulcinea's journey is destined as she opens the seal of each step; on the other hand, since the stories are in her head, they are also sealed from the world. Our journey through the seals is a journey into the mind. Lois Parkinson Zamora suggests that contemporary writers use the Book of Revelation for its "wonderful complex of images of historical process, and also of the act of writing itself . . . because it can be endlessly interpreted but also because it addresses the problem of interpretation itself."[24] Dulcinea's thoughts can at times be chaotic, visionary, and symbolic. Zamudio affirms that references to the Apocalypse both highlight the confusion of dreams and reality and prefigure Dulcinea's own death.[25] Naomi Lindstrom suggests that Dulcinea connects the end of the world to our modern sins: technology and the destruction of the environment.[26] Dulcinea tries to give these thoughts order, but as Muñiz-Huberman writes, "The writer who loses his birthplace penetrates into the apocalyptic terrain: Paradise has been sealed: evil forces give birth to destruction. His only hope will be to find a niche where order prevails amidst chaos."[27] I will argue later that this intertext highlights the role of revelation in a Jewish mystical discourse. However, at a more secular level, it could be understood that exile feels like a world coming to an end, a bitter story that you have to swallow, the suffering of loss and change like charging horses, the pain of witnessing destruction. And it can feel like a quest to open the seals of new stories, new ways of understanding, and perhaps a prayer for the kind of revelation that comes from voices on high.

Derash

There have been several studies of *Enchanted Dulcinea* that have sought to interpret (and explicate) the text. From its very beginning to its very end, the novel is open to many ways of seeing its protagonist, her actions, and the meanings behind her words. Taken together, these studies show that Muñiz-Huberman crafted a novel that wrestles with some major questions of our times: the experience of exile and identity formation, the workings of

---

24. Zamora, *Writing*, 14.
25. Zamudio, *Exilio*, 119–20.
26. Lindstrom, "Narrativas visionarias," 8.
27. Muñiz-Huberman, "Exile and Memory," 96.

memory, the notion of time, the role of language in shaping our lives, the question of reality, and the theme of death.

Most scholars of *Enchanted Dulcinea* look primarily at the experience of exile since it is at the heart of the major plotline of the novel. Most agree that all the other aspects of the novel are the results of Dulcinea's, and Muñiz-Huberman's, experience of exile. Judith Payne has noted that, "The unusual nature of her perception of her life has generated a body of work that is difficult to categorize in any respect: lexically, nationally, generically, and thematically."[28]

When speaking about her identity as an author, Muñiz-Huberman and others have used the term "Hispano-Mexican," a fusion of her identities as both the child of Spanish exiles and someone who has lived in Mexico most of her life. In the novel, Dulcinea questions if that is also her identity and, if so, what that means. Payne also writes about Muñiz-Huberman as part of the "nepantla" generation in Mexico, using the Nahuatl (Mexica) word to mean people who are neither from here nor there, located between two worlds.[29] Many scholars acknowledge Muñiz-Huberman's Jewish identity, referring to her place in the larger Jewish diaspora, as well as her double Spanish exile, first from her Sephardic practices (post-1492) and second during the Spanish Civil War. In this way, Muñiz-Huberman takes the ambiguity of not belonging to a single place as a space for creativity.[30] Certainly Dulcinea's resistance to having only one story, since she creates multiple stories of Dulcineas, expresses the freedom and creativity of not being tied to one national narrative. Diana Castilleja proposes that Muñiz-Huberman's Hispanic-Franco-Cuban-Mexican Jewish identity is reflected in the hybridity found in the language, genre, and themes of her texts.[31] What is without a doubt is that Dulcinea and her mental novels defy categorization as she presents the state of exile as something fragmentary, disordered, and chaotic, while at the same time liberating, full of possibility, and profoundly internal (her inner world).

Although scholars agree that Muñiz-Huberman's works do not fall into simple preestablished categories, some have attempted to define her writing style. Zamudio claims that *Enchanted Dulcinea* is a neo-Baroque novel. Citing Severo Sarduy, she highlights the world in crisis and uncertainty, characterized by "confusion; *tremendismo*; horror of the void (filling space to avoid emptiness); polysemy; use of antithesis; critique of that which is balanced, univocal, universal, unmovable, and values that are arbitrarily

---

28. Payne, "A World," 50.
29. Payne, 49.
30. Payne, 49.
31. Castilleja, "Angelina Muñiz-Huberman," 22.

made by groups in power."[32] Zamudio affirms this argument by showing that many of Muñiz-Huberman's intertexts come from time periods preceding and including the Baroque, thus *Enchanted Dulcinea* may be seen as a contemporary rendering of Baroque thematics. I would argue that many of these same characteristics fall into the category of postmodern literature, which questions notions of truth and reality through language, including silence and the breakdown of language; through a playful use of metafiction, highlighting the process of writing itself; and, at times, through the use of multiple voices and/or a fragmented narrative voice. Both categories defy a nationalist, realist approach to semi-autobiographical writing. Additionally, Payne highlights Muñiz-Huberman's idea that literature written in exile shares certain textual and thematic characteristics: nostalgia, an apocalyptic sense, characters who are cynical or who feel insecure, writers who create new worlds or inner worlds, detailed descriptions in slow motion, intertextuality used as camouflage, and a writing style that will not necessarily reflect that of other writers in their nation.[33] Zamora argues that apocalyptic literature "is fundamentally concerned with our human relation to the changing forms of temporal reality, not with static simplifications."[34] Through all these techniques, Muñiz-Huberman reflects the difficulty of revealing the exile's complex experience of life where the crux of the dilemma is how to "harmonize a shallow reality with the depth of absence," what one lives in the exterior world while communicating what has been lost within.[35]

Muñiz-Huberman wrote extensively about her thoughts on exile in her book *El canto del peregrino* (1999) where she proposes that humans have lived in a state of exile since Adam and Eve were cast from the Garden of Eden. Since then, humans have addressed various states of exile through memory, imagination, and literature.[36] Memory attempts to recall what was lost, imagination fills in the gaps, and literature both records and influences these (imagined) memories. Thus, exile can create a circular movement of remembering, imagining, recording, and beginning again. It is no wonder that Dulcinea circles the Periferico highway as she engages in this process of remembering, imagining, and writing a mental novel that can be stopped, modified, and "rewritten" at any time. Muñiz-Huberman writes that exiled writers have a "magic wand of enchantment" that allows them to create and

---

32. Zamudio, *Exilio*, 88–89, translation mine.
33. Payne, "Writing," 434.
34. Zamora, *Writing*, 13.
35. Muñiz-Huberman, *Canto*, 182, translation mine.
36. Muñiz-Huberman, 65.

destroy (new) worlds with language, even if only in their own minds, to represent their experiences.[37]

Yet, Muñiz-Huberman links the experience of exile to more complex questions regarding the problematic role of memory and language in constructing one's life story. Dulcinea laments her ability to have her own memories, having spent much of her life immersed in the memories of her parents who impulsively pass on their idealized image of a long-lost Spain. Although Dulcinea has some vague memories of wartime Spain, she has not felt free to define herself based on her own memories alone. She feels the gaps in her own ability to remember the past as well as the overwhelming influence of other stories she has read, pictures she has seen, and others' memories she has heard. Payne reminds us of Muñiz-Huberman's assertion that the children of Spanish exiles "constructed their lives in the air. . . . Dulcinea laments her parents' need to identify her as Spanish instead of fostering in her the Mexican identity that was hers by right of her life in that country."[38] Like puppets held in the air by their parents' controlling arms, their children internalized the narrative of Spanish identity from the time they were learning language, thus forming their earliest memories. Through the coining of her own term, "pseudomemories," Muñiz-Huberman underscores the role that imagination and fiction play in memory formation, especially in children, thus discarding simple categories such as autobiography and fiction.[39] No text is free from the influence of others. Likewise, Dulcinea resists any notion of knowing the absolute "truth" of her life. As much as she desperately seeks the comfort of order and assurance of memory, she affirms that it is impossible. Instead, language and memory are used to create a narrative, or multiple narratives, to entertain, to enjoy, and ultimately to claim, fiction and all, as one's history/story.

The novel's fragmented structure and narrative style encourage readers to contemplate the nature of our modern, fragmented lives. In its more basic form, Dulcinea's fragmented voice reflects the postmodern notion of the impossibility of the unified subject. When confronted with narrating her life story, Dulcinea is incapable of seeing herself through one, univocal narrative. Furthermore, Dulcinea's status of exile is only one way of showing how individual identity is never a coherent whole, but rather a conglomeration of different inheritances and experiences from which we draw our knowledge. Thus, the fragmentation of the text mirrors the fragmentation of memory, which cannot function as a unified whole. Filer notes that Dul-

---

37. Muñiz-Huberman, 70.
38. Payne, "A World," 57.
39. Castilleja, "Angelina Muñiz-Huberman," 25.

cinea "perceives her identity as broken in fragments, incapable of restoring itself or of meaningfully arranging the dispersed images that she collects indiscriminately."[40] Therefore, the goal ceases to be to unify or order the parts, but rather to express the fragmented reality that the modern subject inhabits. Perhaps the goal is not to seek unification, but to examine our own fragments to better understand our place in the world. For others, Dulcinea's fragmented mental novel moves beyond that of exploring personal identity to observing the world around her as also fragmented. Zamora posits that Dulcinea's many fragmented stories "represent this century's storm of progress" and the "need to resist the buffering winds of modernity" which may promise a coherent narrative of purpose, but that never manifest as such.[41] Interestingly, several scholars who examine Muñiz-Huberman's writing note that her protagonists ultimately seek to unify their narratives by weaving together the fragments, like first-person bread crumbs that the author pieces together, crumb by crumb.[42] Castilleja concludes that Muñiz-Huberman's narrator-authors reconstruct their lives as they seek to define them by combining the pieces according to their will.[43] Filer asserts,

> While Muñiz's works offer a remarkable account of a struggle for unity within a multiple cultural identity, they attest, at the same time to the power of language to bring together what was separated by life and history. . . . To construct her own self, without renouncing any part of her heritage, is the personal and literary project to which she has committed her imagination and her intellect.[44]

Therefore, the irony often found in Muñiz-Huberman's texts is present in the theme of fragmentation—readers can see it as an unfortunate reflection of the chaos and disconnect of the modern world, or fragmentation can be seen as the unifying factor that helps us to reflect and construct the complexity and depth of our modern lives. Although language may be used to separate us, even from aspects of ourselves, it can also be used to make sense of our multiple layers and to resist any essentialized notion of self.

Time is a complicated subject in *Enchanted Dulcinea*. First, Dulcinea inhabits several different times through her stories, thus suggesting that while we are rooted in a certain time, our lives mirror others. The twentieth-century Dulcinea who sees Mexico for the first time is duplicated though the nineteenth-century Dulcinea who travels through a new country with

---

40. Filer, "Integration," 275.
41. Zamora, *Usable*, 159, 158.
42. Castilleja, "Angelina Muñiz-Huberman," 26.
43. Castilleja, 32.
44. Filer, "Integration," 275.

the Marquise. In this way, Dulcinea does not need to conform to any one set of historical or social definitions. This layering of time is also related to memory and imagination, which does not constrain itself to linear boundaries, and which Castilleja associates with pseudomemories and the inclusion of visual cues, such as photos.[45] In fact, Dulcinea describes her memories like photos or films, wishing that she could see all people's memories like films running simultaneously. This suggests that memories don't capture a moment, frozen in time, but rather play continuously in our minds as we lay down new memories and narrate our lives. Therefore, past, present, and future can become intertwined. In fact, the novel circles, literally on the Periferico beltway, and thematically through the repetition of stories and themes. The reader can feel the circularity of time as Dulcinea dialogues with herself. Muñiz-Huberman herself states that "memory is obsessive and moves in circles."[46] And yet, the novel does evolve. Dulcinea advances her stories at the same time the car passes neighborhoods in its movement around Mexico City. In fact, the character of Blizmanah, meaning "without time" in Hebrew, stands in contrast to Dulcinea. As she spends time with Amadis and Dulcinea, Blizmanah begins to lose her timelessness and becomes affected by the human experience. Her ability to know all outside the limits of time is not the same as Dulcinea's repetitive foray into memories and stories in her head. Ultimately, the car leaves the beltway and comes to a stop. Again, like much of her novel, supposed binaries coexist in Dulcinea's existence. She can exist both within and outside time. Her mental novels largely layer and move seamlessly around different times, whereas her physical experience is still framed by an apocalyptic sensation, rooted in time.

Another characteristic of Muñiz-Huberman's writing is the treatment of transgression. Muñiz-Huberman chooses to include themes and techniques that transgress taboos and boundaries, where, as Muñiz-Huberman writes, the darkness that so many carry within can be examined naturally.[47] This can come in the form of incest, for example when we find out that Amadis may be Dulcinea's brother. Conflating the pain and love Dulcinea felt for her deceased brother with Amadis, the reader never knows if Amadis is simply part of Dulcinea's imagination, whether he is separate but associated with her brother, or whether Amadis is truly Dulcinea's brother. The sexual act between them becomes a unifying force, a way to find connection among all the chaos of the world around them. Several times, they see their own reflection in each other, thus implying that our own personal fragments

45. Castilleja, "Angelina Muñiz-Huberman," 28.
46. Muñiz-Huberman, "Exile," 84.
47. Payne, "Writing," 436.

connect us to ourselves and are connected with others, especially those closest to us. Life itself is renewed through transgression. Payne also notes that Muñiz-Huberman sees her rewriting of classical figures (through intertexts) as an act of transgression that highlights the experiences of writers in exile: "such attitudes do not affirm traditional ways of viewing myth. . . . They tend to imply imminent disaster, the existence of ulterior motives, the reverse of every coin, the vulnerability of established boundaries, and the mutability of structure."[48] Thus, Dulcinea imagines instead of being imagined. Her shift from an idealized Golden Age Spanish literary figure to a creative, twentieth-century Hispanic-Mexican writer-narrator shows exactly that kind of reinvention. Zamudio similarly asserts that Muñiz-Huberman's playfulness and irony transgress our familiar readings of well-known texts, such as the Bible, and especially the Song of Songs; chivalric characters, such as Amadis; and fairy tales, such as when she cites Dulcinea, who states that as a child in exile, she never heard "Once upon a time. . . ."[49] These rereadings of familiar literary references decenter canonical interpretations and instead center alternate voices, such as those living in exile. Just as writers in exile transgress national boundaries through their existence, they transgress literary boundaries—through style, genre, language, themes, and intertexts—as a way to carve out space for difference, for new ways of seeing the world.

This new way of seeing the world is key to interpretations of Dulcinea. When faced with interpreting an overarching interpretation of the novel, many scholars have highlighted Dulcinea's unique characterization. First, Dulcinea transgresses the very purpose of storytelling by insisting that she is only "writing" for herself through her "mental novel." The irony that we are reading a written text by an author-narrator who abhors written texts is the first indication that Dulcinea inhabits a world with which the reader is not familiar. Her profound silence with others amid the proliferation of words in the book the reader holds only further emphasizes the metafictional disconnect between protagonist and reader. Yet, Dulcinea dialogues openly and continuously with herself. So, how do we make sense of this apparent contradiction, this transgression of normative written and oral communication? Howard Mancing writes, "Rarely has the enchanted world of autism been so movingly and authentically evoked, and the intertextual Cervantes connection deeply enriches an extraordinary literary achievement."[50] Dulcinea's rich inner world suggests that what people know is not limited to what they are able to say aloud or write.

---

48. Payne, 437.
49. Zamudio, *Exilio*, 85–87.
50. Mancing, "Dulcinea del Toboso," 60.

Another critical interpretation we see repeatedly is that Dulcinea is insane, either because of a mental illness, such as schizophrenia, or due to the trauma of exile. Payne suggests that the novel is a "bid for psychic survival and the affirmation of displaced identity."[51] Dulcinea lives alone in her inner world, unable to function in in the world around her. In fact, Muñiz-Huberman has suggested that, in one possible interpretation, the car in which Dulcinea travels may be taking her to a psychiatric hospital.[52] The novel itself has been publicized for its "schizophrenic world" or, in Muñiz-Huberman's words, its "literary schizophrenia," due to the many stories and dialogues the narrator continuously plays in her head.[53] Zamudio links Dulcinea's schizophrenic insanity both to her inability to distinguish her identity from her literary namesake and the "insane" actions of the people around her.[54] Much like Don Quixote, Dulcinea would rather inhabit her fictionalized world than follow the ridiculous and sometimes horrific "reality" of the people around her who insist on superficial social interactions and whose body language betrays their false words. Dulcinea is unable to see herself as an integrated subject according to the ways in which others would understand her. So she refuses to try and inhabit what others call "reality." Muñiz-Huberman writes that the novel "embodies madness through the multiple voices of exile" wherein "the fragile line between sanity and insanity has ceased to exist: these planes become confused and interwoven. . . . When everyone else denies reason and justice, only one formula remains: the rationality of the irrational. As a person in exile, you have to choose that category."[55] Therefore, sanity is defined by the majority—someone who cannot fit into that reality is deemed mad. The result is that the exiled person turns to other ways of surviving the madness of not belonging.

In contrast, Zamora suggests that Dulcinea's "undifferentiated mental state might imply schizophrenia, or at least acute depression. Rather, Dulcinea suffers from what [Walter] Benjamin diagnosed as the twentieth-century's sickness, the storm of progress" that accounts for her multiple stories and her need to connect them all, ultimately creating a storm that is "personal, political, and aesthetic."[56] Therefore, Zamora sees Dulcinea's fragmentary and potentially "insane" inner dialogue as a reflection of our modern lives, seeking to balance the varying histories, narratives, expectations, and social norms that characterize a more global world in which wars

---

51. Payne, "A World," 46.
52. Angelina Muñiz-Huberman, pers. comm.
53. Muñiz-Huberman, De cuerpo, 35.
54. Zamudio, Exilio, 114.
55. Muñiz-Huberman, Canto, 173, 185, translation mine.
56. Zamora, Usable, 159.

and injustice, among other things, create situations where people inhabit complex spaces, both externally and internally. Dulcinea's unusual narrative is a way to address such complexity within her own aesthetics.

Despite Dulcinea's quest for knowledge, the end of the novel leaves that journey open to interpretation. Several different explanations have surfaced, each one trying to resolve the question of how or whether Dulcinea leaves the circularity of the beltway, her stories, or her exile. Payne writes that the madness of exile drives Dulcinea to suicide or death as a way to "point zero" or her own apocalypse caused by her "disenchantment."[57] Yet, Payne links this endpoint to both death and the potential of a new beginning. On the one hand, she argues that the ending could emphasize the ourbouros, an unending circle and Carl Jung's symbol of individuation.[58] However, consistent with other parts of the novel, conflicting resolutions occupy the same space: "It is undeniable that Dulcinea leaves the Periférico (the circular thinking that torments her), whether en route to death, madness, a new life, or any other possibility divined by the reader."[59] Zamudio also interprets the ending ambivalently. She references the Book of Revelation and concludes that the seven seals, seven being a perfect number to represent a complete cycle, like the days in a week, represents the completion of Dulcinea's cycle of her mental novel, signaling completion.[60] But she also states that considering Muñiz-Huberman's proclivity for circularity, we must keep open the possibility that everything will ceaselessly continue repeating.[61] Dolores Rangel highlights the angry and vengeful tone of the Apocalypse that Dulcinea also feels inside, which only abates at the end of the novel when it is destroyed by Dulcinea's death by suicide. However, she also sees this apocalyptic writing as cathartic and revelatory, in which Dulcinea processes her exile through a silent, introspective process. Therefore, her death is symbolic, literary, and "in the process of death, Dulcinea emerges, finding peace and apparently a reconciliation with herself and God."[62] On the other hand, Zamora writes, "Perhaps at the end of *Dulcinea encantada*, there is a revelation of nothing— 'the nothingness of Revelation.' . . . Dulcinea is a messenger without a message; her indeterminate revelation is offered, perhaps as an antidote to the storm of progress."[63] Zamora sees the novel as ultimately destructive, perhaps something never to be recovered, or perhaps" (rarely) the reader may glimpse

---

57. Payne, "A World," 59–61; Payne, "Writing," 455–57.
58. Payne, "A World," 59.
59. Payne, 61.
60. Zamudio, *Exilio*, 139.
61. Zamudio, 122.
62. Rangel, "Creación," 132, translation mine.
63. Zamora, *Usable*, 163.

a means to redeem the wreckage."[64] Without doubt, the ending of the novel does not lead the reader to a certain message. Dulcinea's quest, whether it ends in the moment of the crash or continues on, turns into the reader's quest. We must pick up the crumbs and make sense of the novel. In its last sentence, the doors have opened—do we go through them?

Sod

The last sentence of the novel references doors, but it gives us a hint that they aren't just car doors.[65] Muñiz-Huberman put the words "of heaven" in parenthesis. Suddenly a moment that seem rooted in a very physical act suggests a more spiritual meaning. Dulcinea's car trip does not end in the car, but rather in a possible ascension. And the mystical crumbs that have been scattered throughout the novel now seem to be the key to understanding the end. This final section of my introduction focuses on the representation of mysticism in the novel, specifically the Apocalypse, the figure of the Shechinah, and the traditional imagery of Hekhalot and Merkavah literature.

Several scholars, as well as Muñiz-Huberman herself, have noted that her work did not follow the style of many Mexicans authors when she began publishing in the 1960s and 1970s. Rather than a nationalist-realist literary style, Muñiz-Huberman employed characters and themes from medieval Europe in a way that, for her, seemed perfectly logical in Mexico "where anything was possible."[66] But it was mysticism that most interested her: "a mysticism of rupture, of a heretical nature, in which the *vías iluminativas* were my processes of intra and retrospection."[67] In this way, exile is a space of mysticism, one that ties personal and historical experiences to the divine. Catherine Caufield credits Muñiz-Huberman with originating the concept of "neomysticism" in a Mexican literary context, which Caufield then develops in her study of Mexican Jewish neo-mystical writers: "Set in historical contexts where exile is an element, neomystical texts are concerned with connection and reconnection, and with gaining a sense of the whole of life in continuity with an ineffable presence as well as an historical past and present . . . literature that refers to medieval mysticism from a lived position in the contemporary world."[68] Additionally, many mystical concepts rooted in Kab-

---

64. Zamora, 163.
65. The word "puertas" can mean both "doors" or "gates" in Spanish. Therefore, the last sentence may refer to the doors of the car, other doors, and/or the gates of heaven. In the translation—in the last line of the novel—I chose to use the word "doors" to highlight the multiple interpretations possible.
66. Muñiz-Huberman, *Canto*, 188, translation mine.
67. Muñiz-Huberman, 188, translation mine.
68. Caufield, *Shmiot Fugue*, 9.

balist thinking are Sephardic, dating back to pre-expulsion Spain. Therefore, Muñiz-Huberman can make a connection between Jewish mystical thought (that was also exiled from Spain post-1492) and her secular lived experiences as a journey toward the divine.

As we have seen, one of the intertexts for the novel is the Book of Revelation. Apocalypse in its most literal sense means "revelation," which, according to April DeConick, forms the basis of most Judeo-Christian mystical experiences.[69] Dulcinea experiences several revelations as she works through her mental novel, including the very first, authorizing her—here the relationship to "author" is intentional—to record her own memories and thoughts. Although not all apocalyptic literature emphasized eschatological themes, end-of-world imagery, including destruction and retribution, was common amid the trauma of oppression and exile; however, DeConick also points to this literature's equally important objective of personal transformation through the revelation of God's mysteries.[70] Caufield also contends that mysticism responds to the void people experience in exile, which is not only physical, but can be filled through spiritual experiences.[71] Therefore, as Dulcinea journeys though lands and her mind, she searches for an understanding of life, knowledge, belonging, and personal meaning rooted in the cosmos, beyond a simple mortal understanding. We can see this especially clearly with the medieval Dulcinea, who seeks the meaning of her story from a hermit and later the ethereal and immortal princess, Blizmanah. Both of these figures are traditional conduits to divine knowledge. In fact, we can look at her loyal companion, Amadis, and his name that could mean "loving God" ("ama a Dios"), as a reflection of her soul, which yearns to unite with God. In this way, Dulcinea shows a sustained effort to reach God, and the ending offers the open doors of divine revelation and connection.

Blizmanah is an interesting character because she evokes different concepts and images rooted in Jewish mystical thought. First, she is reminiscent of the concept of the Shekhinhah, the female aspect of God who is present with Jews in exile. In another text, Muñiz-Huberman takes this Talmudic understanding of the Shekhinah and, in her poetic style, paints an image of her as a maiden or a princess stripped of her lands who has been made blind from crying, but who sees by means of the light from within and whose tears are the "water of salvation."[72] She understands the suffering of those in exile and provides comfort:

---

69. DeConick, "Early Jewish," 1.
70. DeConick, 18–19.
71. Caufield, *Shmiot Fugue*, 174.
72. Muñiz-Huberman, *En el jardín*, 173.

Most likely she is the invisible point of the communion between heaven and earth. The emanation of divine breath that protects her dispersed people. Their consolation in exile and a concealing cloak that protects from danger. The divine dwelling that will one day be reached, when everything is consumed at the end of times.[73]

The quote reminds us that God is with us in the most vulnerable of places: the limbo of exile, our earthly world, in ourselves when we don't feel rooted. The cloak evokes the sukkah shalom, or shelter of peace and safety that Jews pray for in evening prayers. The divine dwelling, called Malchut or Shekhinah, is the lowest of the Kabbalistic sefirot, from where we may feel God's presence.[74] Blizmanah similarly comforts Dulcinea and Amadis. In her cave, they are well cared for and, ultimately, she offers them some peace. Although meeting Blizmanah is not the end of their journey, Dulcinea sees in a new way. Blizmanah helps her to understand her journey better. It is after Blizmanah helps Dulcinea and Amadis with their story that the car crashes, leading the reader to wonder if it is not merely a car crash, but rather the end of times.[75]

Both medieval Dulcinea and Blizmanah are princesses. In the Jewish Kabbalistic tradition, the Zohar uses the metaphor of lovers, like a knight and his princess, to represent the relationship of man to God through the Torah.[76] Like a princess whom the knight can only glimpse in her chambers, the divine knowledge of the Torah is revealed to its readers in glimpses:

He knows that out of love for him
she revealed herself for that one moment
to awaken love in him.
. . .
This is why the Torah reveals and conceals herself.
With love she approaches her lover
to arouse love with him.[77]

---

73. Muñiz-Huberman, 174, translation mine.

74. Kabbalists developed a system of understanding the aspects of God through ten sefirot, or vessels, that contain Godly emanations or energy. As the lowest sefirah, Malchut or the female form, called the Shekhinah, is closest to humans. Muñiz-Huberman describes the Shekhinah as "the release of divine breath that protects the people in their dispersion." Muñiz-Huberman, En el jardín, 174, translation mine. For an introductory reading about Kabbalah and the sefirot, see Matt, The Essential Kabbalah.

75. Interestingly, some scholars have interpreted Cervantes's Dulcinea as a symbol of the Shekhinah since she is never seen but is always with Don Quixote. See McGaha, "Hidden Jewish Meaning," 175, 182.

76. The Zohar is one of the principal texts of Kabbalah. Written in Aramaic and attributed to Simeon ben Yohai, it was discovered by Moses de León in thirteenth-century Spain, although most academic scholars now believe de León was the author of the text. Comprised of several tomes, it is a mystical commentary on the Torah and one of the most important sources of Kabbalistic thought.

77. Matt, Essential Kabbalah, 141–42. This citation is from the parable of "The Old Man and the Ravishing Maiden" from the Zohar (2:94b–95a, 99a–b, 105b, 114a; Sava de-Mishpatim). See Matt's

Knowledge is both revealed and concealed, always there, but mostly concealed at first. The true scholar of Torah engages in a quest for revelation through his dedication. This seductive play between the maiden princess and her lover is replicated many times in the novel. Dulcinea's stories are all about finding true, deep love, sometimes through a search for Amadis and sometimes (or always) for something beyond the two of them. Like the lover-knight, Dulcinea finds love only in glimpses. Muñiz-Huberman rewrites the same story in "Repeated History," in which the princess (or Torah) states, "Now you understand its true meaning and how many mysteries were contained in that sign with which I called you that first day?"[78] The lover who truly understands the mysteries is the one who loves the Torah, who dedicates himself to understanding the words of the Torah through that divine love. In this case, that lover is Dulcinea, and it should be noted that Muñiz-Huberman creates a female mystic within a historically masculine tradition. Dulcinea is not only a princess, but a lover seeking signs and understanding, from her first revelation in the beginning of the novel, through her journeys and love for Amadis. And while the Torah itself is never explicitly mentioned, Dulcinea uses excerpts from and references to the Song of Songs to highlight the motif of the lovers, and ultimately the relationship between God and (wo)man. Throughout the novel, there are glimpses of mystical understanding, but it is at the end that true ascension to God is possible.

The medieval Kabbalistic imagery of the Shekhinah and the metaphor of the mystical lovers are not the only ways to interpret the novel. In fact, we can find imagery from earlier Jewish Hekhalot and Merkavah traditions, which reinforce that Dulcinea's journeys are not only historical, but also mystical.[79] Imagery in *Enchanted Dulcinea* evokes mystical traditions that begin with the Book of Ezekiel and other apocryphal writings.

Hekhalot literature is concerned with the journey to understand and experience God through ascension through divine palaces, often in multiples of seven (like the number of seals in the novel). As mystics progress, they may see and experience many things, all of which bring them closer to God: "Before visions are granted and attained, adepts are expected to expand their perceptions beyond an ordinary human perspective and to gain awareness."[80] In the novel, Dulcinea goes through a process of turning inward, gradually

---

notes about the parable on pages 210–12.

78. Muñiz-Huberman, *En el jardín*, 202, translation mine.

79. There are debates about from when Hekhalot and Merkavah literature date. Some date it back to the first century CE while others date it later in the rabbinic period. See chapter 1 in Arbel for more on the origins and authors of these early mystical texts. See also April D. DeConick's *Paradise Now*.

80. Arbel, *Beholders*, 29.

losing the desire to speak and interact in the human world. In fact, Muñiz-Huberman writes that Dulcinea "gives in" to revelation, and as she loses herself to the mystical process, she moves closer to "un-representation" (just like Don Quixote's Dulcinea, who is never truly represented in the text).[81] Through a mystical lens, Dulcinea begins to separate herself from other people and to see the human world with new eyes as she opens herself to understanding something bigger than herself.

Although it is through a twentieth-century perspective, we can see several references to palaces and caves that allude to Dulcinea's process of discovery. Medieval Dulcinea leaves her own palace, where she seems to have everything she needs, to begin a quest for what she doesn't know. In each of the seven seals, Dulcinea, through her different stories, progresses in her journey. The most obvious mystical experiences happen to the medieval Dulcinea, such as when she and Amadis ascend mountains to try to find the hermit, but are not yet able to "see" the signs right before their eyes. They also explore Blizmanah's palace, which exists in a cave.[82] There Dulcinea and Amadis experience something other than the earthly world they know. Blizmanah's ethereal presence is reminiscent of the angels found in Hekhalot literature and Dulcinea and Amadis seek her messages and guidance.[83]

But one could argue that the other Dulcineas also have journeys that spark otherworldly experiences: nineteenth-century Dulcinea visits a convent, a cave, and a psychiatric hospital. In each of these spaces, she searches for Amadis, or love, in the shapes and faces that surround her and she is transformed; for example, after leaving the caves with the Marquise, Dulcinea feels as if she could fly, or ascend, a common characteristic of this mystical literature. Twentieth-century Dulcinea inhabits a car for the duration of her mental novel, and when it stops (or crashes), she finds herself in front of a castle, or the final palace. And it is this car that connects the Hekhalot imagery to the Merkavah imagery in the novel.

---

81. Muñiz-Huberman, *Canto*, 184, 186.

82. Symbolically caves are often sites of deep introspection, associated with (re)birth and/or death. Returning to *Don Quixote* as intertext, is should be noted that when Don Quixote enters the Cave of Montesinos in chapters 22–24 in volume 2 of the novel, he has visions that alter the course of his adventures, including the revelation that his beloved Dulcinea has been enchanted, appearing as a country peasant. Ironically, Dulcinea's "enchanted" appearance was the most realistic vision of the woman Quixote had first seen as the illustrious Dulcinea. After Quixote's disillusion in the Cave and his subsequent failure to break Dulcinea's spell, the knight returns home melancholic, himself disenchanted. The Cave becomes the catalyst for Quixote to consider his own perceptions of imagination and reality and his place in the world.

83. Payne reads the ending of the novel according to a more Christian mystical journey, including the castles: "the castle corresponds to St. Teresa's *Castillo interior*, the abrupt rocks to the *vía purgativa*, the light to the *vía iluminativa*, the eye of God to the *vía unitativa*, and the open doors to the journey's end." Payne, "Writing," 455.

Merkavah literature is connected to Hekhalot literature in that many of its stories utilize throne imagery stemming from its first manifestation in chapter 1 of Ezekiel. Known as a foundational mystical text, the Book of Ezekiel describes the prophet's vision of the chariot-throne upon which God sits. Ezekiel's vivid description of the spinning wheels held up by mythical creatures and the magnificent throne of God influenced many later mystical visions, and his imagery introduced the concept of a God who travels with Jewish people in exile.[84] In *Enchanted Dulcinea* we also see thrones, chariots, and even God (on a throne) from the Book of Revelation.

Although other scholars have studied Muñiz-Huberman's use of the Book of Revelation in the novel, none have connected it with the Hekhalot and Merkavah traditions. However, if you look at the two citations Muñiz-Huberman uses in the first and second seals of the novel, they each include descriptions of God; in the second one, God is clearly on a throne. In fact, Cameron Afzal uses the same exact citation we find in *Enchanted Dulcinea* to make a case for reading the Book of Revelation within the Merkavah tradition, arguing for "an emerging Jewish *Merkabah* mysticism" in which Jewish and Christian apocalyptic writings overlap, and in the case of the Book of Revelation, show evidence of Merkavah exegesis.[85] This connection between *Enchanted Dulcinea* and the palace/chariot literary traditions suggests that the inclusion of the Book of Revelation is not only another clue linking the novel to Jewish mysticism, but is also the key to a further layer of interpretation.

It is here that I would suggest the ultimate revelation lies: as Dulcinea travels the circular Periférico, she mentions the sound and feel of the wheels spinning. She even refers to herself as one in a long line of family members who travel in carriages and even chariots. The repetition of circles evokes the spinning wheels of Ezekiel's mystical chariot. Arbel notes that wagon or chariot images stemming from Ezekiel are ways in which "the spiritual-contemplative journey becomes concrete."[86] In this way, Dulcinea is able to use the car as a metaphor for both the movement of exile and the vehicle of spiritual ascension. In the end, the car seems to crash and she has the opportunity to ascend, but what if the crash is the ascension itself? I would suggest that the entire journey in the car was a mystical journey—the

---

84. Ezekiel's mystical vision occurs while he and other Israelites were living in exile in Babylonia after the destruction of the First Temple of Jerusalem in 586 BCE. While Jewish life centered around the Temple where it was believed that God dwelled, Ezekiel's visions suggested that God could travel with the people of Israel in their dispersion and, therefore, both God and Judaism were not tied only to one geographical space.

85. Afzal, "Wheels of Time," 196.

86. Arbel, *Beholders*, 83.

mystical journey—that takes her to the final palace, the palace where God is sitting on a throne. Her inner journey, where she peels back the layers of her earthly existence, lead her to true love, divine love.

Ultimately, *Enchanted Dulcinea* is a novel about revelations. It both reveals and conceals. Dulcinea herself, seeking revelation, is like the rabbis in Pardes: in one interpretation she dies—her situation is simply intolerable, and she is unable to process it. In another, she circles in secular thoughts, anxious to find a sense of belonging, perhaps finding a way through her own narratives in a form of rebirth in the end. Another reading would see her as lost in her own insanity, perhaps of failing to conform or lost in the trauma of war and displacement. But in another interpretation, Dulcinea ascends to God, finding transcendent meaning and love. Muñiz-Huberman certainly does not tell the reader what to think. We are on our own journey. So let us return to Pardes for insight. Perhaps one interpretation of the story of Pardes is not about four individuals at all, but rather about reader response. We are all those readers, and at any given time, we may travel one path over another, seeking insight. In the novel, meaning is both concealed and revealed from seal to seal. In fact, it is the framework of seals that holds the key to the text:

> The significance of the seals displayed by the descenders to the Merkavah . . . may be understood in light of the original function of the seal in the ancient Near East, and its depiction in narratives. Emerged as a legal mark of ownership or contractual obligation by an individual, it has been suggested that the seal represents and comprises the "essence" of a person. A similar concrete depiction seems to be suggested by the Hekhalot and Merkavah descriptions. Qualified adepts who can demonstrate their merits and "essence" by showing the seals can pass unhindered and enter God's palaces.[87]

By framing her text as a series of seals, Muñiz-Huberman points directly to her "essence," and we, the privileged readers, catch a glimpse of her revelations. Whether we take a mystical journey with her, or whether we come to understand exile as a space of freedom to inscribe who we are, free from the narratives of others and carefully crafted with the infinite possibilities of language, we can see that the novel takes us through a process of transformation. It is this process of transformation and rebirth that ties the work together and, like mystics, in a quest for knowledge and understanding, we can explore our own layers that we may have been concealed to others and even to ourselves.

---

87. Arbel, *Beholders*, 94.

Finally, in fully exploring the "essence" of the text, I return to the metaphor of this novel as similar to a crypto-Jew. *Enchanted Dulcinea* never explicitly points to its Jewish context. A reader could read the entire novel and never think of Judaism since so much of its Jewish content is merely evoked or coded, and more suggestive of a process than furthering a plot; however, as I have sought to show in this introduction, through a close reading, it is clear that Muñiz-Huberman reveals the novel's profound Jewish roots and, with *Enchanted Dulcinea*, contributes an important text to the canon of Sephardic women writers.

Rebecca Marquis

Enchanted Dulcinea

~

THE FIRST SEAL

The border between the interior and the exterior is minimal.

—attributed to Paul Klee

One day, riding in a car on the Periferico,[1] barely listening to the words of the other passengers, the revelation comes to you. Yes, the revelation. The revelation or feeling that you've discovered something. You thought you didn't remember anything, you thought you lacked memories. Because you just lived off those that had been passed on to you, those you'd been told. But suddenly, among the words in the background that you barely understand, the revelation occurs: yes, you have memories. Your own memories. Belonging to you. To no one else. Yours. Exclusively yours.

Your parents and your teachers had taught you so much. Not "so much." Everything. You were indebted. What small memories did you possess? Not one. Not a single one. Confronted with the grandeur of History, who were you, humble being who looked upward? Toward God? No, toward your parents, toward your teachers. Enormous personalities. Who would tell you everything, and you listening, listening, spellbound, not like now when conversations slip away from you amid the background noise.

In other words, yes, you possessed memories. Yes, I possess memories. Not the glorious ones of my ancestors. But they're also good memories. I won't be able to pass them on because I'm not familiar with the art of speaking. But I'll be able to think them. I'll be able to splice them together inwardly. Words overflow in me, they pile upon each other, I don't know what to do with so many of them. But don't compel me to speak, don't ask me anything, because I will only be able to respond yes or no. Within the speaking world, I'm reduced to those two brief words. Still, the most important of all. The most feared and the most frightening. Yes. No. They belong to the external world. The one that doesn't count. I remain in the internal world. I don't know what the passengers in this car will say, but if I tell them a yes or a no, they will be content. Anyway, those who speak only hear themselves. As long as you keep silent and look them in the eyes, it's enough. They consider you the best of listeners.

---

1. The Peripheral Highway, also called the Peripheral Ring, is the outer beltway that encircles Mexico City.

So, memories reside within. Any memory. Every memory. Because in addition to my memories, other memories are added. Those that so many times I heard or read or invented.

Behold Dulcinea who inhabits a stone castle atop a high hill. Tall turrets and the spacious courtyard of the tower keep. Interior gardens with fountains of clear water and birds that sing among the branches. Rose gardens of pink and red and yellow and white blooms. Golden cages for birds from exotic lands. A well of sculpted stone. Carved benches. In the four corners, orange trees with perfumed blossoms.

Dulcinea strolls along the paths. As she walks, she breathes in the fragrances and enjoys the freshness of the air that brushes her skin. Her ample garments float lightly. She carries a book and is searching for a place to sit and read. She heads to her favorite corner where there is no wall because the steep cliff replaces it, over which she can see the sea below, breaking against sharp rocks, and where on the cerulean horizon she occasionally glimpses the sails of distant ships and dreams of sailing away.

Dulcinea doesn't yearn to live in another era because she lives in that era. She doesn't yearn for a castle because she lives in a castle. She doesn't yearn for land or sea because she has them. She doesn't long for time to be slow and unmeasured because she knows no haste. She doesn't long for peace because nothing disturbs her.

Her world is enclosed within her rooms and the grounds that surround the castle. And there below, the sea.

Halls, chambers, and bedrooms. Hallways and corridors. The library is large and warm, the armchairs are comfortable, and the large, carved mahogany table invites one to rest a book on it, or, even better, to write. The big leaded glass windows open to a view of the sea and even the faint sound of waves, at this height, arrive softened and lazy. In winter, the great fireplace warms the room even more and distracts Dulcinea, who spends countless hours contemplating the playful flames and jumping sparks.

I am Dulcinea. In this car, on the southern section of the Periferico, not listening to the other passengers. Sifting through my memories. Discovering them. But without saying a word. I won't say a word. People say such strange things. It's not like in books. No, it's not. I have a book here with me. A book always accompanies me. Wherever I go. A book is good company. The best. It doesn't talk. You read it. Anywhere and anytime.

Do you remember the day you first arrived in Mexico, Dulcinea? Yes, I do remember. It was raining, do you remember? Yes, the train had stopped at the Balbuena station. Big black umbrellas were waiting. But I also remember the stagecoach from Puebla, the muddy road and the persistent hail. It took a few days of travel, with the danger of being robbed while we passed through Rio Frio.[2]

Dulcinea, Dulcinea, search for your memories and don't invent them. I'm not making anything up. It's like this. Everything I've read I carry within me. Therefore, it's mine. The castles. Castles I've never seen or I'll never see. But castles I know very well. Because I've been there.

Dulcinea lives alone, but noble knights guard and revere her like the high princess that she is, owner of lands that cannot be crossed in a day's riding on a fast steed.

When it rains, it rains softly. From the tall leaded-glass windows, Dulcinea sees how the water runs down the leaves and trunks of trees. Dressed in black velvet and a high, white lace collar, she enjoys the rain, the sound of raindrops hitting the glass, and the liquid trickling transparently on transparency.

It's pleasurable to see the landscape from inside, the warm sensation of feeling protected, safe from the lightning yet glimpsing its momentary luminosity.

As a child she'd escaped the castle to feel the purifying rain on her face and body. She'd raised her face to the sky and savored drops of water, while in the distance, gargoyles with terrible mouths spewed the elemental liquid.

The raindrops are drumming on the roof of the car and the windshield wipers are unable to separate the water from the glass. It doesn't matter where the car is going. Dulcinea has time in front of her. Above all, since she decided not to speak. Only to herself. Just to think, nothing else.

Along with the revelation, she transforms the art of memory into the art of writing. She's going to create a book inside her head. It will be neither oral nor written. It will be a mental book. The first to be composed. An internal book, in perpetual creation. A book that is repeated or resumed at any point.

---

2. Río Frío, about fifty miles from Mexico City, is a popular stop on the mountain pass of the famous Camino Real (Royal Road) between Mexico City and Veracruz. Río Frío was made popular by the novel, *Los bandidos de Río Frío* (1889–1893; *The Bandits from Río Frío*), by Manuel Payno, which paints a picture of early nineteenth-century Mexican society.

One that is redone and never the same. That exists and does not exist. That will live in her and last as long as her life. That if it were to be published would take years to read, and no one would know which was the definitive version. It would span all styles and would begin like Snoopy's books: "It was a dark and stormy night." Or better yet: "It was night and nevertheless it was raining."[3]

A book produced without haste. Words appearing and disappearing in the very process. Without remorse, omission, or error. Perfect. As if written in sand or sea.

Dulcinea accompanied Madame Frances Calderon de la Barca on many of her travels through Mexican lands. As she was traveling by stagecoach, from Puebla to Mexico City, she was excited about what she would see and learn when she joined the Marquise. She'd left her homeland of Toboso when the Marquise selected her to be her lady's companion.

Dulcinea was fourteen when she arrived in Mexico in April of 1948. She'd disembarked from the train in the Balbuena Station, tired and sick to her stomach. Her next memory is the journey through the streets. With the rain drenching everything and the roads flooded. People with pants and skirts rolled up and shoes in their hands. And her excitement or feeling of adventure at having just arrived in a new country. Leaving behind European wars, death, bloodshed, bodies and feelings torn apart.

But the day will come. The end of days and the revelation will come. As it has been declared, so it will come. Your neighbor who sells cakes, exquisite Viennese tortes, proclaims the coming of the millennium with every cake you buy from her. Behold—it comes with clouds and every eye will see it. I am the alpha and the omega. The beginning and the end.

His head and his hairs were white like wool, as white as snow; and his eyes were as a flame of fire;

And his feet like unto fine brass, as if they burned in a furnace; and his voice as the sound of many waters.

---

3. This sentence in Spanish is ironic due to the non sequitur "however" or "nevertheless" and mocks low-quality literature, lacking both logic and clarity. It has shown up in Snoopy cartoons in Spanish in which the famous dog aspires to be a writer.

And he had in his right hand seven stars: and out of his mouth went a sharp twoedged sword: and his countenance was as the sun shineth in his strength.

And when I saw him, I fell at his feet as dead. And he laid his right hand upon me, saying unto me, Fear not; I am the first and the last:

I am he that liveth, and was dead; and, behold, I am alive for evermore, Amen; and have the keys of hell and of death.

Write the things which thou hast seen, and the things which are, and the things which shall be hereafter;[4]

What are the people traveling in the car with Dulcinea saying? What are they murmuring? What are they whispering? Nothing, they're not saying a thing. Because they're saying what's happening around them (they say, for example, how it's raining) and this is the same as saying nothing. When what one ought to be saying is what is not happening. What has never happened and what will never happen. That's the only reality and the only possible reason for breaking the silence. What you are thinking is worthy and therefore, you will never say it. You do your best to make it seem trivial.

Hence, Dulcinea doesn't listen to words. Words aren't even like the drumming of raindrops on the glass. Neither unique nor fresh. Of course, they trickle with impunity. Spoken words. Fleshy words. Other words aren't like that: unpronounceable and hidden words: silence.

That's why Dulcinea has gradually lost the ability to speak. Why speak? If no one listens or understands. If no one notices that someone isn't speaking. Eternal monologues without meaning. Moreover, nothing has ever happened to me, nor do I remember what people tell me about others. I don't talk about the weather because saying it's raining when it's raining or it's cold when it's cold is so obviously Cartesian, it's not worth it. Mentioning the latest film you saw is to subject yourself to such contrary opinions as someone liked it a lot and someone else didn't like it at all. As for books, books, books—what's that? Who reads them? Who believes in them? Me, only me. I'm the only one who reads, who knows there are books, who has them, who keeps them, who treasures them. Who carries them with me. Here in my bag—and I open it once in a while to check—is the one I'm reading now. I caress it and feel it. I couldn't live without it. I'm a "bookist": I believe in books and I love books.[5] Chivalric novels. I collect chivalric novels. Sir Tristan of Leonis,

---

4. Rev 1:14–19 (King James Version).

5. Here Muñiz-Huberman underscores Dulcinea's love of books by evoking Fernando de Rojas's *Celestina* when Calisto proclaims his enduring love for Melibea: "I am a Melibean, I adore Melibea, I beleeve in Melibea, and I love Melibea." Rojas, *Celestina*, 26. Both Rojas and Muñiz-Huberman create neologisms to highlight the intensity of their characters' love.

Sir Olivante of Laura, Sir Palmerin of England, Sir Belianis of Greece, The Famous Knight Tirant lo Blanch, Sir Florismarte of Hircania, Sir Florisel of Niquea, The Knight Platir, The Knight of the Cross, The Great Conquest of Lands Beyond the Seas, the Knight Cifar, The Adventures of Esplandian. And, above all, Sir Amadis of Gaul. He is my guide and model, as he was for Don Quixote. With the advantage that I've fallen in love with him. And he with me.

One day I met him, years ago, and what we experienced together did not appear in his novel, but I carry it written within myself.

After the rain stopped, Dulcinea threw a thick wool cape over her shoulders and walked toward the pine forest that descends to the beach. As she continued walking on her favorite paths, beneath the canopy of branches or over the terrain cushioned with ferns and dead leaves, she felt a presence behind the trunks or thickets, sometimes high up and sometimes down low. Crackling noises and labored breathing. A vanishing shadow. Almost a whisper. Perhaps a shape or something moving. Something sliding. Something stopping. Not wanting to hide, rather wanting not to frighten. In a clearing in the pine forest rather close to the sandy waves, she wasn't too surprised to see him there waiting for her. Leaning on a tree trunk, dressed in the ways of other lands, a foreigner of uncommon features. Straight blond hair. Protruding cheekbones. Almond-shaped eyes. A straight nose. Thin lips. Tall and slender. Dressed in black with a dagger in his belt. (A Bergmanian character. Amadis von Sydow.[6]) His arms are crossed in front of him and one foot is resting on a fallen rock. He seems to be waiting. Dulcinea moves toward him and he is her mirror image because he doesn't speak. (Even then she spoke very little. In that era.) Each one wonders if the other is real. Both feel the desire to touch each other's faces, feel their skin.

At that moment, it begins to rain again. Swift, heavy drops of water strike their bodies. At first, they don't notice. They don't care. Until Dulcinea grabs the foreigner by the hand and runs, guiding him to a cabin in the middle of the forest, a refuge for wayfarers. Inside, Amadis lights a fire and Dulcinea sits on a bench.

---

6. This is a playful refence to Ingmar Bergman's film *The Seventh Seal* (1957) and its main character, a medieval knight, played by Max von Sydow. Here Amadis is the knight. Both the film and this novel allude to the Book of Revelation to explore theme of silence and death.

The stagecoach could have been robbed in Rio Frio, but the driver had con-served the horses' energy so when they arrived at the dangerous area they could cross as quickly as possible. He succeeded.

Dulcinea contemplates the volcanoes.[7] Their perfect shapes and the low snow at this time of year.

In fact, on the Periferico you can think of several novels, not just one. But they aren't novels. It is life itself happening. The people traveling in the car talk and talk. They don't stop talking. They are life itself escaping through words. Because every word pronounced is time. Lost time. For me, on the other hand, time does not pass. I don't speak, I don't lose time. It's another secret I've discovered but won't be able to transmit.

Who is the person driving? Amadis? He has Amadis's long, straight neck. It must be Amadis. The other passengers are difficult to identify and yet they seem to know me. Just because they call me by name doesn't mean they know me. No. Only that they know my name. But they don't know me. If they knew me. If they knew that Amadis and I. If they knew that Amadis. If they knew that I.

To drive along the Periferico is to travel without a view. It's a rumbling of cement. It's throbbing asphalt. It's the tiger without a tree to climb. It's cloudy skies and opaque glass. So, better to think about the Cuernavaca highway.[8] The first highway I got to know, shortly after arriving in Mexico. Back then I imagined I would be taken by stagecoaches, with dangers and adventures. The plains before Tres Marias, with their high pastures, belonged to me.[9] Not to mention the highest pines. And the needles and pinecones carpeting the ground. I would press my forehead against the hard glass of the window of the shuttle in which I was traveling. The van, that now nonexistent shuttle van that used to make the rounds on the Mexico City–Cuernavaca–Mexico City route.

---

7. Dulcinea would be contemplating the famous volcano Popocatepetl whose name in Nahuatl (the language of the Aztecs, or Mexica) means "smoking mountain," due to its frequent activity. Known affectionately as "El Popo," this volcano figures prominently in literature and the daily lives of Mexicans. To its north lies another volcano, Iztaccihuatl, meaning "white woman," referring to its shape of a sleeping woman. There is a popular legend, a love story much like that of Romeo and Juliet, about the two volcanos who represent an Aztec warrior (Popo) and a princess (Izta). Izta was told by a jealous rival that Popo had died at war. Overwhelmed by grief, Izta dies before she finds out Popo is really alive. The gods turned them into volcanos, covered in snow, eternally at rest near each other. Their unrequited love is the reason for Popo's frequent eruptions. See Orozco, "Legends."

8. The Cuernavaca Highway, the "old highway," was replaced by a newer, modern one for quick travel. However, this scenic highway is popular for Mexicans who want to get away and take vaca-tions in cabins in the woods along this route between Mexico City and Cuernavaca.

9. Tres Marias is a very old, small town on the Cuernavaca Highway.

How nice that I can speak of disappeared things. Of things that no one knew and will never know. In other words, I have my own memories. I don't depend on the memories of others. I have my own life. Corners that are exclusively mine. Will I finally be myself?

Dulcinea remembers those first trips to Cuernavaca. The landscape was very important. On the old highway, of course. That highway that cut a gray path through pine forests and fields. Fighting against the grass and undergrowth. Dulcinea, what were the colors? The colors were green and brown and sky blue. Mostly. I don't remember the others. And the smells, do you remember? Yes, if I opened the window, the smell of pine and wet leaves. Sometimes burnt hay. What else? Keep asking me. I like it when I ask myself.

Cuernavaca's main square: you would sit on the wrought iron benches. Of course, I remember. You would see and hear birds returning to sleep on thick branches. And I loved it. The dark and cool corridors of the hotels. Hotels whose names you no longer remember. Some I do remember: the Iberia, the Marik, Los Canarios. Others, I've forgotten. But not the hallways and black and white tiles, the big flowerpots on either side, the dining room, the half-remembered kitchen, the bedrooms. Because hotel rooms aren't interesting. So different from the room I would want. With so many ghosts imprinted there. Nude bodies on the walls. Stains that are no longer there. Saliva. Blood. Semen. Sweat. Urine. Feces. You notice the presence of everything. Imagined absence. More terrible because of your imagination. Since childhood you felt disgust. Yes, since forever. You would stop eating if you felt disgust. Your throat would close. When you went on the train with the other Spanish kids, you wouldn't eat the bread made of potato peels and preferred to remain hungry. When they took us from the wooded area of Monino to Saratov, the region of the Volga Germans. Hitler's soldiers were penetrating into Russian territory and the children of the International House were taken farther from the danger. Do you remember, in the train they gave you that inedible bread and a greasy sausage? Which I wouldn't eat. I only drank cup after cup of tea with a bit of sugar. And you slept crowded in with other children and there were lice and bedbugs. You kept yourself apart and didn't speak. You weren't speaking even before then. Since the day your parents said goodbye to you on the boat that would carry you from Spain to Russia with the other saved children. Why speak? Salvation is silence.

People always say the opposite. Here in the car, what do the people who are accompanying Dulcinea say? Anything. Anything that is something else. Not anything she comprehends. Or apprehends. Or intends. Or tends. For example, for her, words don't indicate a conversation to follow, but rather from one of those words, distant and foreign memories unravel, or simply become a stream of sounds. As if she were in a third room and, on top of what she was saying to herself, she was hearing conversations from the first two rooms at the same time.

Dulcinea arrived a little after the Marquise, finding her already settled and complaining of the cold. She'd ordered some thick woolen carpets to be brought and, because there was no fireplace, had placed braziers in the main rooms. The house was spacious, with a nice garden filled with a plethora of flowers, fruits, and birds, but the inside was dark and damp. At first, Dulcinea didn't care for the high beams in her room and she shivered from the cold. She went about removing the long, heavy dresses from her trunk and placing them, with the help of a servant, in the polished pine wardrobe. Suddenly, she felt scared about leaving behind familiar places and finding herself in strange lands. She almost wanted to pack up and take the stagecoach back. And the idea of so many unfamiliar people terrorized her even more. Of having to greet and speak to them.

Dulcinea dislikes Dulcinea's life in Mexico at the end of the nineteenth century. She's going to have to make substantial changes. She can't choose a dream life that is unpleasant. She sticks with the Middle Ages. The advantage to writing in your head is that you can discard whatever isn't working without regret. The recorder goes in reverse and everything is erased.

Where were we going, Dulcinea? Dulcinea, come back. I don't know what to do with my thoughts. With this waterfall—and this is no symbol—of thoughts. Because they're piling up and I don't know where to begin. I pass the days in silence, tranquil, trying to bring order to this "wordalanche." But it's not possible: I jump around, I digress, I get sad. I don't forget a thing: I accumulate and accumulate, deaf sounds, unpronounceable syllables, sentences, stories, novels. All literature. I don't know who I am now. But I repeat to myself from within. I am me. I am me. I am me. And if not, I start reading. Which is the same. Or rather, the opposite. I am not me. I am Penelope. I am Orlando. I am Rodrigo Diaz of Vivar (not Lady Jimena, such a boring lady), I am Dulcinea, I am Saint Teresa, I am one of the Brontë sisters, probably Emily. Oh, I am also Elizabeth Browning, via Virginia Woolf. But I could also be some Jewish-Hispanic cabbalist from the thirteenth century. Some famous mariner from the sixteenth century. Or some character from Walter Scott (maybe Rob Roy), or Joseph Conrad (Lord Jim?).

The truth is you're having fun, Dulcinea, you're having fun. You can't complain. No, look, I'm not complaining. Yes, I'm having fun. It's the others who aren't having fun. How boring are these people here in the car. Poor fools, they don't stop speaking. For them, words are sounds. Poor things, if I can catch something they say, for example "madness," it's not real madness. What do they know about madness?

Madness like that of the Angel of Ephesus: the one who holds the seven stars in his right hand, who walks among the seven golden candelabra, saying things like:

I know thy works, and thy labour, and thy patience, and how thou canst not bear them which are evil: and thou hast tried them which say they are apostles, and are not, and hast found them liars:

And hast borne, and hast patience, and for my name's sake hast laboured, and hast not fainted.[10]

Madness like that of the other angels: the Angel of Smyrna and the Angel of Pergamon, the Angel of Thyatira and the Angel of Sardis, the Angel of Philadelphia and the Angel of Laodicia. Sublime madness. The madness of God.

The madness of man? Nonsense. A parody of madness.

Dulcinea, after the long trip from Russia to Mexico, after having arrived ill, and after coming face-to-face with her parents, barely recognizing them, continued, little by little, to lose her ability to speak. She spoke less than in the train and the International House. But thinking: ideas bubbling. Her refuge and her solace. Enclosing herself in a wardrobe, on the floor and in the darkness, thinking and thinking. Shrunken figures, without faces and bodies. Those children from her memory, dancing about in limitless space, with nothing to support their feet. Among them, she too, a weightless,

---

10. Rev 2:2–3 (KJV).

plucked feather. Her parents? Were her parents really her parents? She didn't remember them. She didn't know who to look for among the people waiting for the travelers, and in order to hide that fact, she pretended to arrange her luggage and the jacket on her arm and her purse. Let them find her, she thought, while avoiding a glance in search of God only knows who. A disconcerted glance, confused, one that should instantaneously transform into recognition. Yes, it's them. Yes, it's her. So, Dulcinea lowered her eyes and continued adjusting and readjusting her luggage, her jacket, her purse.

In her parents' car, finally on the way to what would be her home, it occurred to Dulcinea to ask: and what if they are not my parents?

Doubt was taking root in her more and more. Those two people were strange beings. Unreal beings. They were speaking of unfamiliar things. They were asking her if she remembered the doll they had bought her just before she left Valencia for Odessa, and she was sure she never had a doll. They called her Dulce because that's what they had called her when she was little and yet no one ever called her that. In contrast, they asked her about that scar on the middle finger of her left hand, unaware she had gotten it gathering firewood in Monino. Nor did they know how much she'd enjoyed picking strawberries, mulberries, cranberries and blackberries in the region of Saratov, furtively bringing the occasional one to her mouth.

They didn't know her, nor did she know them. Their past was not the same. It was difficult to find something in common, a tenuous cord that would still unite the three of them.

No, they weren't my parents. How could it be that the first thing they asked me, still in the car, was about my brother? Why weren't they asking about me? Why were they speaking and speaking about him and not me? Was I not there sitting in the car? They were his parents, not mine.

Dulcinea kept seeing that stranger in black, by the name of Amadis, every time she would go to the forest or the beach. Without speaking, as in dreams, Amadis and Dulcinea get to know their stories. A beautiful not-line of unconnected successive points. A beginning that one senses is doomed never to end.

The stories they tell each other get longer and more perfect as the days go by. Stories each one gradually learns in silence because the words are words that do not make sounds, words you say from within, words that can reach the highest heavens. All words, all new.

Dulcinea runs on the beach with Amadis. They take off their shoes and wet their feet in the shallow waves. Fine sand slips through their toes. Warm sun bronzes their skin.

They could be siblings or they could be strangers. Two siblings who may have fallen in love.

In the distance, Dulcinea could see the fireworks in Moscow. She doesn't remember the date, but her brother was still with her. And she would most likely never forget those fireworks. Surely they were the first fireworks she saw. Sometimes, before going to sleep, she rubbed her eyes hard because she'd discovered this was also a way to see fireworks. Fireworks on the inside. And this is a good thing. Everything should be internal. We were a small group of children who went to see the fireworks. It was a very large, very green field. We leaned on a fence of thick trunks. In the distance, Moscow and the fireworks. Multicolored. All colors. So fleeting, with cascades that vanished. The white ones were almost like water. The red and blue ones hurt my eyes. Just like when sleeping. Those fireworks penetrated me without me knowing where. But my fireworks, those from within, I would always stir up and, without effort, they would explode over and over in even more beautiful and unusual forms. They would appear and reappear, escaping my field of vision. I could not capture the shape I liked, since it would rapidly transform into another. Its beauty was its brevity. Its unrepeatability. Its uniqueness. So the only thing left was the memory. Yes, I kept them in my memory. Even though I think I didn't actually see the fireworks in Moscow. It was my brother who saw them and told me about them. When I found out that by rubbing my eyes these points of light came to me, those from Moscow faded and those from inside stayed. Those from within, parading in darkness and silence.

The ones in Mexico aren't like that. The first time I heard them, I thought it was the war again. That Nazi sniper who'd caused so many deaths, perched alone in a tree. When they brought him down, the peasants battered him with sickles, hoes, and picks. Mexican rockets, firecrackers, palomas, whistlers, M-60s, moon rockets, poppers, sparklers, Roman candles, screamers, snappers, strobes. And later, the fireworks: cascades, castles, flaming bulls, wreaths. A noisy country. How it made me panic to walk the streets. I would cover my ears and blink. I didn't dare go out when they were setting off fireworks. Gunshot, from a rifle, a pistol, a machine gun.

Do I continue or not with the story of Dulcinea from the nineteenth century? I am so many stories that sometimes it's difficult to choose which one to follow. In other words, which one I am. It doesn't matter. I can keep trying. Let Dulcinea unpack and not return to her homeland. In Mexico she will get to know new landscapes. New flowers, new fruits, new birds. New faces. New clothing. (*Rebozos*—Mexican shawls.) New customs.

Her first walk through the Chapultepec woods and Castle with the Marquise provided her with a contained happiness.[11] To be able to forget the streets and instead, enjoy yourself in the diffused light between the leaves of the Mexican cypress *ahuehuetes* and smaller bushes. Different kinds of trees with Spanish moss hanging from the highest branches. They reminded the Marquise of her distant homeland and a certain druidic tone. The tranquility and solace of the wilderness, the plants heavy with wild fruits. Melancholy that is not sad but welcoming. Taking interior paths in the woods and, almost without expecting to, arriving at the lake. The silence of still water. The questioning swans: a few black swans among the white ones. Reflections of clouds, of branches, dissolving in the concentric waves formed by the swimming of the swans. ("Loose garlands of foamy roses."[12]) Sitting on the shore and giving in to lightly wetting your fingers in the water. Liquid crystal. Later, the way back, slowly, toward the carriage that would take them up the steep ascent to the castle.

That day, December 31, 1839, Frances Calderon de la Barca wrote:

From the terrace that runs round the castle, the view forms the most magnificent panorama that can be imagined. The whole valley of Mexico lies stretched out as in a map: the city itself, with its innumerable churches and convents; the two great aqueducts which cross the plain; the avenues of elms and poplars which lead to the city; the villages, lakes, and plains which surround it. To the north the magnificent cathedral of Our Lady of Guadalupe, to the south the villages of San Augustín, San Angel and Tacubaya, which seem imbosomed in trees, and look like an immense garden. And if in the plains below there are many uncultivated fields and many

11. This famous castle is located atop a hill in Mexico City's Chapultepec Park and offers a beautiful panorama of the woods in the park and the city surrounding them. Constructed from the eighteenth to the nineteenth centuries, it has been home to the national military academy, the Emperor Maximilian and his wife Carlota, and numerous presidents, including Porfirio Díaz. By 1940 it was converted into the National Museum of History, exhibiting works of art and objects from across Mexico's history, as well as salons as they appeared during the residence of Maximilian and Carlota.

12. Translation mine, from the Spanish translation of Proust as seen in *Dulcinea encantada*, 27. Moncrieff's English translation is slightly different: "moss-roses in loosened garlands." Proust, *Swann's Way.*

buildings falling into ruin—yet, with its glorious enclosure of mountains, above
which tower the two mighty volcanoes Popocatepetl and Ixtaccihuatl, the Gog and
Magog of the valley, off whose giant sides great volumes of misty clouds were roll-
ing, and with its turquoise sky forever smiling on the scene, the whole landscape as
viewed from this height is one of nearly unparalleled beauty.[13]

As long as we're speaking about landscapes, I'm content. It's what I like. Not
this gray Periferico. What is there on the Periferico? Wherever I go, it feels
as if I've been there before: factories, smoke, asphalt, cement, faded and run-
down buildings, broken glass. When will I see a tree? I never get a chance
to see a tree. The people behind me don't stop speaking. Neither do those
in front. What can you say in a closed car? If only it were open and the air
would take their breath away. Mouths would remain shut and flies would
not enter.[14]

Dulcinea and Amadis had a dream, the same dream. They should go in
search of a hermit. A hermit who would give them a clue. And that was the
whole dream. That vague. But the two of them dreamt the same thing on
the same night.

They could ignore the sign. One must understand that a sign is a sign.
Because it may not be one. Or it's possible it doesn't announce itself as one.
There must be a desire or a predisposition to recognize a sign. A pre-sign.
A light that exposes the darkness. A ray that illuminates. Then the sign is
recognized.

Whoever wants to find signs will find them. Dulcinea and Amadis decide
to set off on new paths, abandon the perfect enclosed world surrounding
them. To go in search of a hermit. As in a fairy tale they would have to con-
front what many centuries later Vladimir Propp would name as the thirty-
one functions of a fairy tale:

I Absentation, II Interdiction, III Violation, IV Reconnaissance, V Delivery, VI
Trickery, VII Complicity, VIII Villainy, IX Mediation, X Beginning counterac-
tion, XI Departure, XII The first function of the donor, XIII The hero's reaction,
XIV Provision or receipt of a magical agent, XV Spatial transference between
two kingdoms, XVI Struggle, XVII Branding, XVIII Victory, XIX Restoration,
XX Return, XXI Pursuit, XXII Rescue, XXIII Unrecognized arrival, XXIV

---

13. Calderón de la Barca, *Life in Mexico*, 116.
14. This is a play with the very well-known idiomatic expression, "En boca cerrada, no entran
moscas," which warns people against speaking indiscriminately and getting themselves in trouble.

Unfounded claims, XXV Difficult Task, XXVI Solution, XXVII Recognition, XXVIII Exposure, XXIX Transfiguration, XXX Punishment, XXXI Wedding.[15]

Because one of our great concerns is to find names. We think that without names nothing exists. We, emulators of God, Who named His creation. Name = substance. Noun. Substantial. Essential. Thirty-one functions that would not be fulfilled in her case. Dulcinea, the unfulfiller.

Dulcinea's story flows through many channels. It's water that escapes. Alongside Amadis, she walks on paths, shortcuts, woods, and meadows. They must reach a mountain. A mountain far from stony ground and rocks. A mountain with a cave. A cave that is difficult to access. In it, a hermit. A hermit of few words, strange humor, threadbare clothing, and a long beard. Hermit, sorcerer, wise man, prodigious magician, attentive herbalist, great man of prayer, expert in penance, master of metaphors, paradigm of the symbol. So unaccustomed to the sound of words resounding thunderously in his interior. From the silence, only the echo of a stone thrown into the steep abyss, dragging, unsuspecting, its haphazard grazing against little bits of foliage and sprigs with scant roots, adding to the noise like repentant scratches. Sounds the hermit breaks down into their possible auditory fractions, their fusions and derivations, straight lines or curves, slippery paths or anfractuosities, according to the way the rock tumbles on its descent. Ever-changing sound because space is beyond reach, and time devours itself.

The hermit knows nothing but the distance between himself and the divine mantle. The in-betweens, concessions, and support points have disappeared. It is the hermit and his soul, God and His immensity. Thus, neither doubts and they encompass one another.

This hermit could be a sage. He may know many signs and signals. For him they are clear: they've appeared so many times in his dreams, in receiving words from heaven, in his silent dialogues. In his solitary strolls, when there were portents in scattered feathers, in the twisted branches of an old tree, in the only flower on a dried hawthorn. He deciphered this language: it was no longer secret or inscrutable. He swam in it. He floated. Pirouettes and never-before-seen leaps. Twists and contortions that elevated each minute meaning. The animal world and the vegetable world were being reinterpreted. The hermit was a detached and living rock.

---

15. Propp, "The Functions of Dramatis Personae," 25–65. The words here are listed by function, cited from the "abbreviated definition in one word" of the thirty-one sections of the chapter. After each abbreviated definition, the function is explained with examples.

Dulcinea and Amadis will be able to walk all the paths of the world. They will even be able to find the hermit. By then, the hermit will be mute.

Like me now. How nice. I like people who don't speak. I no longer understand the words of others. They don't even make a sound. They only open their mouths, separate their lips, pucker them, move their eyebrows and their eyes too, their nose a little, and their hands a lot. This is speaking. How strange. How strange it is. Sometimes you see their tongues, naked and moist; the teeth, maybe teeth with fillings; and with luck, surely bad luck, the uvula. There are some people who spew little drops of saliva. How disgusting. It's disgusting to speak. A humiliating spectacle. Better to dance. Many things can be said through dancing. Better to dance. Or paint. Many things can be said through painting. Making sculptures, as well. And, of course, there's also music. Write? No. Not that. Again, you bang your head against a wall. Why? Because of damn words. They're words that don't make a sound: even worse, when they're recorded. And they're not anything. Absolutely nothing. Arbitrary and variable signs, representatives of horrid speaking.

I will not pronounce a single word and whatever I write will be from memory. Forever and ever. The little old pastry chef believes in the end of the world and this encourages her to live. That and the wonderful pastries she will make for the day of the final judgment. Every daybreak she improves her recipes, since she doesn't want to be unprepared. I do hear her when she speaks because she believes firmly and announces the final destruction.

We pass the Escandon neighborhood.[16] The Periferico is so ugly. There, below, is Escandon. How sordid. How run down. I who used to dream of rivers and trees. Why must I be trapped here? Are the others trapped? Do they realize they're trapped? An enormous prison. I escape. I fly away. I open the door and fly away. It's so difficult to return later.

Someday I won't return. It so happens that some people don't return. Someday, I won't return.

Moreover, that is my goal in life. Not to return.

The bad part is I have to unlearn what I've learned. Forget all the routes. Erase what is familiar. Abandon the world of reason and sanity.

For the time being, I no longer speak. If only the internal words would fade away.

---

16. Places in Mexico City are often referred to as *colonias*, or neighborhoods. Escandon is a small neighborhood situated to the southwest of downtown Mexico City.

I know it's a grand aspiration. I aspire to the extreme and disdain the Golden Mean. Ah, but I shouldn't judge. Everything is a guess. Because there will be those who guess. There will be a place for everyone. Even for me. So as not to become crazy, I recommend that you think about mundane things. Yes? Like what? Ah, like those two yards of English tweed you would like to buy yourself. To make myself a *rebozo*? Yes, exactly, to make yourself an English tweed *rebozo*. Splendid, this really excites me: no one has an English tweed *rebozo*. Do you see—do you see? Mundane things are different.

Ah, so this is what it's all about. Making the mundane different. Of course, not that what's different should become mundane. But really, once you stop speaking, it's no longer important. You've already taken the big step. Because speaking is the mundane. Do you realize how many times you've said good morning, good afternoon, good evening? Speaking makes you mundane. Only silence is unpredictable.

Silence is the imagination unleashed. When you don't hear anything, you bring forth everything from within yourself. Rhythms of words inundate you. That's how you learned, not only to be alone, but also to be alone among others. Alone among children, alone among adults. Immensely accompanied by yourself. Alone in Spain, alone on the boat, alone in Russia, alone in Mexico. Alone in this car traveling along the Periferico. Who is driving? Is it Amadis? It looks like his neck. And those who are traveling with me? Do I know them? Do they know me? Are they my parents?

The truth is I didn't love my parents. Nor did they love me. It was an obligation on both parts. They got rid of me and I got rid of them. That's why I made up those stories, being a princess in faraway lands, rejecting them: no, they weren't my parents. I was born through spontaneous generation: on some cliff, among wolves, amid the sprigs and mallows.

Because I don't resemble my parents. And if someone tells me something of mine resembles them, I immediately erase it. No way. I don't look like them. Not even as a joke. Ever since I returned to them, I've made an effort to observe them and then myself, in the mirror, to banish any possible traces of resemblance. Nothing. Not even a mole, not a hair, not a tooth must be the same. Not a color, not a sound, not a movement, not a gesture. Nothing. I am not their daughter.

And all of this because they wanted to pass their memories on to me. How many times I had to hear their stories. Their stories, those of their parents, their grandparents and great-grandparents. In order to impress upon me that I came from there. (Which raised my suspicions.) With a meticulous eagerness to make me feel envious and insignificant they highlighted the big differences of other countries and eras. Back then it was better. What was here and now wasn't worthy. Spain. Spain. Spain. And I liked the name. It sounds good. And I loved it. Everything in my imagination.

It was then that I discovered imagination is the only reality. Consequently, I also owe this to those who call themselves my parents: they alienated me. Yes, I became distanced. Not that anything human was alien to me, but rather I was the alien. That is, I was on the other side. Literally: on the opposite side of the Atlantic Ocean, above the African coast, crossing the Strait of Gibraltar. Yes? Did you find it? There, in Spain.

But. You were living in Mexico. You live there now. A good case for a psychiatrist. Ah, no. I'm not crazy. Definitely not. You're not.

My memories will stay with me. I won't tell them to anyone. I won't do what my parents did. I stopped speaking for a reason. Good timing. I like to review memories alone. On a cold winter day. In front of the fireplace. It's snowing and the snowflakes settle on the window frame. From my house in Mixcoac, the snow, white and silent.[17] Lake Chapultepec must already be frozen. I could go there in the afternoon to skate. I digress: my memories: they must not escape from me. My memories tied on a thin thread, like beads on a necklace.

I answer in Russian to people who insist on making me speak. That way, we both remain silent.

I used to speak a little with my brother when he would come for me and take me into the woods in the afternoons. But just a little. He was also of few words. We would walk together. We picked strawberries . . . and sentences. Also, mulberries. We would collect pine needles. We saw curious squirrels. All of this is very precise and I see it so well. Later, I believe I remember, under a tree, just like that, he seduced me. (And to be clear, it was seduction, not rape, because we were bewitched, immobile.) We became even more silent. And surprised. Neither one of us knew what it was about. It happened. Like that. And two days later, that German sniper killed my brother.

The silences have steadily accumulated in me. Why speak if I have so much to contemplate within myself? My parents never found out and my brother's name always stayed on their lips. Good. Let those who do not know speak.

---

17. Mixcoac is another neighborhood further south. It used to be an Aztec neighborhood located a distance from the capital of Tenochtitlan where Aztec artists who were known for the creation of elaborate headdresses lived. Muñiz-Huberman, pers. comm.

~

THE SECOND SEAL

It's not raining on the Periferico now. The raindrops no longer hit the roof or the windows. The windshield wipers have stopped. The last few houses and factories of Tacubaya and Escandon are disappearing. The train tracks from Cuernavaca have separated and run into the distance. The next exit is for San Antonio. If Dulcinea were going to her house, this would be the exit. But since Dulcinea doesn't speak, the car doesn't move toward the exit and continues in the middle lane.

She could also exit at Mixcoac. But the car continues on. If Amadis is the one driving, why doesn't he say where they're going? Dulcinea doesn't remember exactly when this trip began. Only that she was already in the vehicle. Just like she doesn't remember when she was born. Only when she was already alive. They are absurd situations that don't worry her. Unpronounceable as well. Just like she also doesn't know exactly when she began to write her mental novels. She was already in the middle of them. *In medias res*. Within them. In them. With them. Image after image. They had to be ordered. But order was not to her liking. Images meeting and separating. Sometimes due to similarities. Sometimes due to differences. The advantage of the mind is that it allows several paths at once, without the limitation of paper, a hand, a pencil. The words one by one. The advantage of the mind is polyphony. To put something in writing is monophony. No, not even that. Monography.

Dulcinea's room in the Marquise Calderon de la Barca's house gave her chills. But it wasn't the room that was scary. It was Dulcinea who made it that way. Dulcinea specialized in drawing conclusions from the shadows. In the dim light, everything moved to a different rhythm. The curtains, the abandoned clothes on the chair, the piping on the quilt, the embroidery on the sheets, all were hiding something. The scarce light and the thick darkness altered shapes and thoughts. The ceiling beams were falling down and the bed was floating unsupported. Beings lay in wait in the corners. Men capable of murder. Bloody daggers suspended. Hairy hands. Decapitated heads. Snakes with striking tongues. Demons that crawled around in the mattress. A heart driven crazy, an unrestrained mind. Panic. Cold sweat. Death. An ancestral fear of the dark, when in the cavern any unexpected animal could spring forth, any unbidden ghost. The inheritance of fear along with all other inheritances. The darkness of death, beneath black earth. Every night beginning again. Wanting rest and trembling in imagination.

This scene with Dulcinea reminds me of the nights in the International House. How strange. I used to feel the same fears. But what would appear before me was the head of the Generalissimo Francisco Franco. Only the head, with the ridiculous angular hat that seemed even more ridiculous when I saw bricklayers in Mexico wearing the same one but made of paper. Franco's head would threaten me, jumping from corner to corner of the room, climbing on top of the wardrobe and settling in between the suitcases, hanging from the light cord and swinging on the curtains. What I didn't want was for it to get close to my bed, because there was always a moment I felt his panting breath on my skin.

So, it was I who put fear into things. Fear that did not need darkness. It could arise in broad daylight. When entering a house and thinking a murderer was behind the door. Because fear is of death or violence. When crossing a street, even an empty one, and feeling like a car is hurtling into your fragile body. Being enclosed in an elevator that might never open its doors again. Being in this car on the Periferico going I don't know where, this car that could crash any second. Extreme fear of other people: being in a room with a torturous, deafening murmur and not knowing anyone and losing yourself, not even recognizing yourself. Who am I? Who am I? Not being part of the amorphous mass, but also not being able to scream until you tear your throat and make the silence bleed. Not knowing if you're really alive or dead. And it's scarier not to know than to be dead. Not recognizing humans: who are those beings who grimace and gesticulate? They're not animals— they have long arms with strange long fingers and nails at the ends. But are they animals? Like animals, are they animals and don't realize it and am I the only one who does? What happens is that men (and women with paint on their faces) scare me more than any thing or any other animal. Except for cockroaches. Cockroaches definitely scare me. Disgust. They disgust me. With those rapid movements and that viscous crunching should you step on them in the darkness.

But returning to men and women, what extravagant beings when seen from afar. Because, lacking the agility of true animals, they move heavily. Each one a different color, without feathers or fur. They walk poorly, with difficulty, sadly. Never free, with their hands always clasping something, even a steering wheel.

I'm not like them. Undoubtedly, I'm not. On the outside I seem like them. I seem a lot like them. But inside, not at all. I don't need to speak, and they don't stop speaking. Things happen to me in dreams, I mean, the really important things. Not to them, because either they don't dream or they don't believe in dreams. I'm always thinking. I doubt that they are.

I remember everything. I remember, for example, a dream I had about the Borda Garden in Cuernavaca.[1] In it, I can be the same Dulcinea who accompanied Madam Calderon de la Barca, just like that. The two of them must have gone to the Borda Garden, right? At least Dulcinea must have. In the dream I was leaving the palace, which was not in ruins, but inhabited, and I climbed down the stone stairs that actually were in ruins, with grass growing through the cracks. I would descend to the pond, which was rather more like a lake, and there I would stop. Below, Amadis was waiting for me, with his beautiful black woolen cape. Hence, I no longer know which of the two Dulcineas I was. Or rather, which of the three, because I could be the other Dulcinea, the earliest one. The medieval one?

Anyway, what I remember now is the first time I was in the Borda Garden, soon after arriving in Mexico. On the other side of the pond (the one that was not in my dream), under an age-old tree, was a man weaving straw bracelets he would later overlay with multicolored silk threads. He would go along, leaving empty spaces and that is how he formed letters. When you figured out the letters (at first they seemed like decorations), you could read the word "Cuernavaca." What else do you remember? Your enchanted memories enchant me, enchanted Dulcinea. Well, memories are like the Golden Age. Do you remember Don Quixote's address to the goat herders?[2] Of course, of course I remember. And do you remember who gifted you that bracelet embroidered with cherry-colored silk threads spelling "Cuernavaca" that you kept so very many years? Of course, I remember: Joaquin Xirau gave it to me.[3] And it surprised me a lot because I was only looking at how the man interlaced the threads he was weaving and I never thought about having the bracelet. And, suddenly, the bracelet was in my hand. A present from a philosopher. An extraordinary thing. There was a smile on his face and I

---

1. The Borda Gardens are located in Cuernavaca. Originally constructed in the eighteenth century by the silver magnate José de la Borda, the property grew to include a vacation home, lake, and botanical gardens. Its beauty was renowned, and among its famous inhabitants were Maximillian and Carlota who chose it as a summer home. Today visitors can stroll through the many gardens and visit the mansion that is now a museum.

2. In this famous speech by Don Quixote, he praises the "Golden Age," referring to a mythic period during the first human age when peace reigned, life was idyllic, and humans were immortal (volume 1, chapter 11). The Greek poet Hesiod was the first to write of this utopian paradise. Don Quixote invokes the content and style of pastoral literature of the Renaissance in which innocence and idealism contrasted with the reality of city life and unending wars. The goat herders' inability to understand his words reveals the irony of idealizing their way of life.

3. The Spanish philosopher Joaquín Xirau (1895–1946) was part of the "Barcelona School" and a student of José Ortega y Gasset and Manuel García Morente. After the Spanish Civil War, he was exiled to Mexico, where he taught at Mexico's National Autonomous University (UNAM). He is most known for his thinking on the metaphysics of love.

had to put on the bracelet. Didn't you like the bracelet? No, but I kept it for many, many years. Because of the smile? Yes, because of the smile.

Sometimes, on the street, I smile at everyone. But they get scared. They get scared of a smile. Scared that someone may have penetrated their solitary walk and made them see they're not alone. Scared of the intrusion. Of the separation from themselves. Of my insistent, here I am, and that's why I'm smiling. In fact, it's a form of power. I spy on others and dominate them—I force them to smile at me. And if they're scared of me, even better: I dominate them all the more.

I also enjoy staring fixedly at people until they look away, alarmed. I have done this since I was a child and it's a challenge I always end up winning. Actually, all the others are cowards. What can an unwavering stare mean?

Are people afraid of eyes? Yes, people are afraid of eyes. You can learn a lot from eyes. Above all, you discover secrets. Intimacies. Hidden things. It's a source of learning. Animals also don't like to be surprised by an unmoving gaze. Nor do humans like to be intently observed by an animal. It indicates the possibility of danger. Of destroying that which is most profound. Of offending. Or of humiliating. Of penetrating the cave. There are those who say love is born from sight and others who say loss is also born from sight. Everyone has different tastes. Guzman of Alfarache knew about the Platonic theory of sight and love:

She had a lively, vivacious wit and her eyes were full of life; they were so joyful they brought forth laughter wherever she set her sight. My eyes gazed into hers and it seemed like the visual rays from them both, centered within, struck our souls. I felt affection for her and she believed me. She robbed me of my soul and my eyes spoke for me.[4]

Dulcinea, Dulcinea, why do you forget that you should continue writing your two novels? Oh, no, I'm not forgetting. They're there, rumbling around. The only thing I have to do is give them order. Sometimes a certain languor keeps me from it. I have to think about exercising willpower.

It's easy to give up. In every sense. It's much easier than anything else. What would be natural would be to live like a caveman, not having to get dressed or comb your hair, only having to grab a club and leave. Instead,

---

4. Alemán, *Guzmán*, 567, translation mine with Miriam Huberman. The quote is taken from the well-known Spanish picaresque novel, *Guzmán de Alfarache*, by Mateo Alemán (1547–1615?) from book 3, chapter 4. Muñiz-Huberman uses a fictional descendent of the original *converso* author, now Mateo Alemán II, in her novel *El sefardí romántico: la azarosa vida de Mateo Alemán II*, which takes place in the twentieth century and follows his modern picaresque adventures.

there's the whole ritual needed for going out in public. In other words, to be seen. We've become dependent on the ill-concealed gaze of others. Not how we see ourselves. The suit. The tie. The blouse. The skirt. For others. On the street. In the office. On the television screen.

How awful. This is exactly why I write. On my *tabula rasa*. In order to return to living in the beautiful medieval times.

Dulcinea and Amadis continue traversing lengthy fields, among wheat and poppies. They resemble the primeval couple that went in search of other fruits, other birds. They've seen the mountain for a while, but they can't manage to draw closer. Every step toward the mountain keeps them at the same distance. It's a mirage. It's a will-o'-the-wisp. It's a reality that does not exist.

Dulcinea and Amadis, who seem to be two, are one. When they take each other's hand, the same blood flows through the veins of one to the other. They lose the notion of skin as barrier and become one skin. The rhythm of their steps is monochord. Their language and all their words are one. So, with one single thought they converse. A double heartbeat makes them imagine they've arrived at the foot of the mountain. They ascend in search of the hermit's cave. There are no paths or traces of footprints in the undergrowth. Free will guides them. They climb wherever there is the gentlest ascent. The agile foot knows to hold on to the most secure rock, the strongest root. Eyesight signals and leg muscles know whether to contract or to lengthen. Jumping from rock to rock, leaving the slippery terrain untouched. Some brook had bent to impede the quest and only managed to refresh it. Tall thickets and trees standing trunk to trunk don't obscure the slender outline of their two bodies. Gnarled branches, nettles and thorns—nothing detains them. Even vines and ferns don't trap them. They are blinded neither by excessive light nor thick foliage. They walk among things as if things don't exist. And it's most probable they don't. The aroma of plants, of fallen leaves, of damp earth envelops them. They appear to pass the same places in concentric circles, but a little higher. Strange golden flutes vibrate bird feathers. It's a melody that returns in an internal echo. The movement of living beings keeps step with the sound of the music. Mountain lions glide along branches. Fawns hide in shadows. Dulcinea and Amadis aren't distracted, which surprises the animated forest. If the figure of an elf or a fairy were to be faintly detected, they wouldn't try to get closer—it would only serve as a clear sign. The more haze, the more certain they are of their path. Curtains and thickness offer the most clarity. A web of light and darkness is glorious lace. Brilliant spiderwebs vibrating with transparent drops descend from the latticework. There are forgotten marble columns that are now trunks for climbing plants and ivy. Immersion in the high passes of the mountain: what seems to open up does not. At any moment Dulcinea and Amadis will arrive at the summit.

It's so calming to be able to imagine and inhale that landscape, even in a car on the Periferico. Because what can you do inside a car except rise to the sky. Push a button and rise to the sky. Escape from your cell after opening the window, and let your soul, step by step, ascend in search of the Great Encounter. And if not, return to reviewing your memories. And if not, return to imagining your existence.

When you were getting ready for Christmas in the Marquise de Calderon's house, back then you were a faithful Catholic and the holiday was meaningful.

The invitation was straw-colored and printed in gold letters. Mass would be at nine o'clock in the morning on the twenty-fourth of December 1840, in the Parish Church of the Tabernacle of the Cathedral. Dulcinea had chosen her best clothes and unfolded the mantilla she kept in a chest. She'd aired it out for the previous few days and the wrinkles had disappeared. The smell of quince that perfumed her chest had almost evaporated. Between her fingers, the smooth texture of lace was very pleasing.

She tried on the mantilla: how to drape it around her head so that it did not hide her profile or the waves of her hair, how to fasten the Spanish tortoiseshell comb, how to lay the mantilla over her shoulders and back, and which folds to let fall over her chest.

At nine o'clock on the dot, Dulcinea and the other guests were in the choir. Everything gleamed with the recently hung adornments, fresh flowers, and polished gold. The smell of incense and myrrh. Semidarkness and a spiritual atmosphere. In the choir, Dulcinea stood out with her distinct voice, its depth, emotion, rich tones, and sweetness. If applause had been permitted, she would have been applauded after her solo. The celebration lasted a few hours, and the sermon was very long.

That same night, Dulcinea was invited to join a *posada*.[5] Among the singers illuminated by the lighted candles each one carried as they walked along asking for *posada* at the door of every house, Dulcinea repeatedly saw

---

5. The ritual of asking for *posada* (lodging) is a very old Mexican tradition re-creating Mary and Joseph's search for lodging in Bethlehem. In this pre-Christmas celebration, people dress as Joseph and Mary and walk along with attendants and musicians in a procession, moving from house to house

the figure of a gentleman who was also looking at her. The first time she saw him was in the reflection of a mirror and for a brief moment she thought it was her face and not that of another person. So, she smiled and received a mirrored smile back. Then she raised her hand to her cheek as if to recognize herself and the gentleman did the same, inspired by an identical impulse. She should have spun around to face him and yet she didn't. Their two faces no longer smiled and they contemplated each other intensely. It was a double image that was reflected. The same features, the same faces, the same hair. They both tried to move their hands in front of the mirror to see if they would erase the reflection, and their hands became intertwined. They both were startled and moved away. Those who were asking for *posada* had entered the room, and she and the gentleman were not together again.

Later, when she recounted it all to the Marquise, Dulcinea thought it wasn't true, even though she'd seen him again from afar and their gaze always found each other's eyes. However, the Marquise did believe it, even though she never saw the gentleman. She assured Dulcinea that she would ask around to find out who he was.

That night, Dulcinea dreamt about the same scene with the mirror. And not only that night, but also the following ones. Her dream was so real she forgot reality, and she came to believe not the lived image but rather the dreamt one.

When much later she came across Amadis, she didn't consider him real, but rather like the reflected image. A reflected image, just like her.

It would be a while before they met again and during this period when they didn't see each other, Dulcinea dwelt in her made-up stories:

She arranged dates with him and they loved each other. But they didn't speak. They never spoke. What would they say? Impossible to speak.

They loved each other in basements and they loved each other in attics. And one time in the Desert of the Lions Park, on a layer of damp leaves beneath the tall pines.

They would ride in the carriage and there they also made love. To the rhythmic trot of horses, with curtains drawn and in the half-light.

They didn't ask each other anything. Being together was enough. They never tired of each other, and exploring each other's skin was a novel exercise.

Their faces told it all. Eyes pronounced and cheeks smiled. Hands. Extraordinary hands. In order to know all, to learn all.

---

asking for lodging. At each house, people in the home invite everyone in to sing carols and re-create the Nativity scene.

But what insanity. What remorse. Eclogues aren't for me. Impossible to conceive of idyllic love. I become agitated. I shudder. They say it's a fit of madness. But what do they know if they've never experienced it? This hoarse scream that surges from the caverns of your chest, that alters your pulse and makes you spew foam from your mouth. Your legs tremble and your arms falter. Your throat burns from the wounded scream. I will scream and scream. I won't do what the others tell me to do. No. No. No. But nobody tells you anything. That's a lie. I don't know if they say anything, but they expect something. They wait in hiding. And I don't want them to expect anything. Nothing from me. To be a simple vegetable. Oh, what a great relief. Definitely not an animal. Animals are too sensitive, too close. A vegetable. A green vegetable. That's what I aspire to be. You aspire, but you won't be one. This is why I scream, I scream, I scream.

They say you scream. But what do they know of silence? Given that your scream doesn't make a sound. It's a deaf scream. That irritates your throat and hurts. That isn't heard. Because if it were to be heard, it would crack walls and shatter glass. It would be a scream that would move God. But them, how dare they? And you, what do you know about screaming? Maybe your scream makes a sound and it's you who doesn't hear it.

You feel as if you're entering an unending space. Somewhere so big you can get lost. But not lose my way, rather lose myself. In other words, I may no longer be myself. Because I might be part of everything else. Because the internal breaking off might carry me to black abysms, never reaching the bottom. What is this sensation of darkness? This never finding my way. When I look back, everything is confusing. I forget myself. What I remember are the other Dulcineas. Is it them or me? And, yet, someday there will be light. I know. I know.

That murmur of the others: what they speak or what they say. Words spin and I don't understand them. Here, in the car, they're speaking and in other cars they're also speaking. I see their mouths move, and the muscles in their faces and, sometimes, their hands. Without a sound. At most, an unintelligible sound. As if in front of every person there were a closed window.

It seems as if the people traveling in this car know me. I think it must be Amadis who's driving. His neck was like that. His head. The color of his hair. He also does not speak. Now we are two who do not speak.

He that hath an ear, let him hear
what the Spirit saith . . .[6]

---

6. Rev 2:17 (KJV).

My parents never stopped speaking about my brother. The comparisons were unending. He was this way, I was that way. If he had lived. If he had returned. If he were at their side. If he, if he, if he. Whereas I, who didn't even speak.

But it was all the same to me. Nothing mattered to me. No one can know what is inside of me. The others are so distant. They don't understand any-thing. They get shocked. They get upset. They get worked up. They yell. They stop at the surface. They don't see or go deeper. Impossible for them to know anything about me. Impossible for me to know anything about them. For this reason, I don't recognize the people who ride in this car. They might be who I suspect they are. But it doesn't interest me.

I read only one book in the tepid afternoons in Saratov. At the start of au-tumn, when the leaves were already turning yellow and a few were beginning to fall. I would sit near the window to see the trees and the only book I read, the only one I remember having had, was *Heart: Diary of a Child.*[7] I read and reread it. And I cried like I'd never cried before. Because I only cry when I read, never in real life. In real life, you have to act; only in books can you truly live.

For me, the title of my only book was: daily heart of a child, which is to say, the daily beating of a child's heart.[8] I didn't know what a diary was; I did know what the heart of daily life was.

There, sitting next to the window, I would see the other children go to-ward the woods to collect fruits or flowers. I enjoyed staying by myself. Why do we want others? They're very bothersome. Yes, others are very bother-some. They're the ones who spoil everything.

I was reading and crying. Reading and crying. I would go back and read the same story and cry again. I soaked the page. I would put the book aside and run to look for a handkerchief so that I might continue crying more com-fortably. Crying is such a pleasure. So calming and pleasant. Such a warm sensation of tears trickling down your face. May these Gongorine pearls

---

7. In 1886, this well-known novel in the form of a diary was published by the Italian novelist, poet, and journalist Edmondo De Amicis (1846–1908). The novel was based on his sons' lives and was popular for teaching moral values. The title in English is my translation from the Spanish. Exist-ing translations in English use different wordings. See De Amicis, *Cuore* for one version in English.

8. In Spanish the word *diario* can mean both "diary" and "daily." The narrator plays with the double meaning by changing the semantics of the title.

bejewel us.[9] May the clear mucus, the liquid salt crystal, find relief in falling away and purifying us. A grand lachrymose ritual.

If I raised my eyes from the book, it was to contemplate the landscape. I have always needed a landscape. Not so much to see it, but rather to imagine it. It can be a flowerpot or a mental image. If there's no water or greenery, remembering the times there was.

Back then, I did have woods and a river. I would look through the window and force myself to memorize them, for when I might be confined inside and would no longer be able to see them. I half-closed my eyes and retraced the landscape. Every tree. Every branch. Every leaf.

When they evacuated us, I kept thinking about that landscape and, through the train's window, I did not see the trees gliding by, but rather the others appeared in my mind, those that had stayed behind. I never forgot that day. I had seen the children go into the forest, but after the German planes bombed the area, few returned. And those who did, returned scared and hurt. I didn't cry. I had already cried earlier, with the book.

That same book made me imagine other things. I especially liked the story that was called "From the Apennines to the Andes" because I'd heard that at the end of the Civil War many Spaniards had taken refuge in Mexico, on the same continent as the Andes. What I didn't know was how close or how far that was. Perhaps it was the place where my parents could be found. Someday I would receive a letter from them and someday they would call for my return.

I loved my parents, I hated them, and later, I was indifferent toward them. Like what happens with anyone. The only difference is I never knew for sure whether they were my parents or not. I was rather inclined to think they were not. Or I wished they were not. Since parents don't choose their children (which sperm or which egg will they be?), there should be no pledge of reciprocity or interdependence or false affection. It all depends on chance. So, why settle?

Since I didn't feel that my parents were my parents, I decided they were not. Of course, I made that decision after I saw them, upon my arrival in Mexico. They could be a couple like any other. How could I be certain they

---

9. Luis de Góngora y Argote (1561–1627) was a famous Baroque poet from Spain's Golden Age whose works were known for their complex syntax and metaphors. This literary aesthetics (*gongorismo*), often seen as an exaggerated adornment of language, defined an artistic style known as *culteranismo* (based on the word *culto* or cultured). Here Muñiz-Huberman uses "Gongorine pearls" as a metaphor for tears. The Spanish Golden Age, or *Siglo de Oro*, refers to the period between the sixteenth and seventeenth centuries at the height of Spain's literary production. Poetry, drama, and the novel flourished through well-known authors, such as Góngora y Argote, Francisco de Quevedo, Garcilaso de la Vega, Lope de la Vega, Miguel Cervantes Saavedra, María de Zayas, and mystical writers such as Saint John of the Cross and Saint Teresa of Ávila.

were the ones who had conceived me? Certain I wanted to have been conceived by them or certain they wanted to have conceived me? For the time being, I decided they were not my parents. Instead, I had something more original in mind: I was the daughter of royalty, at the very least. A thought I could modify at my convenience: those people were the ones who picked me up, but I continued to be the daughter of royals. In this way, I calmed my desire to have had a miraculous birth. One to which we all aspire. Before and after Jesus Christ.

The children came and went. We weren't always the same. The mix of children changed with the houses to which we kept being taken. I never had my own place, instead: the urgency of transitoriness, the different roommate, the borrowed clothing, the scarce food. I was, undoubtedly, an enchanted princess. The day of my disenchantment would come. They would bring the crown for my head, the long dress, the ermine cape.

It seems I have always loved Amadis. His name indicates it.[10] I wonder what it is to love? I think it's nothing. As unattainable as any other human enterprise. (Everything we attempt, we don't achieve.) As utopian as utopia. As melancholic and frenetic as empty and desperate. Impossible to attain. Who can say they love? It is theory and an abstraction. It's another thing to make love, feign love, imitate, invent, imagine. But love, no one has known it or experienced it. Because to love would be to die. It would be knowing the absolute and after knowing the absolute, it is impossible to live. It would be knowing God. It would be the mystical experience that would end in the same moment of being, without transferring to word or poem or sound. Undoubtedly, it is untransferable and indefinable. Sometimes we invent words: to love: it sounds good, very good: but nothing more. We are more phonetic than semantic.

Love doesn't exist, just as meanings don't exist. Just as God doesn't exist. Everything is beating around the bush: never facing the facts. The only way to understand is to keep silent. And to not draw conclusions.

Now you're understanding, Dulcinea. Now you really are. So, what do you think: did you love Amadis or not? Yes, I loved him, but I didn't die. Yes, I loved him and, yes, I kept quiet. Did I actually love him? I just had words

---

10. Several times throughout the novel, Muñiz-Huberman plays with the etymological possibilities of Amadis's name. The various names for Amadis play with the Spanish verb "amar," meaning "love" and "Dios," meaning "God." "Amado" also means "beloved."

and that's not the way to love. I was silent. Maybe I was on the way to loving him. Did you love Amadis or not?

If I had loved him, it would have been among thistles and squalor and putrefaction, and I wouldn't have noticed. Among flies and trash and stenches. And I wouldn't have noticed. Among flat tires, nails, and rust. And I wouldn't have noticed. Among pins, needles, and scalpels. And I wouldn't have noticed. In mud, in swamps, and in marshes. In suffocation and in vomit. In choking and in the throes of death. And I would never have noticed.

But no. I loved him comfortably. Aesthetically.

You did not love, Dulcinea. You did not love.

If I did not love, no one loved. Probably.

That's right.

You did not take the plunge. You did not love.

The real story would escape me, not the imagined one. Because loving isn't real: what's visible isn't exact or true. You must pass through the layers of skin, continuously stripping away, until you reach the core and even going past the core, reaching the clarity of emptiness. Then, in emptiness, loving.

It's not the water from this shore. Or the effort of crossing it. Or the other shore. It's to be in the center of the abysm, but without a point of reference, without time or space. Thus, being unaware of the center. It is nothingness.

If we were able to imagine nothingness, this would be love.

Only mystics were the ones who got closest.

Hence, death is what most resembles love.

Lovers kill and lovers kill themselves.[11]

---

11. This section is a direct reference to the mystical journey in which love and death are linked. The mystic must shed his or her earthly ties to be one with God. Not a literal, physical death, this death is about being able to let one's soul escape the confines of the earthly body. Saint Teresa

I dream a lot. But when I dream I don't want reality to invade my dreams. Lately I've been dreaming about my parents. It's an unpleasant feeling. Since I've rejected them. They don't belong to me. How dare they enter? I also dreamt about them in Russia. But those were real dreams. But you liked dreaming about them. But back then I didn't know them and the dreams were made up. But the dreams from now are also made up. They aren't real. But they seem real and that's why I don't like them. Dreams are for dreaming. In Russia I would dream that Nazi soldiers had captured me. They would take me to an ancient fortress where they already had lots of prisoners and make us go to an upper floor and from there they would throw us down to the patio. I would fall on top of bodies, but I did not die. I pretended to be dead, but the soldiers would discover me. They would take me back up and throw me down again. Again, I would not die. Again, they would figure it out and throw me back down. With the same result. I wanted to die as I was in agony from my shattered body and I couldn't bear the suffering, but it was useless. I never ended up dying.

Those dreams didn't matter to me. They were interesting and I would always remember them. But dreaming about my parents. How common. And moreover, to see them doing what they would do awake in everyday life. What a lack of imagination. So, your rejection became a real presence. How disgusting.

Since the end of the world is drawing near, I would like to repeat these prophetic words:

After this I looked, and, behold, a door was opened in heaven: and the first voice which I heard was as it were of a trumpet talking with me; which said, Come up hither, and I will shew thee things which must be hereafter.

And immediately I was in the spirit: and, behold, a throne was set in heaven, and one sat on the throne.

And he that sat was to look upon like a jasper and a sardine stone: and there was a rainbow round about the throne, in sight like unto an emerald.

And round about the throne were four and twenty seats: and upon the seats I saw four and twenty elders sitting, clothed in white raiment; and they had on their heads crowns of gold.

(1515–1582) wrote the line "Muero porque no muero" ("I die because I do not die") in her poem "Vivo sin vivir en mí" ("I live without living in me"), expressing the angst and difficulty of letting go of earthly connections. Teresa, *Obras completas*, 713–14. This topic is also treated by Sigmund Freud, who linked eros and thanatos (love and death). Muñiz-Huberman implies that where there is life (or love), there is also the impulse of death.

And out of the throne proceeded lightnings and thunderings and voices: and there were seven lamps of fire burning before the throne, which are the seven Spirits of God.

And before the throne there was a sea of glass like unto crystal: and in the midst of the throne, and round about the throne, were four beasts full of eyes before and behind.

And the first beast was like a lion, and the second beast like a calf, and the third beast had a face as a man, and the fourth beast was like a flying eagle.

And the four beasts had each of them six wings about him; and they were full of eyes within: and they rest not day and night, saying, Holy, holy, holy, LORD God Almighty, which was, and is, and is to come.

And when those beasts give glory and honour and thanks to him that sat on the throne, who liveth for ever and ever,

The four and twenty elders fall down before him that sat on the throne, and worship him that liveth for ever and ever, and cast their crowns before the throne, saying,

Thou art worthy, O Lord, to receive glory and honour and power: for thou hast created all things, and for thy pleasure they are and were created. [12]

You tell me if that isn't a dream. Who could believe that? Undoubtedly, it's a dream transcribed exactly as it was. But it was believed, and is still believed, and will continue to be believed. The cycle must complete itself: beginning, middle, and end. The destruction was going to be in the year 1000. It didn't happen. Fine, it will be in the year 2000. Maybe it won't happen. Well, then it will take place in the year 3000. What? The world will still exist in the year 3000? And in 4000? And 5000? Because someday the end will come, right? Yes. Tomorrow.

Then don't come to me with your questions. Before you realize it, a delicious bomb will explode and you'll go flying into pieces and reintegrate into the space of creation. Transformed into rock, you'll be another small world that will begin to revolve around itself. In a while, Adam will be created from your rib and from his, an Eve. And back to the beginning again.

No. No. That's very boring. It's better to finish forever. Hence, we desire the end so very much. We're screaming for it to happen. So many protests, so many protests: to hasten the final breath.

---

12. Rev 4:1–11(KJV).

At some point Dulcinea and Amadis will reach the summit. The hermit will be waiting for them up there. The hermit who no longer speaks. The hermit on the tall rock. Petrified. His body embedded. Concave. A trace of a fossil.

From the peak, Dulcinea and Amadis will look into the distance, but they won't linger on the markings on the rock. They won't see the hermit at their side. They won't rest their loving gaze on what they were looking for most and what they had closest to them.

By not having delighted in close contemplation and in contemplation of only one essence, they were lost in the enormity of the scenery. They never discovered the rock that mattered, the touchstone. They weren't humble enough to decipher the porous gray and preferred instead the distance of the unattainable. At their side, the hermit remained silent.

Whoever doesn't want to find clues also won't find meanings. Whoever doesn't want revelation will not receive it. Whoever arrives at the summit and looks down has forgotten the goal of elevation. Whoever isn't familiar with the next step sinks even more precipitately. There's no pity for wasted opportunities.

Dulcinea and Amadis initiate their descent. The hermit won't ever separate from the rock. His last hope has been his last deception. If Dulcinea and Amadis try harder, they will find the secret in themselves. If once they have descended, they can remember and describe precisely what they didn't see, if when in silence they hear words, they will be able to see what they didn't see and learn what they didn't learn. The hermit will then leave his rock and say what he needs to say.

Meanwhile, Dulcinea and Amadis cross enchanted lands and grief-stricken lands. They carry the echo within, even if it doesn't make a sound.

This is my favorite story. It gathers together so many memories I've kept. It's like telling myself fairy tales to rescue the forgotten. It's re-creating childhood to my taste. It's telling my own story. It's inventing myself. It's coming alive in third person. It's living what I imagine. No one can comprehend the joy of mental books, continually being created and being undone. Never finished. Never definitive. Favorable to any change. Adapted. Renewed. Always beginning.

It's stupid for you to cling to these dull stories. It's continuing the deception: for a moment we're going to live in another era. Can't you seal off the past? Has anything good ever come from the past? Have you inherited anything good from your parents? Nothing. People only dwell on the negative. It's a tradition that's alive and well. All people feel shame in the face of evil:

they convert it into hypocrisy, into cowardice, into ambiguity. Those people who talk so much and it's just spit they spew. Do you realize how absurd human activity is? Only one question remains: for what?

Well, to calm down a little I tell myself my novels. If it weren't for that, I would open the car door and throw myself onto the pavement right now. But you don't do it, you never do. You think about it, but you don't dare do it. You don't even dare to write your novels. Oh, no. Not that. This I will not tolerate from you, since the reason I don't write them is because I don't have a tie to the outside world. I'm not going to give anything to a world that has not given me anything: even worse, that has made me live in it. My novels are for me. The only pleasure that exists is making them up. The imaginative process is the only truth. And this process is mine alone. Would I like to see a completed work? Never. Any completed work is death. One should produce works that are not finite so they may then be infinite.

But. We are always struggling between beginning and end. When what little we do is in the middle. The beginning as obscure as the end. I hate the middle: it's the only possibility of living, which is to say, of not-living. Which is to say to drag through mediocrity. Which is to say, of salivating hypocrisy.

Dreaming is the proof of existence. I elaborate a theme freely: I appear and disappear: I'm me and I'm the others. It's the same when I write my mental novels: I see landscapes and I express myself verbally: I feel even higher than the highest peak. I enjoy the act of dreaming. I'm in the process of writing my dreams: as I dream them. I foresee and I have premonitions. It's a fountain of knowledge. Undoubtedly, it's a fountain of knowledge. I've known ecstasy and revelation. I was traveling by car, a black Ford from the thirties, with a high roof. Amadis was driving. The highway was wide. Only one car was passing us and I was scared because I thought there were criminals inside. The highway ended in a desert with smooth golden sands. Amadis put an arm around my shoulders to protect me. I no longer saw the other car, it wasn't there anymore. The desert advanced, in waves. A slightly elevated limestone wall blocked the right lane of the highway. We got out of the car and took shelter by the wall. It was a wondrous moment. The end of the world. Pressed against the wall, we felt an enormous black shadow pass over our heads: the wings of a giant bird. Amadis continued with his arm around my shoulders, squeezing me closer to him. The golden sands of the desert were now pinkish-orange, like a sunset. They came closer and closer toward us without frightening us, but unyielding. The sands. We knew it was the end of the world. It was beautiful and calming. There was no longer anything that could be done. But Dulcinea and Amadis, we were together.

And then, I think, why the end of the world? Isn't every day the end of the world? Yes, dear Dulcinea, but the others don't know it. The world builds and destroys itself at the end of a day and a night. Even though no one wants to admit it. It goes too fast. There's no time for anything.

Now I understand. The end of the world happened for me before. It occurred in childhood, when my parents sent me to Russia, when the war ended, when I arrived in Mexico and an identification card awaited me, a card that no one would forget, for the rest of my life, even if I wanted to forget it. I would forever be exiled, without a country and without a home. Exiled, out of place, tolerated, never integrated. Without the desire to put down roots because some day would be the return. I lived in rented houses (the idea of buying a house never occurred to my parents, ever) and we moved residences for any pretext. In fact, if we didn't move every few years, I missed the change. And if you were not moving, Dulcinea, at least you moved around the furniture, and one chair would go from the living room to the bedroom and a carpet would be turned in the opposite direction. It astonished me, Dulcinea, your anxiety to move or move things. But this is how it is, and every time I visit a house, I imagine myself living there and the changes I would make. On the streets, I go looking for flyers announcing houses or apartments for rent, and often I go see them. Every day I look at the want ads in the paper and mark the most suitable ones. I call and get upset if one has already been rented. I buy myself decorating magazines, from *Better Homes and Gardens* to *Design from Scandinavia*, preferring the latter. The pictures I see in these magazines also help me imagine that I live in those places. I especially look for those that have fireplaces. (The habit has stayed with me since the Middle Ages.) And libraries or studies or bookcases. Decorating magazines are for me what pornography is for others. I need them intensely. Another manifestation of the exile in which I live.

And did I enjoy being exiled? Well, yes. I can't deny it. I know there were some who suffered, cried, and lamented. It's true, it was their lot in life to do so. But for me? What was my lot or what was expected of me? Meanwhile, I defined myself through indefinition. I was nothing: neither Spanish nor Mexican. Because the comfortable position, that of the majority, was hybridization: we are Spanish-Mexicans. We are ambiguous, we are conciliatory: we love Mexico and we love Spain. Not me. I settled into hate. Here in the impenetrable labyrinth of my brain, I can think what I want and nobody will find out: it's the only free space I know, the only land of freedom: my brain. There's a reason I don't speak: speaking is lying, it's protecting yourself, it's distorting. Hence the truth is that my elders promised our return to Spain and its virtues and its marvels so much that when it never happened I reverted to hatred toward them. Which, in reality, was hatred toward myself: I also did nothing to return. And, on top of everything, I became mute. Passivity had to be taken to the extreme. Exile was imposed on me: as a girl sent to Russia, later sent to Mexico, later to who knows where. (Well, to shit.) In reality, I always felt like an unclaimed postal package.

But no. Don't believe I suffered so much. There's a good side to being exiled: others feel sorry for you, they treat you with care, and the foolish ones even admire you. Your advantages are not committing yourself, remaining in ambiguity, erasing ambition. Above all, you carry a halo of saintliness: you are untouchable and unpronounceable.

Oh, Dulcinea, you're forgetting something. No, I'm not forgetting it. My terrible conflict, my true conflict, is that I'm no longer exiled. True, I'm not. How can I keep calling myself an exile? If since the day Franco died (another stupid passivity: Franco had to die from a natural cause) you could have returned to your promised land. Then rid yourself of that exile label. So what am I: an ex-exile? Resign yourself to not being anything at all.

You're afraid of lacking a nation. You need the support of a land. An inherited exile, a condemned exile, had never been seen before. Because your parents were definitely exiles and did have a reason for thinking about Spain. Their cruelty was transmitting their failure and disillusion to you. Wanting you to continue defending their instability and emptiness. You were asked to live off nothing and you remained that way: nothing but angry. Your only country will be the earth in which you are buried.

~

THE THIRD SEAL

And I saw in the right hand of him that sat on the throne a book written within and on the backside, sealed with seven seals.

And I saw a strong angel proclaiming with a loud voice, Who is worthy to open the book, and to loose the seals thereof?

And no man in heaven, nor in earth, neither under the earth, was able to open the book, neither to look thereon.[1]

Exactly. The book should not be opened. It cannot be opened. They would have to break open my head just to read the book. They would have to open it layer by layer: skin, bone, meninges.

Finally, they would arrive at each of the cerebral centers, and even further, at the microscopic level, the fine histological sections would not reveal the book that's there. Whoever removed the book's seals could not explain the mystery either. Likewise, the divine word lacked order and was never fully understood.

The book cannot be opened. Who would be able to understand and unlock it? Who, with their eyes on the pages, understands the signs, deciphers the words?

What is in each book does not stay written. The true book remains in those cerebral convolutions that do not reveal even to a microscope what they hide. The true book cannot be opened, cannot be read, cannot be written.

I don't know who sent the torn and bloody scrap of shirt. I don't know. But they received it. And they didn't tell me right away. They waited patiently for me to adjust to Mexico. For me to get to know them. For them to tell me about the years we were separated. I should have seen it coming: a gesture, a word that seemed to allude to some secret. But they were so alien to me I couldn't imagine it. I didn't understand their private gestures. Their quick glances, the slight blink of an eye, the imperceptible trembling of lips, the barely noticeable furrowing of brows. What did it all mean?

Until one day they could no longer remain silent. They told me on the way home, after picking me up at the Luis Vives Institute.[2] "We want to show you something." And what they showed me was the scrap of bloody shirt. I didn't know what it was: a piece of cloth stained with coffee: an unpleasant dirty rag: a frayed and wrinkled piece of fabric. They showed it to me

---

1. Rev 5:1–3 (KJV).

2. The Luis Vives Institute was founded in 1939 in Mexico City to serve the children of Republican Spanish Civil War exiles, many of whose teachers were also Republican exiles. The Institute is named after the famous Spanish Renaissance philosopher, humanist, and *converso* Juan Luis Vives (1493–1540).

and fell silent. I had to guess what it was. I didn't know what they expected of me, but I saw a perfect round hole in the cloth with the coffee-colored stain spilling out around its edges.

And I didn't speak. Even though the stain began to stir my memories, I wasn't going to speak. I didn't feel like pleasing my parents. I now understood that I would never mention the obvious. If they needed threads and stains to maintain an absence alive, I, conversely, would resort to silence and strip away any ties. I went around tossing my clothes in the garbage and was left naked. I lit them on fire and delighted in contemplating the flames as they rose into the air.

It took a long time for Dulcinea to see Amadis again. She was accompanying the Marquise to pick up a necklace from the jeweler on Plateros Street. She saw all the people passing by on the street reflected in the mirror in front of her. And then he passed by. He passed her and, disappearing from the mirror's view, took her by the arm and carried her away with him. They walked around Alameda Park.[3] The tall trees and rose gardens. Dulcinea, feeling confused, was unable to guess what Amadis was thinking. That desire for clarity and the penetration of secrets that do not belong to her. That desire to be able to erase boundaries: to stop being herself in order to be the other. Coveting plurality: what can be in other minds? What opaque and obscure thoughts? Are we all the same or are we all different? What is Amadis like? What might he be thinking? Most of all, what is he thinking? It's exasperating that there is absolutely no way of knowing what Amadis is thinking. Especially since his face doesn't reveal what's inside him. Since he doesn't speak and doesn't look at me, only his hand presses into my arm. And even if he were to look at me, how would I understand his gaze? And even if he were to speak to me, how would I interpret his words? How would I know if his words are the same ones I use, or if they mean other things to him? What if he expresses himself with ironic or solemn tones, nuanced in ways I can't manage to understand? What if he surrounds them in ambiguity, yet they seem precise to me? What if they're too curt and I judge them full of maturity? What if they carry some other meaning that escapes me? What if

---

3. Known as Alameda Central, this popular park in downtown Mexico City is one of the oldest parks in Latin America. Originally a marketplace in the Aztec (Mexica) capital of Tenochtitlan, it was later used by the Inquisition to burn heretics. After Mexico's independence it was made into a park, filled with poplar trees (*alamedas*), and today is known for its gardens, fountains, monuments, and cultural events.

they are simple and I find them wise? What if they are heavy with emotions of which I am ignorant? What if they are simply words?

No, words are not simple. They are learned and repeated sounds, never fully understood. Who can define them? Define them with other misunderstood words?

Neither Dulcinea nor anyone will ever know what Amadis thinks. Not the naïve Marquise, trying on the necklace with Dulcinea still at her side. Dulcinea and Amadis have not been seen walking through the Alameda.

And this is as far as I go with this story. I don't know why I'm telling it to myself. I don't think it has a good future. I don't like it and I'm not interested in it. But you should do it. You've been very lonely. You don't have anyone to talk to. What would you do then? I've already told you. You, you bore me. I cut and add stories, don't you see?

The lives of writers are so desperate. So solitary and so dependent on others. But not me. No. I'm fortunate enough to avoid all this. I don't want anyone at my side. I don't need anyone. I make up everything, even love. Every once in a while, I scream. But that's all.

Do you have many hidden recesses in your soul? Ah, yes. It's a pleasure for me to penetrate those recesses. A never-ending story. An enchanted forest. You could describe it this way: First I start thinking, and thinking is always dark: hidden recesses are dark. I penetrate them over and over: they're interminable and I never get to the end. In the beginning, I don't know which of the paths to follow. But I always end up picking one. And I go in. I feel as if I'm looking for something: there's an endless black lagoon I can never come to know. The secret lies in its depths. Darkness surrounds me. I dare to submerge myself in the waters. I don't find it. I don't find what I'm looking for. There's a stirring of thick liquids, an immeasurable sluggishness, a caressing weariness. Waves come and go. I want to reach the bottom and I don't want to reach the bottom. But I continue. I have to discover it. It's very unsettling. It is the origin. If I could know the origin. My origin. My moment of birth. Or even earlier: my fetal state. Those dark waters. Horrible dark waters, so similar to those hidden recesses in which I lose myself. Could I arrive at the beginning? I must. It's my duty to arrive. There must be some path. I must understand my birth, just as I must understand my death. For now, all I can do is think and think. Enter into those depths, even if my only progress is to fall from abysm to abysm. Staying there, not wanting to leave, even if the morass continues. Preferring to live here inside. Inside myself. In order to understand gestation. When does memory begin? It must have begun then and been erased then. Since there were no words, it could not be remembered. Therefore, I must reconstruct gestation by penetrating into my soul. And, in the end, I'm left with my imagination. Just as I make up my life. Because we do make it up, right? Or we intuit it. Intuition shapes invention. That's what counts. Adjusting the external world to the true internal world. Even better: erasing the external.

This neck of the person driving the car. I'm familiar with this neck. This neck that I like so much, that I contemplate and that distracts me. No, it's not Amadis. It must be Amadeo. Beloved of God or he who loves God. Wolfgang Amadeus Mozart. This is the real Amadis. I remember and see his naked neck. The line of his shoulders descending toward his arms. Naked. Completely naked. Why is he driving clothed now? It's so strange. I only remember him naked. Those shoulder blades that could be angel wings. To raise him to heaven. Amadeo. No, I don't like Amadeo. Amadis, yes. They are one and the same. Amadios-Amadis.[4] Those ancient knights of God. About whom Ramon Llull wrote the rules:

1. *The knight is a man who procures peace through force.*
2. *Since ancient times, the knight is a man elected to be a better man than another.*
3. *The knight has a sword for justice and a steed due to his nobility.*
4. *Since humility is elevated, the knight should be humble.*
5. *The knight is well dressed because he is honorable.*
6. *Cloth vestments are not as noble as those of virtue.*
7. *The knight has insignia so that he may be recognized by all.*
8. *A bad man should not ascend to heights just so that he may be known.*
9. *Pride lowers a man.*
10. *One ascends through virtue; one falls through vice.*
11. *A peasant who becomes a knight offends his horse.*
12. *A vile knight should only mount an ass.*
13. *Honor and possessions belong to a knight.*
14. *The world would be better if its lords were a good clergyman and a good knight.*
15. *Great is the company of a good clergyman and a good knight.*
16. *No one is more vile than a cowardly knight.*
17. *No one falls as low as he who falls from great virtue.*
18. *Fear the humble knight, but not the proud one.*

---

4. See footnote 9 in the "Second Seal."

19.   *The knight is stronger by his virtues than by his spear and sword.*
20.   *The world judges knights through their deeds.*[5]

And the Knight Zifar was also the Knight of God and ascended a ladder of light, walking on air, to reach Him. And so many other splendid knights: Sir Tristan of Leonis, Sir Belianis of Greece, Sir Olivante of Laura, Tirant lo Blanch, Palmerin of England, and even Orlando the Furious himself. I loved them all.

But returning to Ramon Llull, I have developed my art of memory from his *Liber ad memoriam confirmandam.*[6] That is why I don't need to write. Nothing manifests on the exterior if it hasn't been created previously in the interior.[7] Only in the interior does the true effort of understanding come to fruition. Memory gathers and contains everything. It's the mother of the Muses. Mnemosyne for the Greeks. According to Albert the Great and Saint Thomas, memory should be cultivated as a religious exercise. It's the basis of Kabbalah, which is transmitted orally. It became more intensified in the occult philosophy of the Renaissance, in the treaties of Camillo, Bruno, and Fludd. And in Rosicrucianism.[8]

I remember Llull's engraving of the ladder of ascent and descent. Each step corresponds to a degree of perfection: *instrumentativa, elementativa, vegetativa, sensitiva, imaginativa, homo, caelum, angelus, Deus.*[9] At the top is the divine castle with the door ajar. The sun faces the door. Below is the mystical circle and the seeker begins the ascent. Each step corresponds to an element: stones, fire, trees, lion, man, heaven, angel.

And I return to the memory of Amadis's neck. It's the first thing I remember about him. Circle, square, and triangle, in Llullian style. The neck seen from behind. It's a straight neck, with exact proportions, handsome and harmonious. A neck that responds to memory, intellect, and will. A neck that

---

5. Llull, *Libro del orden*, 96–97, translation mine. This list is from the chapter titled, "Estos son los proverbios de caballería" ("These are the Chivalric Proverbs") in Llull's *Libro del orden de caballería; Príncipes y juglares* (c.1274–1276).

6. The Latin translates to the *Book for Strengthening Memory.* Attributed to Ramón Llull (1232–1316). One can find the *Liber* in the Appendix of Rossi, *Logic.*

7. This sentence is inspired by Paul Klee's ideas about the exterior and the interior. See *The Diaries of Paul Klee, 1898–1918.*

8. In this paragraph, Muñiz-Huberman recalls the work of the English historian Frances Yates (1899–1981), an avid scholar of the Rennaissance, especially with regard to esotericism and the occult. In this list of Rennaissance philosophers, Muñiz-Huberman nods to Yates's final book entitled *The Occult Philosophy in the Elizabethan Age.* Yates also wrote *The Art of Memory*, in which she studies mnemonic systems from the ancient Greeks to the seventeenth century.

9. In English, "Instrumentative, elementative, vegetative, sensitive, imaginative, man, heaven, angel, God" (my translation). You can see the print in Llull, *Liber de ascensu.*

could be an architectural column. Or that could have been from the Globe Theater. An Elizabethan neck.

Of course, they (and sometimes it seems like they're the same people traveling in this car) didn't understand the burning of my clothes. They grew worried and even horrified. I would have settled for a fireplace. But I never had a fireplace again. The last ones were in Russia. More accurately, they were stoves with mosaics. So I was left with this taste for seeing flames rising and everything being swallowed in the tongues of fire. Heat on your cheeks and eyes aglow. Blackened pieces of wood collapsing on each other. Your body comforted. Orange and blue fire. Crackling. Sparking. Ashes. Embers. Llull also must have loved fireplaces throughout his Catalan lands. It would be so pleasant to take refuge from the cold in front of the convent's kitchen stove.

And since I like to live through my memories so much, another fireplace that I have appropriated is from *The House of Ulloa*.[10] I take what I like from it and eliminate the rest. In other words, as I do with all my memories: I arrange them and put them in place, I perfect them, I adorn them, I change them. What happens with a memory that ceases to be a memory? It becomes a new memory and you come to believe it. So that some things happen to you and others don't, but you believe them all. Of course, the best memories are the ones that didn't happen. And if nothing that I remember is true? If they were all stories like those of Amadis? How do I know what has actually happened to me and what I've made up? It doesn't matter. Even made-up stories have happened, just as vivid as those that actually happened. Both are remembered. And so there's no difference. Hell was ever-present for the ancients. That's why Thomas Aquinas recommends exercising the art of memory. Vices, virtues, the road to hell and the road to heaven. And by repeating, you come to believe it. Llull says that what reinforces memory is constant repetition. From which I deduce that by repeating my stories, they will become true. What's the difference between my stories and the one about hell? Don't we all believe in fairy tales as children and even substitute ourselves for the characters?

People, what I say is true. Of course, of course, Dulcinea, no one doubts it. It's the truth. Great. Let's move on to something else.

---

10. In Spanish, *Los pazos de Ulloa* (1886). A well-known Spanish naturalist novel by Emilia Pardo Bazán (1851–1921).

Through enchanted and mournful lands, Dulcinea and Amadis walk in silence. Their feet planted firmly on the ground, it's their heads that fly, and fly so high that sometimes they stretch their arms to reach them so that they won't completely fly off. Their capes fill with air and their fear is that should their feet rise from the ground, they will definitely begin the ascent. Because this has happened before and they remained on top of a tree the whole night, and only when the calm of sunrise returned did they descend and return to their journey.

Consequently, evil tongues begin to murmur, teeth begin to chatter, and the cochleae of ears welcome perjuries and heresies. Those two people are strange beings, from who knows what enchanted place, cursed by some fearful prophecy. They're sibling lovers. They won't be accepted by honorable people. What hangs over them could attract misfortune. Better to avoid them, not to meet their glance or acknowledge their words. Let them continue their senseless wandering.

One afternoon, under the shadow of an apple tree, the thick heat and the insects' slow buzzing lowered the curtain of dreams over them. So, they dream. They both dream the same dream.

They dream that, in the distance, against the horizon, Death takes all by the hand to dance: rich and poor, gentlemen and rogues, old and young, maidens and matrons, emperors and popes, those who are sad and those who are happy, those who are good and those who are bad.[11] Death rattles her bones rhythmically and effortlessly brandishes her scythe. A dance that cannot be stopped. Eternal movement. Eternal harmony. *Perpetuum mobile*. Impossible to grieve. The maiden smiles because she gives her hand to the gentleman. The boy and the old man, their fingers intertwined, are no longer alone. The peasant would never have imagined dancing between an emperor and a pope, or a rabbi or an alfaki between a priest and an archdeacon. This was not the stuff of life; rather, the things that result from dreams of Death.

Against the horizon, the figures that Death drags along fade out in grotesque leaps. On the other side remains the abysm. Dulcinea and Amadis dream it. That is how they know. On the other side of the abysm, bodies will not be bodies. All will float in the pleasure of oblivion. The crossing will be easy and so quick that no amount of time can measure it. There will barely be a deep breath. After all, Death is compassionate: she puts an end to pointless suffering.

---

11. According to medieval lore, the Dance of Death shows the universal reach of death that affects everyone, regardless of social status. Combining poetry, music, and dance, people from all walks of life hold hands and dance around a tomb.

When they buried her brother, Dulcinea wasn't afraid. She felt relief at being alive. At having remained. At being more free. Dulcinea never wanted to have ties. Never having someone watching over her or telling her what to do. She put on a sad face because everyone had sad faces and because she knew how to fake sadness. Inside she repeated: it's the end and I won't see him again, someday that will happen to me. Consequently, sadness was not so important. She felt good: the laws of nature were being fulfilled. Things were happening according to an order. Death was harmonious. It restored. It reintegrated. It returned. The darkness of the soil and the blows of the shovels against the casket couldn't stop it. Dulcinea couldn't stop time. She had the calmness of one who accepts futility. She didn't cry. She didn't know how to cry and it's difficult to fake tears. It surprised her that other kids cried—what right did they have? Only she was his sister. And so she drew a conclusion: sisters don't cry.

Her sense of freedom was growing. Growing and giving her another feeling: of rising into the air. Of weightlessness. Of lacking a body. Of having eliminated earthly concerns. Of developing an internal world that was exclusively hers, so private and so inviting. Where she could continue speaking with her brother. Where she could return to the woods to gather wild berries.

That was when she found music. There was an old phonograph in the dining room and she would listen to the chorus of the Red Army. Those Russian melodies almost brought her to tears, if she had only known how to shed them. A kind of deep sigh she also never managed to express. Something located in her core. And the desire to remain still, very still. Listening. Nothing more. That was music. Feeling vocal cords vibrating with reverberating sounds as if they came from the echo of a cathedral. Losing yourself in a void without thoughts, without words. Letting the melody physically penetrate you in order to glide through an unlocated internal world. In any case, in rhythm with the circulation of blood. A flow of sonorous pleasure that invades the body and stirs it from within until you can no longer take it, ending in an orgasm of cosmic equilibrium.

From that moment, Dulcinea had to listen to music daily in order to survive. It was a physiological necessity. Eating or drinking weren't important. That she could leave aside. Listening to music was true nourishment.

Later, in Mexico, she arrived punctually for the concert season in the Metropolitan Theater, and every Sunday, hungrily, she would get her fill of music. She salivated, chewed, swallowed, absorbed, and distributed her ration of proteinaceous sounds. She acquired energy for the week and made it last until the next Sunday. She organized her subsistence in this way. Between books and music, she was well nourished. One day her parents saw her tearing off the corner of a page from a book, tasting it. It tasted like a field of Garcilaso.[12]

She tried other things after her return from Russia. For example, cologne. She thought it was for drinking and she would take a swig of it every now and then. Rose petals also attracted her and every time there were some in a jar in the sitting room, she would take a few for dessert.

She would dialogue with her brother. Her brother was inside her, never again to leave. She felt that when he had penetrated her, he had stayed there. The sniper shot and burial were incidental. She had swallowed him. He wasn't buried. He was in her. She had cannibalized him and turned him into flesh of her flesh. With time she stopped feeling he was separate, stopped marking his entrance into the dialogue. Either she forgot about him or it didn't matter. The mere grammatical game had lost its interest. The boundaries between the three—I, you, he—had collapsed.

Of all the children at the International House, her only true friend was Leninito. Leninito, whose name was not of a dogmatic origin, but rather derived from what he named himself, perhaps meaning "little boy."[13] The others made fun of him. They stole his food, hit him, and threw him to the ground. So Dulcinea immediately became his defender. Now she could right wrongs and pursue scoundrels.[14]

Leninito followed her like a puppy dog everywhere. Until Dulcinea, whose solitary space could not be invaded, sent him away. When Leninito tried to speak, no one understood him. When he tried to be playful, he was taken seriously. When he sang, he was out of tune. He couldn't memorize multiplication tables. His drawings were enigmatic stains. He cut paper up into strips, but couldn't cut out a shape. He loved to move beans from one pot to another and back again.

He was an ideal companion for Dulcinea. They didn't speak and were simply together. Dulcinea observed him, trying to guess what he was think-

---

12. This reference is to the poet Garcilaso de la Vega (c. 1503–1536), credited with bringing Italian Renaissance poetic forms to Spain. He was one of the poets foundational to Spain's literary Golden Age.

13. The use of the diminutive "-ito" in Spanish, when added to the end of nouns and adjectives, denotes smallness and/or is used to express affection. Here Muñiz-Huberman plays with the sounds in Spanish of "niñito" ("little boy") and "lenin-ito" ("little Lenin"), also ironically recalling the larger-than-life Russian political figure and contrasting him with Dulcinea's small and solitary friend.

14. The words in this last sentence in Spanish, "desfacer entuertos y perseguir malendrines," evoke the words and imagery from Don Quixote in which the fabled hero fights battles for his beloved Dulcinea. In Muñiz-Huberman's intertextual playfulness, it is Dulcinea who fashions herself as the quixotic hero.

ing. I wonder what you are thinking, Leninito, what you're feeling, what you see and what you hear. What words or images do you bring together in your internal ramblings? Do you ramble? Or is your internal wandering something else? If only there were no words, no images. A different way of expression. You can remain in a corner for hours without doing anything. How do you plunge into your depths? Suddenly you're in another world. And nothing makes you come back. You haven't forgotten your fetal pulse. The abysmal waters become entangled in your fingers. The tenuous cord binds you. Your lungs remain collapsed. Your heart terrifies with its beating. Blind eyes. But attentive ears. You move or glide with the one who carries you. You're uncomfortable and spin around. The cord gets in your way. Your fragile fingernails almost pierce it. The cord is taut and your heartbeat thunders within it. A world of round harmony. You feel neither heat nor cold. Neither hunger nor fatigue. You float in liquid without hues. You absorb without effort. An alchemical hermaphrodite. An athanor that is never extinguished. How could you possibly leave? How could you dare to begin the abandonment? From the summit to the abyss. It's called the Fall. From Paradise to Earth. But you weren't the messenger angel: you remained inside yourself. You enveloped yourself in your nest so as not to forget your origins. That's why you're so introverted. You distance yourself. You're silent. You half-close your eyes, eyelids heavy. Things look blurry through your eyelashes. Chiaroscuro. You cross to the realm of sleep. You sleep without feeling it. When you awake you ask me with your halting words to tell you a story. And this is the only thing I can definitely say out loud. For you, I can definitely tell stories. You aren't familiar with logic, and the more fantasy, the more order to your thoughts.

I've been directing my mental novels to you, Leninito. My dear Leninito. You remained in Russia. No one claimed you. Where did you end up? At least I hold on to memories of you.

There is a view from Tacubaya that Dulcinea never forgets and likes to recall from memory.[15] Along with the Marquise Calderon de la Barca, she compares memories and almost in tandem they write a page. The summer homes of Tacubaya are large, with ancient gardens and stone fountains. A certain

---

15. Tacubaya is a neighborhood of Mexico City that has been inhabited even before the Aztecs. Its Nahuatl toponym referred to it as a place where "water was gathered" because of its rivers and proximity to lake water. Noted for its wealth and beauty in colonial times, it was popular among the elite who had summer homes there. The Marquise Calderon de la Barca lived in one of those summer homes. Over time, Tacubaya has transformed into a more urban, working-class neighborhood.

touch of abandonment, an unkempt yard with flowers in disarray, empty rooms, tall walls, all contribute to a feeling of life not lived. Of artificiality. Of disillusionment. Of doing things because that's the way they've always been done (in summers one must go to the summer home in Tacubaya). A repeated pattern. Worn out.

Dulcinea interrupts her memory of Tacubaya. She now understands what she can no longer bear: life alongside the Marquise. The way it has turned into a daily routine. Dinners. Meals. Visits. Dances. Protocol. Days at the club. Walks. Meetings. How horrid. Enough. Dulcinea can't bear it. The perfect diary of the Marquise. Her impeccable grammar. Her restrained weariness. Her orderly world. Dulcinea screams. She screams in the summer home in Tacubaya. The glass window panes vibrate and the volcanoes in the distance seem to crack. Amadis, come for me and take me away. Far, far away. Far from the routine of the masses.

Amadis carries her away toward Michoacan. Or so she thinks.

Horrible. I can't continue with this story.

In the car, Dulcinea looks at the stifling houses that face the Periferico. Their dirty windows. Some broken. Without curtains. Or covered by newspapers. In any case, the invading noise. The constant background noise, almost like waves, never in silence. Doesn't even God command silence?

And if everything was a mistake? If my brother died in a bombing in Madrid? Then I went to Russia alone. My parents didn't want to see me. They were getting rid of me. They were the ones who carried my brother's bloody clothing in exile. From Spain to France. From France to Cuba. From Cuba to Mexico. No one sent it to them from Russia. They always had it.

The thing is, I don't remember a brother. I know some things because they told them to me: I don't remember him. I've seen his photo on the beach. A summer in Hyères: I wasn't there.[16] I don't know if it was true. That's what they said. You begin by believing every story. It's repeated and believed. And later it becomes the truth. It's true.

But I don't believe it. I keep redoing the story. The story has no foundation. It's pure imagination. Who died in Russia? It wasn't my brother. Might it be Leninito? Not him either. No one claimed him and he went to a home. To a shelter? What kind of shelter? Just a shelter. You don't even know if

---

16. Birthplace of Muñiz-Huberman, Hyères appears in several of her novels.

you had a brother. And the bloody clothing? I saw it. And your brother? I don't know. I have to believe. I cling to him. You no longer care about your brother. You believed he mattered to you. He never mattered to you. It was a story you would have liked to tell. An old story. A story for which there are no witnesses.

You were calm. Restrained. Very prudent. You didn't risk a diverging opinion. You wanted to make a good impression. You may have believed that. But the volcano was smoldering from within. Someday there would be an eruption. Your internal answers were contrary. They were always the opposite. You never agreed with anyone. But you could not speak.

I know that chaos is God's great raw material. God's favorite material. Nothing would have meaning without chaos. It is the beginning and it is hope. Thankfully there is chaos. The skein is tangled. Disorder exists. Eternity is confirmed. Neither beginning nor end. Chaos is in me. Internal sea. Waves of images that flood me. I don't know where to begin.

The beginning doesn't matter. Picking up, gently, between your index finger and your thumb, any loose end that appears. With the same arbitrariness as God. Thus dismanting the established order: why believe in Genesis and the Great Chain of Being? Why would Darwin come to support evolution? Not chronologies. Nor genealogies.

It's easy to say. First, you start with the idea of order and later you reject it. If you weren't so familiar with it, you wouldn't reject it.

You're wrong. You're wrong. Without chaos I wouldn't move. Chaos indicates pure movement, without indicating anything. It's the fountain of life. Of disequilibrium. Of a single impulse. It drives you to act. To be.

But how do I know that I exist? That I'm alive? I don't know. I can't know. I dig my nails into the palms of my hand and if I feel them, I know I'm alive. Is that the only way of knowing? Yes, I think so. Because I don't recognize myself. Before, when I was speaking, I would ask myself, who is that woman speaking? It wasn't my voice and I didn't understand how these strings of sentences kept coming out. Strings? If I see a reflection in the mirror, I think: who is she? Other people are also unrecognizable. They're strange beings. They gesticulate. They emit sounds. They move their eyes, eyebrows, lips. Sometimes they show their teeth and tongues. Frequently there's a little space between the top two incisors. I can't stop looking at it. As if it were a fault. An error. What's a little space doing there? I don't know. Sometimes the space between the upper lip and the nose is very large or very small. Why? I don't know. The forehead can be wide or narrow. Why? Genetic explanations don't interest me. They don't clarify the mystery. What does it mean? No, no, I don't know. Faces are scary. That's the truth. They're strange and different. I can't look at them. They move away from me and shrink. They escape to the end of a telescope. Or they fall into the depths of a glass of water, as if it were a well. They begin to blur in concentric circles. They stare sternly. They're scary. I don't like them. I prefer the faces of animals. They're beautiful faces, well proportioned, with a pure and direct look. Undoubtedly, they're not scary. Maybe a rhinoceros isn't beautiful, but it's an exception. And it can transform into a unicorn.

Thus, it's hard to know who I am, especially when I don't know the others. The others begin over there, far away, in Poland.

They're so distant, so boring and repetitive and expressionless. The same people I always see on the streets, on buses, in places. If only I could shake them, wake them, slap them. Spit on their cheeks. In a word, make them feel they are alive. So they would be forced to recognize their happiness through horror and scandal. Shake their inertia. Their deep inherited boredom. Their maddening sanity. Their awful good manners. But, Dulcinea, how dare you? You believe in sanity and good manners? Which Dulcinea are you? The one from yesterday or today? Because today there is nothing to believe in. Fifteen thousand Jewish children killed by German soldiers in the Theresienstadt concentration camp. Sanity and good manners. You seem like you're from the eighteenth century, dear Dulcinea.

And the flowers I beheld   all looked and smelt so sweet
That the senses and the soul   they seemed alike to greet;
While on every side ran fountains   through all this glad retreat,
Which in winter's kindly warmth supplied,   yet tempered summer's heat.[17]

Dulcinea and Amadis are familiar with places like those described by Gonzalo de Berceo. They live in them. They continue their pilgrimage because, until they arrive at their true destination and know it's their true destination, they cannot stop. It's as if a curse had set their feet in incessant movement. Their bodies are weary and they cannot stand still. Barely a fleeting rest under a tree or in a haystack. Condemned to exile, they do not know repose. If some compassionate lord welcomes them in his castle, they don't go farther than the kitchen stove, and seated on the wooden benches, they fill their bowls twice with soup from the pot. They eat sizable chunks of still-warm bread and drink red wine. The only thing they know with certainty is that

---

17. Berceo, *Miracles*, 31. From Gonzalo de Berceo's (c. 1195–c.1260) opening to *Miracles of Our Lady* (c. 1245–1260). Gonzalo de Berceo is considered Spain's first poet to write in Castilian. He is known for his four-line stanzas with fourteen-syllable lines, each line with a break between two sets of seven syllables.

they must continue their journey, thinking about finding what they must find. As if they were waiting for a star that would signal the place one night.

Is it the place of contrition or sacrifice they seek? Occult yet wise forces guide them. An inescapable magnet attracts them.

One autumn night, well on the way to winter, in tightly wrapped capes because the cold creeps in indifferently, they arrive at the doors of a monastery that announced itself from afar by the tolling of its bell and a twinkling light in its turret. They arrive, knock on the door, and are graciously welcomed in. They know that many years ago a poet of *alejandrino* quartets had taken shelter there.[18] Maybe he would know where to tell them to go. They ask to be led to his cell. What they find is the shell of a body. In the bed, under the sheet, the old poet is shapeless. He's a shadow breaking into parts. He's skin stretched over bones. Sharp splinters tearing cloth. Misaligned gears. Dislocated joints. Life at a standstill. Irrational words. Involuntary. Incommunicative remains. Each organ separated: no longer harmonious. Hand that doesn't obey and trembles as it lifts sustenance to the mouth. Tongue without teeth or muscles to support it: parody of speech. Pupil that possibly focuses on some vagueness of the imagination. Does he have some memory, an image, a thought? Does he feel at peace or at war? Is he hanging on to life or death?

Dulcinea cannot tolerate the bitter smell. The smell of old. Of sweaty and disheveled hair. Of purulent tear ducts. Of shriveled-up wrinkles and folds. Of splintered bones. Of dried urine and feces. Of the shapeless sexual organ. Dulcinea can't tolerate the view. The pale green of death. Decomposition invading. The hastening reflection of nothingness. Meaningless desires.

They've arrived too late. The old man will not speak to Dulcinea or Amadis. He has moved beyond his melancholy state, as described by the ancients. He's a lamentable shell of a human, a bodily prison whose soul escaped into his poems. Nothing is left of him. Then what is he waiting for? His final breath. The arrhythmic, agonizing scream. The portent comes and the bell punctuates it. In a desperate senile gesture, he stretches out an arm whose stiff and vehement prehensile fingers try to cling to something alive and warm from this world, and they trap Amadis's arm. The old man, with the force of death, pulls and pulls on Amadis to take him along. When his eyes glaze over and the claw weakens, the rasping sound of his throat has spilled out liberating death. Then there is peace.

---

18. Muñiz-Huberman uses the Spanish words "tetrástrofo monorrimo," referring to a kind of Spanish verse with four-line stanzas, each line with fourteen syllables (*alejandrino*) containing one rhyme: AAAA BBBB. The name comes from the *Book of Alexandre*, a medieval epic about the life of Alexander the Great. This poetic form was very popular in medieval Spanish texts, such as Berceo's *The Miracles of our Lady* and Juan Ruiz, the Archpriest of Hita's *The Book of Good Love* (c.1330–1334). Here the poet Dulcinea and Amadis seek is Gonzalo de Berceo.

Later there's the burial. What's a burial? It's leaving a person there inside. One who can no longer leave. Who no longer worries. Who forgets. Or it's having a person always present in a new way, one who always accompanies you even when you abhor his company. Who appears in your dreams or whose unsolicited voice you hear. It's your feeling of guilt at having survived. No, not at all, it's my liberation, this person doesn't matter now, one person less, someone who no longer bothers me, or demands of me, or impedes me. One less mouth. On the other hand, I affirm my existence, I'm luckier, I saved myself (saved for what?), I have more space around me. I'm the heir. It's possible you inherit something, material or spiritual, or that your resentment only grows, doubly alone, and that nothing was your inheritance.

Bones are the inheritance of the earth. They alone remain. What for? Where do you put the bones? What do you do with them? They get in the way and take up space. When living they don't bend, and when dead they take up space. It would be better to burn them, reduce them to ashes. You are dust.

Dulcinea and Amadis continue on without becoming any wiser. They only find desolation on their path. They do not decipher the message. It does not even appear to them. And if they were to miss it?

This night was strange. So strange. Dulcinea remembers it now along with the constant spinning of the car's tires. She awoke at daybreak without being able to fall back asleep. A panting breath was closing in on her bed. A figure was trying to creep up her sheets. A weight prevented her from moving. Something was bubbling. Something hot and dense. Something that was taking up more and more space like a hot liquid flowing. A thick shape that was slowly settling in. A panting that was not threatening. Yes, that's what it was like. That's how it felt to me. An unyielding slow advance. The certainty of immobility. I wouldn't get up. I wouldn't scream. I would let it invade me. Crushing. Drowning. Tamping down. Like tobacco in a pipe. No anxiety, Dulcinea, a simple sensation that is different. Don't worry, Dulcinea, they weren't Freudian echoes that surrounded you. Just your unfettered imagination. You were born a writer, Dulcinea. You make up everything.

Do you remember another nightmare? You would have it in the International House. The first time was when you had that high fever for which they never figured out the cause. A perturbing line of rocks and more rocks in deformed unity. A chocolatey dense black with dark grooves and greenish veins like pinpricks. Deformity in movement. Rocks like convulsing faces. Cavities and growths. Exploding eyes and uprooted cheeks. Broken noses. Peeling lips. The thickening of pimply pores. Creative movement. Twisted and slow, wavelike, superimposing one upon the other. Like face upon face, original and negative, without merging. Copies that slide away. Unmatching. Incongruent.

After this first time, time and time again. Repeated and different. Terrible. Stuck in my head. My favorite nightmare. Without it, I didn't feel right.

There was another nightmare I made up. It wasn't mine. But it matched up with my nostalgia for other time periods. What's more, it could be a scene for one of my novels, the one with Dulcinea and the Marquise. I dreamt of myself dressed all in black silk from head to toe. With both a high neck and cuffs of white lace. I was descending a staircase. Wide. With a lustrously carved handrail. I descended slowly. With good posture. Like a princess. As it should be. The light illuminating me from behind. From some very high windows above. And me descending, fearing what lay in wait behind that door. Taking the last steps more slowly. If only I could freeze in space. Cut off time. Stab the impenetrable. No. The door remains. A door has two sides: it beckons and seals. The hinges are golden and well oiled. The wooden panels soften a half-broken breathing. There is someone behind it. Someone waiting. A messenger with an inevitable voice. I am no longer me. It is Dulcinea. Dulcinea knows it. Surely. Step by step she approaches the door. She will have to open it. There are moments that can no longer be delayed.

The messenger delivers a missive. His face is childlike and sad. He knows. Dulcinea still does not. She will remain with the letter in her hand. Looking at the tall rows of birch trees with shuddering white bark. The interminable park, almost a forest. A crisp breeze of late fall. Some leaves barely whispering on the ground. An inaudible galloping. A throbbing frontier. What Dulcinea fears has occurred: the broken word.

That is Dulcinea's dream. Or it could be a movie. Yes. A movie based on a Chekov story. A Russian movie. Or an English movie (with James Mason, Simone Signoret, Vanessa Redgrave, David Warner) filmed in a Scandinavian forest. No matter. The same strange things that happen in movies happen in dreams. Reality is distortable. We're all transgressors.

The end of the world is coming. The owner of the Bremen bakery told me so. The millennium. We must be on our best behavior. Be restrained. Be cautious. It's in our best interest. No way! Bombs here, bombs there. Shattered bodies flying. Bloody brains. Entrails stuck on glass. Pieces of legs. Amputated fingers. Scalps blown off. Careful—don't walk on the fingernails on the floor. You'll slip on that slimy intestine. You almost burst that swollen bladder. Gather, gather the pieces carefully. Later they will come to claim them. Organized and perfectly labeled in their small plastic bags. Each family will aseptically choose what belongs to them. The distribution will be fair. You won't recognize the liver or gallbladder of your relative, but you will recognize a piece of their clothing or their shoelace. You'll accept it. Because you've always accepted what you had to. And you'll continue to accept things.

The end of the world is announced on walls. Every morning writings appear. Without being seen, someone (God), mysteriously dictates methods of destruction through a hand with a can of spray paint. Death and extermination are painted on all the walls. Never an aurora borealis or Niagara Falls.

Marches are organized. Like in the era of the Crusades, they go door to door and someone rallies the multitudes. The marchers demand things and yell more. There are special marches for children, women, men, homosexuals, prostitutes. Each group has its holy crusade. Even the Marxists have their crusades. And each announces the end of an era. An era? Our era. Humanity is rightly terrified.

For me there is no end of the world. My world was destroyed the day they put me on the boat. Have you forgotten, Dulcinea, what it was like to be in the middle of the ocean in an unsteady boat? Do you remember what you did the first day when the shoreline was no longer visible? I threw my doll (the only one I would ever have) overboard. I did it because my mother had told me to take good care of her. Logically, I threw her away. And then I felt much better. I was never interested in tying myself to anything. Successive deaths—of others, of my brother—have bestowed upon me a joyous freedom. I always envied the time Robinson Crusoe had alone. This is why I aspire to be like God, so rotund in roundness, so circular in solitude. But here's the problem: God did not know what He was doing. All-knowing, the all-knowing God did not know. He sensed loneliness and surrounded Himself with worlds. He possessed the elements for creation and that is what He engaged in. He combined them. And here is the result. However, within chaos God instilled some order: humanity's mortality and the universe's destruction. God also gave toys to humanity: their own minds. Oh, and deoxyribonucleic acid and the genetic code: perfect biological structures. Perfect? Well, scientists are still studying that.

Later came the story of the four horses. Dulcinea knew the four horses since Russia. She had seen them in the fields:

And I saw, and behold a white horse: and he that sat on him had a bow; and a crown was given unto him: and he went forth conquering, and to conquer.

And when he had opened the second seal, I heard the second beast say, Come and see.

And there went out another horse that was red: and power was given to him that sat thereon to take peace from the earth, and that they should kill one another: and there was given unto him a great sword.

And when he had opened the third seal, I heard the third beast say, Come and see. And I beheld, and lo a black horse; and he that sat on him had a pair of balances in his hand.

And I heard a voice in the midst of the four beasts say, A measure of wheat for a penny, and three measures of barley for a penny; and see thou hurt not the oil and the wine.

And when he had opened the fourth seal, I heard the voice of the fourth beast say, Come and see.

And I looked, and behold a pale horse: and his name that sat on him was Death, and Hell followed with him. And power was given unto them over the fourth part of the earth, to kill with sword, and with hunger, and with death, and with the beasts of the earth.[19]

The four powerful horses: the white, the red, the black and the pale green. Dulcinea had ridden them in secret. Nobody had forbidden her from doing so, but she knew they would have forbidden it. That happened when her brother was still alive. She rode the white one and he the black. Or she the red one and he the pale green. They went into the forest and galloped, feeling branches strike their backs. Velocity shattering fear and wind overwhelming their breath. Forgotten memory. Forgotten past, forgotten things. Certainly not foreseeing the future. Galloping in the vertigo of the moment with horses' hooves barely touching the ground. Flying ever so fast. The sweat of the horse's flanks on Dulcinea's thighs. The mane flowing. Dulcinea's hair too. Ungrounded. Horse and rider are one, like a mythical creature. The horse moves effortlessly because Dulcinea propels their ascent. If it rains, the same water sliding down from Dulcinea onto the horse. Both soaked. Tense skin and sharp bones. If mystics had ridden runaway horses, they would have sealed the ways of the soul. Freedom transformed into froth and the sounds of eardrums broken. Ungraspable images and painful touch.

Dulcinea is very familiar with the four horses of the forest. They await her.

---

19. Rev 6:2–8 (KJV).

~

THE FOURTH SEAL

Dulcinea had read other books. They were part of her memory. In other words, part of being alive. Surely part of her transgression. Hence, part of her justice.

Books helped her inhabit her own spaces. Chosen spaces that were always far away. Haunting chimneys. Snow and good shelters. Garden corners. Fallen leaves and the shade of woods. The sun filtering in. Drops of water on the broken stones of a fountain. Crossing a peaceful lake in a canoe. Returning to a little girl's room with toys strewn about. A cabin lying in wait. Always another place. Never this one.

Inhabiting her own time periods. Which meant dressing another way. Like a classical Greek woman. Like a lady at the Court of Love (without the chastity belt). Like a princess in the Medici palace. Even in Napoleonic Empire style. Also, Victorian (although a bit more lively). And with a certain reluctance, she set 1914 as the endpoint. From then on, everything was garbage. And not just in fashion.

Books are good brooms: they sweep away garbage.

So, for Dulcinea, the only things that should be saved in the final cataclysm are books. (Of course, women, children, and old people don't matter: targeting them would be an excess of good aim.)

From books we came and to books we shall return. We live in books. From books. Near books. With books. (In front of books.) (Under books.) Between books. Toward books. Through books. For books. Because of books. According to books (varying them, and this is very important). Behind books (not shielding yourself, but rather pursuing them). But never without books or against books. And certainly never excluding books.

By the way, what do you do? What is your profession? The best of professions (maybe the oldest). Writing mental novels. Both unverifiable and undeniable. Flawless. Unforgettable. I am the very process of creation.

Dulcinea and Amadis don't know where to go after the poet's death. For the time being, they accept the convent's offer of shelter for a few days. Of walking through the orange trees. Under archways and carved stones. Like polished lace. Dotted with leaves when the wind blows. Straight columns that will remain standing when everything around them crumbles and the roof flies away. When the void arrives. When only columns are left.

The columns travel, like Dulcinea and Amadis. In memory, or because they are borne by other men to other places. Yes. I saw those columns of Saint-Michel-de-Cuxa in the Cloisters museum in New York City. And there by the orange trees I sat and listened to Gregorian chants. Surrounded by the perfume of orange blossoms. And the sound of music. And the bluish light. And the gray feeling of porous rocks. In New York City.

But Dulcinea and Amadis don't know this. But because I know it, they live it. But because I gift it to them, they enjoy it. But I enjoy it because it's the first time for them, which is like the first time for me.

Surely that's why I love my Dulcinea so much. All my Dulcineas. Dulcinea: but Dulcinea, you're Dulcinea. Yes, I'm Dulcinea and also Dulcinea and also Dulcinea. I'm glad you're keeping track, Dulcinea. You didn't forget me? Oh no, you're with me.

Once upon a time. How I would love to have someone tell me fairy tales again. Again? Did they actually tell them to you? It's true, they didn't tell them to me. I didn't have a bourgeois mother like the kind that corrupts children and introduces them to obscurantism. And superstition. My parents were enlightened. I never heard, "Once upon a time . . ." In any case, there will be once upon a time. Wipe the slate clean and start over. The Marxist apocalypse, that's what they taught me at the International House. So I grew up without knowing those horrible fairy tales that lie and deceive and foster the imagination and make you desire knights in shining armor and a wolf that eats the invalid grandmother and a witch that savors tasty children.

In the orange grove, Dulcinea and Amadis don't know where to go next. The monks advise them to take the path to Provence.[1] They would have to cross over the Mountains of Fire and they will have to walk for many days.[2] They'll do it. Their legs have strong and elastic muscles. They'll do it. There in Provence they'll hear the songs of troubadours who might know the story they seek.

---

1. Bringing together thinkers from Islam, Judaism, and Christianity, Provence was an important center of religious, mystical, and philosophical thought in the twelfth and thirteenth centuries. It was the site of the school of Kabbalists who produced Jewish mystical texts, such as the *Sefer Ha-Bahir*—and translations and glosses of Maimonides. Other religious thinkers, such as the Cathars, who believed in a dualistic God, the Bogomils, and the Albigenses flourished in Provence until the Church led crusades to rid the region of its these religious movements they considered heretical.

2. Reference to the Pyrenees Mountains.

They walk through mountains and valleys.[3] They find refuge with shepherds and eat their bread and cheese together. They sleep in caves or church atriums. Little by little, they draw closer. They welcome the rain and the snow, the sun and the stars. They make a stop when they reach the islands of Hyères. Pine trees get soaked by the sea. This is where the war between the Greeks and the Romans that Lucan described in his *Pharsalia* occurred.

When they arrive at court, they're well received, like children of nobility. They're led to the baths and find themselves clothed in silk and velvet, chiffon and lace. They eat and drink with pleasure. That night they sleep embracing each other between warm sheets.

Many stories circulate in the palace. Dulcinea and Amadis can choose theirs. Stories of different heresies: of persecutions and killings. Of dualisms and pantheisms. Of new ideas derived from Eastern mysticism. There are those who deny miracles. Those who deny the virtue of baptism. Those who deny the presence of Christ in the Eucharist. Those who deny the effectiveness of praying to saints. Those who deny indulgences, hell, purgatory, transverberation. Those who affirm communalism, detachment from riches and earthly possessions. Not touching women. Not killing animals. Not eating meat. Not procreating and not condemning suicide. The creation of the universe, not by God but by a demiurge, imperfect and incomplete. And yet, aspiring to purity and the suppression of instincts, war, and violence. Loving even your enemy. Caring for the ill and the poor. Hoping that at the end of times God will triumph over evil without resorting to evil. Because every soul will be saved.

Or rather, imagining the Church as the Whore of Babylon and the Pope as the Antichrist. Depicting images of a malformed Virgin, wicked and torturous. Seeing the cross as a simple piece of wood. Loathing adornment, luxuries, artificiality.

Cathars, Albigenses, and Bogomils were all sung by the sweet-tongued troubadours as the new forces that would unmask deceit, betrayal, and hypocrisy.

Dulcinea and Amadis in the midst of a whirlwind.

Is it possible that you're alive, Dulcinea? Tell me, didn't you just feel death?

It's strange, very strange. I know what death is. I've felt it a few times. How do I explain it? It's been in me. I have left myself for a second or an

---

3. Song of Songs 2:8, 2:1. Muñiz-Huberman evokes the connection between nature and love as the two lovers find each other through valleys and mountains.

eternity. I have stopped being me and have glimpsed into a complete void. Into absolute illumination and, therefore, into the loss of myself. And I've said: this is what death will be like. Lacking sensations. Limitless. Infinite time without shades of color. Painlessly white. Maybe transparent. Transparency of the nonexistent. A moment of total silence (without even the internal sounds of the ear). Without sound. Understanding the deaf world. The sudden loss of every sense. The suppression of thought. Sudden paralysis. The internal emptying and escape from the body. Unmoving.

To stop being. For a measure of immeasurable time.
Panic. At the same time as encompassing consolation.
At least nothing hurts now. Nothing hurts.
If only it were that way. What a relief. Yes. If only.
We do not fear death. We know it is repose.
It is transition. Desperation. Imminence. The pre-moment. From knowing I am here to knowing I will not be here. The fleeting consciousness of eternal unconsciousness.

We will have to think about this, Dulcinea. We will have to think about this, sweet Dulcinea.

Speaking of grammar. (What? Were we talking about grammar?) There's a verb tense I can't stand. Pluperfect subjunctive.[4] If the Spanish Civil War had not exploded. If my parents had not sent me to Russia. If I had not arrived in Mexico. If I weren't traveling, at this moment, on the Periferico. If I had not been born. If I had already died.

A tense of impossible hypotheticals. Tense of desire denied. Tense of the most inopportune melancholy. Tense of what could have been but never was. Tense of actions that did not happen. Of all the despairs of man: what if . . . Of all of man's errors: what if . . . Of all forgetfulness: what if . . .

Do you remember that trip from Guanajuato to Mexico City? How could I forget? Was it there that Amadis died? Amadis died? Amadis was driving the car. We were a group of students and professors returning from the first professional exam given in the Department of Literature at Guanajuato

---

4. The pluperfect subjunctive is a tense and mood used in Spansh for hypothetical situations that are contrary to fact. In this section the narrator wonders what would have happened if certain events in the past *had not occurred* the way they did. If the previous sentence were in Spanish, the verbs in italics would be conjugated in the pluperfect subjunctive.

University. It was raining. The car slid and crashed into a stone wall. Only the driver died. Then someone said: what if we hadn't gone today? What if it hadn't been raining? What if the car hadn't slid? Nobody would have died. Nobody would be hurt. And someone else said: your what-ifs are stupid.

Since then this tense doesn't exist. A useless and whiny tense. An immoral tense. Erased.

And the imperfect, Dulcinea? Yes, I like the imperfect.[5] So imperfect. So habitual. So routine. So silky. I used to. I used to do. I used to write. It used to snow. I used to listen. I used to walk.

A tense of habits. Tense of fireplaces. A warm tense on a winter night. Of preparing the samovar and drinking tea.[6] Of ritual and repetition. Of brushing hair and applying perfume. Of preparing for ceremonies. Of telling fairy tales. Once upon a time. Ancient myths. Once upon a time. Memories of childhood. My mother used to tell me.

Happy times and smiling faces.

But if Amadis died in that accident on the highway from Guanajuato, who's driving this car on the Periferico? That neck and the shape of that face are Amadis's. And the haircut. And the color. He doesn't speak. It could be Amadis. And these two people talking so much, who are they? Can it be them? My parents? Why are they with me? Since I don't speak to them. Even worse, since I don't know if they're dead. It's been so many years since I've seen them. Their voices were always intolerable. Their shrieking. Their bursts of little screeches. Like squashed little rats. Pecked words and perforated sounds. Where-is-your-bro-ther? Why-did-you-let-him-die?

What brother? What death? Who cares about brothers? Only the undertakers. It's their reason for being. They wash the bodies. Dress them. Embalm them. Mummify them. What a serene expression. What peaceful hands crossed over their chests. (I will never cross my arms again, I look dead.)

But could these people be my parents? The truth is I don't recognize them. Though they do have a certain air of familiarity. I didn't recognize them when I arrived from Russia either. And they didn't recognize me. So, I had to convince myself: these are my parents, these are my parents, these are my parents. And mash up this idea, crush it, wring it, dry it, starch it, and iron it. THESE ARE MY PARENTS. Like that, a little stiff.

What are they saying? As I don't speak, I no longer listen. What are those sounds that leave their creased lips, their threatening teeth, their raw tongues?

---

5. The imperfect tense is used in Spanish to describe repeated and ongoing actions or events in the past.
6. A samovar is a Russian teapot.

Only other people understand these sounds. I don't worry about it. There were so many years of listening. No, now I don't hear anymore. What for?

Many years ago, they asked me why my brother died. Well, why would it be? Because we must all die. So as not to take up so much space, among other things. Even if one is small and a little boy. Well, that's death.

Dulcinea, go back to the story of your other Dulcinea, the one who is bored with the Marquise Calderon de la Barca in the house in Tacubaya. I don't have any desire to return to her since she is so bored. So, make her have fun. Then I will make her story flow.

Dulcinea is bored. Dulcinea has called upon Amadis to take her away to other places where she can forget. If only she could get to other places without having to move. That would be best. Her mistake was traveling to new lands. It's the same as if she had remained in Spain. She understands that the other place where she wants to go doesn't exist. That if Amadis were to take her there, it would be the same. The emptiness that she was born with cannot be filled. The emptiness. The hole. The blank space. Sometimes she cries and feels compassion for other people, but the well is dry, the water doesn't rise.

She helps the Marquise make lace with bobbins, embroider white linen handkerchiefs, pick out silks and taffetas. And time slips away. The Marquise's enthusiasm lessens the pinpricks of remorse. But later, when she shuts herself in her room, Dulcinea knocks down walls. She tears at the blackness of night. And she doesn't sleep. She lets the stars pierce her head. Wishes her dark eyelids would close over her eyes. Unmoving. Paralyzed. In this underworld of creatures and moans. Of old magic formulas for spells. Of potions and balms. Of eternally sealed doors. Of the shrieking, thickly feathered nocturnal animal. Of the bird beak pecking a collapsed cranium. Of eroded ruins in forgotten deserts. Pyramids that are crumbling. Sphinx made of grains of sand. The pulverization of everything.

The sublunar region is escaping its orbit.

Dulcinea can only compare her emptiness to being submerged in the infinite night. It's the evocation of chaos. It's losing sight and gaining hearing. Her voice resounds from within. Hearing the screams of mute fish. It's a resonating chamber. Where words bounce from side to side, and from the floor to the ceiling. In the silence of night, why do words explode and get tangled in unspoken echoes? Tall walls that hold back dams. Waters that would love to overflow. Her head spins. Dulcinea wants to hold it with her hands, but her hands don't find her head. Dulcinea doesn't know where she is. The room is dark and the black ceiling beams fly away.

Everything is falling apart, reverting to lines and shapes. Everything feels as if it's disintegrating.

The effort of thinking about the nineteenth-century Dulcinea has worn out Dulcinea. Dulcinea nods off in the car. She wants to sleep. She slides down a little and rests her head on the back of the seat. She sleeps for a few minutes and wakes up clearheaded. She remembers other times she has awoken, when she still took naps. Back then, she used to think things were alive. The pillow rippled under her cheek. Beside it, a pillow threw itself over her head. The sheet twisted itself in her hair. The mattress moaned. The legs of the bed started to walk. The carpet flew. The furniture opened its drawers and tossed everything out from inside. The couch slept on the floor. The piano began to play. The flowers in the vase went to take a shower. Lamps turned on and off. Books leafed through one another. The dictionary went onto the balcony for some fresh air. Knives danced with spoons and plates began to hurl themselves from high places. Glasses climbed up walls and fruit hid in corners. Windows flew through the air and the door locked itself in. Paintings lowered themselves to the floor and the colors began running; lines broke apart. Walls cleanly turned back into bricks. Snow crystals formed the smoke from the nonexistent chimney, and snowflakes descended in silence.

The disintegration persists. How to reintegrate it? How to reunify its parts? How to return to God's breast? How to reorganize Picasso's faces? Give tone to the atonal? Re-engrave stone and marble? Impossible. Kandinsky sees spirituality in patches of color. Paul Klee, in the arrow's path.

What is broken is ours. Fractured. Separated. This will be yours, Dulcinea. Dulcinea who left the Spanish Civil War and found herself in the other Great War, always fleeing, only to arrive at your own internal war. My internal war is everyone's.

Dulcinea, if you could pick up the scattered pieces. Tie up the loose ends. String together the beads of an amber necklace. Thread silver needles with silken threads. If in some way the puzzle would be solved for you. If only your story were a coherent and ordered story. If only your life were to appear on a perfect screen for you. If only chronology existed. If only a photo album were to represent a moment of truth.

However, everything has gaps. Memories crowd together. Memory collapses. There's no structure. No time. Dates change. Photos weren't taken. No movie was filmed. No footprints persist. Paper, which contains so much, burns easily. Files get jumbled and the papers fly into flames. How do you find the facts you seek? How do you know they have not been altered or erased?

Do processes exist? Do systems? Do methods? I doubt it. I really doubt it. Unless they exist through their negation. Antiprocesses. Antisystems. Antimethods. Because there is madness in rules. There is. A body destroys itself. Defenses can attack their own side. Blood devours its own order. Cells distort their pattern. The genetic code is deformed. The message gets the code wrong. Soldiers in the same army kill each other. And then . . .

So, the beginning, middle, and end of the story have gotten mixed up and Dulcinea doesn't know where to continue. And if Dulcinea doesn't organize her story, Dulcinea will die. But do we, everyone else, ever have our stories in order? No, we don't. That's why we die.

It is said that total order is found only at the moment of death. It's the chronological key. Absolute harmony. What nonsense.

Chaos is living. It changes. Breaks and corrupts. Bursts in. Moves things around. People are guided by a narrow point of view. Total subjectivity. Nothing matters more than my micromicromicrocosmos. And the world's macromacromacrochaos.

Well, Dulcinea, go back to your work. Sally forth, reap trouble and right wrongs. What else do you remember about Russia? About Russia? I don't know. The thick snow, covering the fields in a smooth white. The day the cook died. His coffin in the middle of the patio and all the serious children together, standing in a line, in their best clothes, hair recently combed, filing past, one by one, to say goodbye to the good cook. The good cook who had made miracles happen so there was enough food for the hungry children. From potato peels he made bread, and from bark and herbs he prepared broths. While children in Leningrad died, the children of the International House still had warm tea to drink. Thanks to the good cook. The children sadly said goodbye. Snow kept falling and, later, in the cemetery, it piled up very high on the gravestone. The calm cleared away the sorrow. It was like a merengue pie the children had never tasted. One, with a quick move, scooped a handful of snow and brought it to his lips. He thought it tasted sweet.

Sometimes Dulcinea tried to memorize a landscape as if she were seeing it for the last time. She would sit quietly, alone, taking in everything she could within her sight. A tree. Another tree. Its branches, its leaves, its colors. Thickets. Flowers. Birds. The flight of insects. She did the same thing with rooms in houses where she had stayed. When she was observing them, everything was clear and she didn't forget a single detail. She thought she would always remember it that way: perfect and complete. Whole. Later, as the years passed, things had fallen to a depth she could not locate: the bottom of a bottomless trunk. Open to the abyss. And all she remembered was some small detail wrapped in a dreamy haze. In grays. In the middle of the field, a ledge jutting out of a partially caved-in wall, onto which the children jumped and practiced standing on one foot. The ledge was mossy and some stones were missing on one part, and it was there that Dulcinea liked to stand. Dulcinea would speak to the stones and tell them that only she understood them, that only she would remember them. She would go to the ledge very early, before the other children, so she could be alone with the stones. When the others arrived she would leave and give one last glance to the place with the missing stones.

It was the same with the tree whose trunk had grown almost parallel to the ground for a stretch, only to grow upright again. She could wrap her arms around that part of the trunk and sit on it. She would think a lot there and it was her refuge when she was sad. Sometimes she cried and the tears danced around on the rough bark. She'd wanted her brother to be alive. Or that her parents hadn't sent her in that ship to Odessa. She felt lost. Hopelessly abandoned. Only the rough trunk welcomed and consoled her.

Another memory engraved in her mind was the wet tiles. Every time it rained, a group of tiles, four or five that had sunk lower than the others on the patio floor, stayed wet for a long time after the rain had stopped. The water was dark and stagnant: it stood out from the rest of the floor. You could only clear the water by sweeping the tiles and using the corner of the broom, spraying the water in streaks onto the other tiles, which then dried quickly. It always happened like this and it always would. This made Dulcinea feel secure.

But security never lasted long for Dulcinea. Those tiles were in the first house. But there would never be sunken tiles on the patio floor again, not in the second, third, or any other house.

When did you begin to lose your appetite, Dulcinea? It was then. After the cook's death, when food was even more scarce. The more other children became hungry (especially Leninito), and the more their eyes sunk deeper and their bodies got thinner and they ate anything they could find (Leninito even ate pieces of paper), the less hungry I felt. My stomach, and then my appetite, gradually shrank. I could only drink tea. A lot of tea. Tea made from any kind of leaf found in the fields.

Did you give your food to Leninito? Yes, I gave it to him and it still wasn't enough. Before they swept the dining hall, I would look all along the floor, just in case some food had fallen. I would even pick up crumbs, pressing my fingertips into them.

(Thank you, Dulcinea, for giving me your food. You left, Dulcinea. I stayed. No one claimed me. I still remember you, Dulcinea.)

Dulcinea, do you realize that you could write a story about Leninito? No, no, enough. It's enough with these stories. If I'm able to finish them.

Nonetheless, Dulcinea will always cherish that truncated and nomadic childhood. It's the only one she had and she holds it dear. She likes to remember. If she had had children, she would have found her voice again to tell them those stories. But since she doesn't have children, she tells the stories to herself.

There is one story from that time that she knows by heart:

Zhili-byli ded da baba
A byla u nikh kurochka ryaba
Snesla kurochka yaichko
A yaichoko ne prostoe a zolotoe
Ded bil, bil, ne razbil
Baba bila, bila, ne razbila
A myshka bezhala
Khvostikom makhnula
Yaichko upalo i razbilos.
Plachet ded
Plachet baba.
A kurochka kudkudakhchet
Ne plach ded
Ne plach baba
Snesu ya vam yaichiko
Ne zolotoe a prostoe.[7]

---

7. Standard transliteration of Russian by Christopher Lemelin. This is an example of a common Russian folktale for children called "Kurochka Ryaba" or "Speckled Hen." Lydia Rodríguez-Hahn, to whom the novel is dedicated, narrated this story to Muñiz-Huberman as she remembered it from her years in the International House.

(Once upon a time a grandmother and a grandfather had a laying hen. The hen laid an egg, but the egg wasn't normal—it was a golden egg. The grandfather tried to break it, but he couldn't. The grandmother tried to break it, but she couldn't. A little mouse came running by, swinging its tail, and the egg fell and broke. The grandfather was crying. The grandmother was crying. And the hen said, "Don't cry grandfather, don't cry grandmother, I'll bring you a regular egg and not a golden one.")

But no one will hear it. Well, it's her childhood. She feels no bitterness about it. It's her life. Her only belonging. Her memory. Exclusively hers. That no one else can possess. It is, therefore, a symbol of joy.

Yes, Dulcinea has helped the Marquise to make lace, embroider white linen handkerchiefs, choose silks and taffetas. And later, in her bedroom, Dulcinea has knocked down walls. Yes, she has done all those things.

The next day, she woke up calm, her anxieties from the night before erased. It would be a new day. One activity sliding smoothly into the next. Saying to yourself: you can live without worries. Forgetting that you're alive. Erasing borrowed time.

So she will happily decide with the Marquise how to spend the day. There are always ways to fill the hours with trivialities. First, order food. What will you eat? To start, a nice chicken soup. Later, Mexican rice. Roasted meat with sautéed vegetables. And finally some tostadas with grated cheese and finely chopped lettuce. For dessert, fruit salad mixed with black sapote.[8] To conclude, spiced coffee, which the Marquise particularly likes.

This first step has begun to order the day. Food is the base. It's what is secure. Stable. Firm. Also delightful. It breaks up the middle of the day, when boredom starts to set in. But before that time arrives, Dulcinea and the Marquise Calderon de la Barca have things to do. They head at once to the Carmelite monastery of Saint Joaquin.

In the monastery, protected by high walls, there's a splendid but slightly wild garden full of flowers and an orchard celebrated for the excellence of its fruits. The prior welcomes Dulcinea and the Marquise along with her attendants, even though he doesn't allow the two ladies to go beyond the sacristy. So they have to resign themselves to barely glimpsing the garden. At that moment, the passing novices are meditating and mustn't be disturbed.

---

8. Black sapote is a fruit native to Mexico that is related to the persimmon.

Dulcinea can't pull her gaze away from one of the novices. Tall and thin, with his hood covering his face, his hands clasped in front of his chest, his way of walking, anyone would say it was him. And he looked toward her, even though it was impossible to really see her. But she is sure their eyes met. Amadis in a monastery? If Dulcinea had wanted Amadis to take her to Michoacan, how is he now in a monastery? Is it Amadis? Was he ever Amadis? In the mirror? In the park? In the back of a garden in a monastery?

The monks have prepared an abundant breakfast for their illustrious visitors. Everything from freshwater fish and different styles of eggs, to rice pudding, coffee, and fruit. But they do not sit and partake with the women. Dulcinea doesn't see the novice again.

They also had a full afternoon, since they decided to visit the Morales Hacienda.[9] There they were able to walk through the gardens and delightfully contemplated the beautiful wading pool: flowers, colors, and smells all around them.

On that peaceful day, Dulcinea feels like screaming, screaming, screaming. Exploding. A hole in your core is a hole that is never filled. Amadis comes and goes. Why doesn't Amadis fill this hole? Does Amadis exist? Is Amadis alive? Because if Amadis doesn't exist, neither does Dulcinea. Amadis, the same as her. In her. Twin brother. Lover. Glimpsed. Where is he?

They had told her that when she was born she had a twin brother who didn't make it. As a little girl she played with his image in her mind. He accompanied her as a missionary to convert nonbelievers in Africa. He accompanied her as a conquistador in the Indies, and he accompanied her as a merchant to China and Japan. Therefore, it wasn't strange to see him in the mirror. It was the same face with masculine features. The same body with men's clothing. In her trunk, Dulcinea kept men's garments and when she was alone, she put them on. So, coming to Mexico had been part of her dreams, expecting to find Amadis

Brushing her long hair in front of the mirror, barefoot in her white batiste nightgown with fine lace from Brussels on the sleeves and high neck, her skin fragrant and perfumed, Dulcinea waits. A light breeze opens the window's half-closed shutters. The candles on the dresser flicker and gradually go out. Only one, revived by the same breeze, recovers a flame and grows strong again. Dusk has taken over the room. The moonlight is steely and distant.

---

9. The Hacienda de los Morales was a colonial hacienda full of mulberry trees for raising silkworms in the sixteenth century. It has survived four centuries and is now the site of a restaurant and is promoted as a tourist destination.

With his hands on Dulcinea's shoulders, Amadis tilts his head to kiss and breathe in the freshness of her recently brushed hair. Dulcinea feels her nipples standing erect and her sex trembles.

The soft bed is theirs. Glorified skin. Lubricated skin. Engorged skin. Full. Delicate. Tense. Hot. Sweet smelling moisture. Accelerated, hot-blooded current. Palpitation and rhythm. Rhythm. Rhythm. Rhythm. Rhythm. Peak. Liquid that fills and overflows. A slow relaxing between the thighs. Little by little, withdrawal, relaxation, loss of self. Muscles released. Nerves calmed. Bones that never hurt. Refreshing dream. The only real dream.

Cars advance slowly on the Periferico. Dulcinea feels as if she has already gone past those places. Not on other days, but today. Red, blue, and ivory-colored cars. A black one with tinted windows. A delivery truck. Large billboards. Apocalyptic: alcoholic drinks and cigarettes. End it once and for all. Destroy your body. Destroy your soul. Lose all taste and smell. The toxic smoke of the city. Insidious. Nauseating. Infectious. Was there ever pure air, where the air was clear, blue skies and white clouds? The walls are gray. The men are gray. The women are gray. The children are gray. Crows' wings above roofs. Vultures on chimneys. Bats in doors and windows. Brownish-gray moths darken neighborhoods. She has seen those walls, those straw figures. That violation of color. Faded. Tossed. Burst.

Garbage. Behold, trash inundates life. Did you realize this, Dulcinea? Of course. Garbage inundates life. Garbage inundates my life. Inside of me are bins and cans, discarded jars and bottles. Rotten food and fermented drinks. Wrinkled bottle caps and crushed Campbell's soup cans. Disfigured and soggy cardboard. Unrecognizable peelings. Discarded leftovers of all kinds of meat. Half-eaten fruits and vegetables. Spit out bits and pieces. Surely, food that was vomited. Plastic all over: in bags, containers, tablecloths, plastic ware. Life itself in plastic. I am made of plastic.

When I realized I was made of plastic, I realized I was garbage. Discardable. Disposable. Interchangeable. (It's all the same: Dulcinea in Spain, Dulcinea in Russia, Dulcinea in Mexico, Dulcinea at the end of the nineteenth or twentieth centuries, Dulcinea in the middle of the Middle Ages.) I came from a factory and in a factory I will end. For you are plastic and to plastic you shall return. (The Horses of the Apocalypse are made of plastic.) (Because of plastic explosives.)

I know this landfill that I see from the left car window, now disappearing out of sight (nothing, not even trash can be eternal). I have seen it elsewhere. No, Dulcinea, don't use clichés. In other words, trash is everywhere. Mountains of trash are going to destabilize the planet Earth and it will tumble out of its orbit. Where will it go? *Qui le sait.*[10] I was wrong—I do know—it will fall *in the middle of nowhere. Newton, Shnewton, abi gezunt.*[11]

In the end, trash redeems. Trash elevates. Purifies. Its presence is because of this ascetic desire that invades me. (Worms and the Duke of Gandia.[12]) Ascetic, you Dulcinea? Yes, me, an ascetic.

Trash can also achieve *la joie de vivre.*[13] Let it dance! Like in the Disney film. The half-opened tomato sauce dancing swing, arm in arm with the crushed Corn Flakes box and the Coca-Cola bottle conducting an orchestra of lids, corks, and beer cans.

Dulcinea, you have never mentioned to me what you remember about Spain. From before you were sent to Russia. Because you must remember something. Or maybe you don't want to remember anything?

The truth is I've never wanted to make myself remember those years. It's a big black hole that I don't remember.

You don't remember anything?

I don't remember anything.

Just try.

I could make some things up, but not remember. I could tell you about the bombings in Madrid. About how people fell to the ground and how grotesque the sprawled bodies looked. How some were alive and others were dead. How I didn't know if I was alive or dead. How that wasn't important. What was important was that in every little piece of land vegetables were grown, because the besieged city wasn't getting food. What was important was to go see the gaping holes of the shells in the City University and if some other child was there playing in the debris. What was important was the loss of daily routines: every day was different and surprising: making firewood from

---

10. French for "Who knows."

11. "Newton Shnewton" is a rhyming play with English to disregard something. Here it is playing with Sir Isaac Newton's famous encounter with a falling apple, or the laws of gravity. Paired with the Yiddish "abi gezunt" ("as long as you're healthy"), Dulcinea uses a common Yiddish expression to mock her interlocutor Dulcinea; in other words, she is saying something akin to, "Who needs gravity as long as you're healthy" or "It doesn't matter."

12. Saint Francis of Borgia, Duke de Gandia (1510–1572) was a noble kinsman of Spain's King Charles V. Upon the death of Queen Isabel II, he was in charge of accompanying the Queen's body as it was transported from Toledo to Granada to be buried with his grandparents, the Catholic Monarchs (Isabella and Ferdinand). Due to the heat and length of the journey, the body had decomposed substantially. Upon opening the casket, which was customary to verify that the body was the Queen's, the Duke of Gandia was so disturbed that he never recovered. Facing mortality, he vowed to live a Christian life. Years later, after his wife's death, he joined the Company of Jesus (Jesuits), and worked diligently under St. Ignatius of Loyola. He was beatified in 1624 and canonized in 1670.

13. French for "Joy in living."

furniture or building barricades with it: burning books or notebooks or documents because of the lack of fuel.

But the truth is, I remember none of that. I make up everything. Everything is fiction. The only reality. The only reality? What is the only reality? What? Is? The? Only? Reality? The one I make up. The. One. I. Make. Up.

The canary stayed in its cage. I left quickly for Valencia with my parents and my brother. We ran down the steps. I screamed: the canary. Be quiet. Someone will take care of him. Do you think so? He didn't have fresh water and I hadn't fed him. I don't remember him either.

You lack the superb memory of Proust. Yes, I do lack Proust's superb memory. Everything is foggy and undefined. Barely discernible. Disconnected and vague. Despicable. Despicable. At the same time memory calls to you, you don't want to recall memory. How much can you control your memory so it doesn't surprise you and catch you off guard? How much do you hide or alter it? And you continue pushing it down.

But you don't always succeed. It has the gift of surprise. And like paper dolls that have been cut from folded and refolded paper, when you unfold one arm, it's attached to the arm of the next and the next and the next and the next, embracing like children in ring-around-the-rosy. And from one memory you go to the next, suddenly, unexpectedly, never ending.

Paper memories. Those pop-up books where you pulled a tab on the edge of the page and it made figures stand out and move around, and again and again you pulled the tab to make them jump out and move once more. "The Gingerbread Man": there was once an old couple who didn't have children. The old lady baked cakes and one day she decided to make little gingerbreads in the shape of boys. One came out of the oven walking around, and it was a real little gingerbread boy, with cherry buttons and a sugar mouth. But he left home and ventured into the fields. He met a dog who barked at him, a cow who charged at him, and a chicken who wanted to peck at his cherries. And on every page you would move the tab several times so that the dog would bark, the cow would charge, and the hen would peck. (Even today you see it with the same clarity as back then.) Meanwhile, the couple was so sad about losing their gingerbread boy. Finally, the boy returned home and the last picture in the book showed all three of them hugging and the cat lifting its paws to hug the boy too.

Maybe Dulcinea's parents were like that old, childless couple that had made her like the gingerbread boy. Because you can be made of gingerbread and one day end up being eaten. By accident. Or not. Yes. Maybe she was made of gingerbread. They would taste a piece and little by little they would become hungrier and they would continue to eat her until not even a crumb was left. Because if parents make children they can also unmake them. They can come back and swallow them. Chronos devouring his children.[14]

After the monastery and the death of the poet, after the islands of Hyères, Dulcinea and Amadis continue walking. They head to the White Mountains.[15] As they pass by wooded trails, it's as if they'd already passed them before. Both of them have the feeling they've been there before. They intuit the curves of the paths, the half-fallen tree limbs, the squirrel sprinting away. And once again, they intuit the curves of the paths, the half fallen tree limbs, the squirrel sprinting away. They've been there. They've dreamt of being there. They walk in circles. They move forward. They leave behind what they've already seen. Because behind them remains the landscape clinging to the early evening.

The White Mountains are distorted flags on the horizon. Dulcinea and Amadis don't know how to describe them. They climb. They twist and turn. They take shortcuts guided by goatherds' footprints, following the goatbells' ringing. Massive rock formations cut into their paths, pieces of wood strewn about, the pointy tips of burnt rocks. Leftover ashes from the fires of other travelers. The vegetation becomes more and more sparse as they ascend. Thorny brush replaces bushes. Trees become more and more scarce. Rocky bluffs become more and more common. Branches are dry. The leaves have stilled their nervation. Transparency of air. Low, thick clouds. The high-pitched whistle of the wind picking up. From behind the rocks, cold gusts of wind steal your breath. Semi-destroyed shrines, a cross of solid gray rock. A small village, the cry of a child, a sheep's bleating, the barks of a herding dog. Moist and musty hayloft. You have to dry the hay by spreading it on the ground. A weathered split rail fence marks the perimeter of the empty corral. Is the flock at pasture higher up? The pleasing smell of smoke from the fireplace promises a stew boiling over hot coals, with bits of good meat, bones with marrow, sausages, greens, and garbanzos all thickening. Everything together, cooking, bubbling liquid, spheres that upon contact with the air that is colder than the surface burst over and over, consistently, though

---

14. This reference to Chronos suggests that time eats everything. It also evokes a famous Spanish painting by Francisco de Goya (1746–1828) *Saturn Devouring One of His Sons*. This painting is known as one of his "Black Paintings," due to its dark and disturbing imagery, from a period toward the end of his life when he was suffering from internal strife while Spain itself was experiencing political and social unrest.

15. The Mont Blanc Massif is a mountain range located in the Western Alps in Italy, France, and Switzerland. It contains Mont Blanc, the second-highest mountain in Europe behind Mount Elbrus.

not in unison, out of tune. And that hot steam whose smell stimulates the comforting craving of even the most shy.

Dulcinea and Amadis are invited in and they rest on the long wooden bench. The dog and her puppies next to the fireplace and its warmth. The youngest children also pressed together with the puppies. The mother dog licks them all. The distinctive smell from the oven begins to promise golden, crusty bread with its dense center, a touch of sour and a little salt. In earthenware jars, milk is curdling at room temperature, a sign of white cheese. Above the fireplace, strings of garlic and onions, dried mountain herbs, aromatic, making one's mouth water.

Dulcinea longs for a place like that to live. Where everyone has his or her job. The man looks after the flock, understands the ever-changing weather, and goes out to hunt. (Hares flee from him.) The woman with her children, the kneaded bread, and jars of food. Outside, the cold; inside, a warmth composed of many smells. Spun wool, dark brown fabric. Straw mattresses. Furniture of thick wood. Minimal windows, with thick curtains so the freezing wind can't penetrate. A precise rhythm of the necessities of daily life. Knowing how to do everything for subsistence. An orderly world. Every thing at its time. In its place. At least, the order of the external world. Of the things we use. Of the things that are useful to us. Of slipping toward death without noticing.

But it's a lie. Dulcinea likes this world from the outside. It gives her peace, but it's not hers to inhabit. Dulcinea is a wanderer. She's a world traveler and an orderbreaker. She could not live without crazy passion. Without pure disorder. Without ascending to other realms of her imagination. Without crossroads that force a choice. Dulcinea of the land, Dulcinea of the stars.

And from the apocalyptic Lamb you also learned, Dulcinea:

And I said unto him, Sir, thou knowest. And he said to me, These are they which came out of great tribulation, and have washed their robes, and made them white in the blood of the Lamb.

Therefore are they before the throne of God, and serve him day and night in his temple: and he that sitteth on the throne shall dwell among them.

They shall hunger no more, neither thirst any more; neither shall the sun light on them, nor any heat.

For the Lamb which is in the midst of the throne shall feed them, and shall lead them unto living fountains of waters: and God shall wipe away all tears from their eyes.[16]

---

16. Rev 7:14–17 (KJV).

THE FIFTH SEAL

Dulcinea, by any chance, did you memorize the Book of Revelation? Yes, I learned it by heart. When I decided not to speak, I had to exercise my memory. I have to keep everything inside in order to speak with myself. To tell myself my novels. That I don't write down. But that flow out of me.

Who would think of memorizing the Book of Revelation? Me. A very good mnemonic exercise. Let's see, can I ask you something? Yes. If I ask you to recite chapter 10, verses 8, 9 and 10, will you be able to? Of course:

And the voice which I heard from heaven spake unto me again, and said, Go and take the little book which is open in the hand of the angel which standeth upon the sea and upon the earth.

And I went unto the angel, and said unto him, Give me the little book. And he said unto me, Take it, and eat it up; and it shall make thy belly bitter, but it shall be in thy mouth sweet as honey.

And I took the little book out of the angel's hand, and ate it up; and it was in my mouth sweet as honey: and as soon as I had eaten it, my belly was bitter.[1]

So now you know, scrolls from angels are meant to be eaten and are at once sweet and bitter. Here Saint John the Theologian was too obvious in his imagery. Bibliophagy is perfectly understood.

But enough. I'm sick of books now. I want to live out my silence alone. You are wrong, so, so wrong. A thousand internal voices call you. Not in monologues or dialogues. But in polylogues. Simultaneously. You're the memory of books. Impossible to separate yourself from them. Moreover, you're not sick of them. You're fasting. Impossible to devour them all. Pluri-literary indigestion.

Dulcinea read *Wuthering Heights* when she was a girl, when she arrived in Mexico. And she cried so much and liked it so much she made a drawing. Air blowing over the cliffs. A threatening cloud escaping in the corner. The leaning tree and the leaves falling, drifting. The shrubs with shrinking, fearful flowers. She stands in the center, her dress flowing, with three deep, distinct pleats. Her hat tied with a ribbon at her chin. A bouquet in her hands.

She kept that drawing for years. For years she kept it. And behold, only a few days ago, looking through the *New York Times Book Review*, she discovers that a painter has repeated the same drawing she painted. David Shannon painted the threatening cloud, the leaning tree, the leaves falling. She stands

---

1. Rev 10:8–10 (KJV).

in the center with her dress flowing, the hat tied with a ribbon, a bouquet in her hands.

She went to look in a forgotten box of papers from her childhood and found it there. Her drawing existed. Her drawing was the same. Her drawing—was it her drawing? She cut out the other drawing from the paper and placed it beside hers. She kept it. How had this happened? How could two identical drawings exist? Can the same mental mechanisms be repeated? In different people at different times?

We're not as unique as we think. We repeat and continue repeating the same things that others have repeated and continue to repeat. The unicorn appears in all regions.[2] Jerusalem is of heaven and of earth.[3] The unicorn roams through China, India, Persia. The Wall, the Mosque and the Cross are in Jerusalem. The unicorn was woven into tapestries.[4] Giotto painted Jerusalem and so did Doré.[5] The unicorn has been reborn, and its image has been adhered to car windows. Jerusalem has been depicted on plates and ashtrays. There are unicorns on paper napkins and also in the deepest part of our souls. Jerusalem travels and Jerusalem is unnameable. Unicorns are glimpsed here and there. Jerusalem is cyclical.

> Every idea comes from its archetype.
> Every image is perfect.
> The circle spins on the compass rose.
> And in the intermediate points.
> Infinite.
> Spheres are the harmony of the spheres.
> Without the circle, there would be no universe.
> Balls are irrefutable.
> The wheel, undeniable.

Everything belongs to us. Everything is ours. Of course, I refer to the inner world. Dear Dulcinea, how you drown from within. You distort faces and

---

2. Unicorns are an ancient, legendary creature whose meaning and symbolism vary across cultures and time periods. In the Hebrew Bible, the figure of the *re'em* (רְאֵם) was associated with unicorns. In Europe's Middle Ages, the unicorn was elusive, drawn to the purity of virgins or associated with the figure of the crucified Christ. Muñiz-Huberman's affinity for unicorns is evident in their appearance in many of her writings, especially *La guerra del unicornio* (1983).

3. Verse 21 in the *Book of Revelation* refers to a "new heaven and a new earth" in the context of a "new Jerusalem." Rev 21:1–3 (KJV).

4. Reference to the great unicorn tapestries in New York's Cloisters and the Cluny Museum in Paris.

5. Giotto, an Italian painter from the late Middle Ages, and Gustave Doré, a nineteenth-century French painter, both painted scenes of Christ's entry into Jerusalem.

you're falling step by step. Like in Saratov when you rolled downhill in the damp woods with the half-decomposed leaves. With the musty smell. You thought it was the end. No one would stop your fall. Behind you, the cries of fright were receding. Your skin was scraped. Your soul was slipping out of its cocoon. Why were white butterflies fluttering so close? Your wrapping was a transparent gauze: a web trapping air: high among the clouds. Rolling. Rolling down the hill. Earth staining your dress. You said. The moment has arrived.

But it didn't arrive.

The capacity to survive is great.

You continue on the Periferico, going in circles. Is it because they don't dare to take you where they are taking you? Will you survive? *Qui le sait. Mozhet byt'*.[6]

You worry about strangers hiding in rooms. Yes. When you arrive home from being out, you go through the house, room by room. In order. From the front to the back of the house. Under tables and couches. Behind the refrigerator. In cupboards. In closets. Behind the headboards of the beds. In the furniture's open spaces. You open and close the curtains. You raise and lower the blinds. Half-open drawers surprise you. (They hadn't been left that way.) A door left ajar—who is behind it waiting to kill you? You hear a slight noise, a footfall, a breath. Your heart jumps. You thought you were safe, but you forgot to check the bathroom. The door to the shower doesn't close all the way and someone could be hiding there. When you go in to wash your hands, they will strangle you. They will leave the water on, so everything gets clean. The window bangs. The lights have gone out. You're paralyzed. It's undeniable, you're going to die.

No. Not at all. There's no one in the house. You continue to survive. It seems like your mission is to survive. Your heart is what tricks you. Your pulse. Your heartbeat. Your imagination is a movie screen.

Stop talking and reminding me. Can't I just be alone for a moment? You invade me. You tire me. You bother me. Go away now. Leave me. That voice that always pursues me. That voice. That you. You. You. You. I want to rest. I want to forget. I can't stand you. Erase the dialogue. Why do you speak to me? Don't you know silence? Who are you? Why are you inside me? Get out now. Don't come back. You smother me. You're going to kill me. Me, who

---

6. The first saying is French for "Who knows?"; the second is Russian for "Maybe."

chose not to speak, and all the voices that pursue me. Go to hell. Alone. Completely alone. That is what I want.

You want death.

No. I have always saved myself. So then you will continue with me. Be quiet, okay? If only for a moment. I don't know when you speak or when I do anymore. Who cares in the end? So, how many are we? Who cares in the end? It's the mirror that reflects.

It's like falling into a pool without water. Has that ever happened to you? Yes. Yes, it has happened to me. Tell me. Once upon a time. It happened to another person, but it's as if it happened to me. Once upon a time. Once upon a time there was a pool full of clean, clear water. It was midnight and the moon was veiled by clouds. I decided to climb up to the diving board (this other person was a swimming champion) and dive into the freshness of the water at night, underneath the starry blanket of the Cuernavaca sky. And I dove (this other person was a swimming champion) and twisted my body into a double flip. I thought: and if there isn't water below? A fatal double flip. I would crash. My body didn't feel the freshness of the water and the cement was getting closer and closer. A fatal double flip. Not even a cry of anguish. Instead, paralysis. My body no longer twisted. I should have felt the foamy impact of water by now. It doesn't take that long to descend from a ten-meter diving board (this other person was a swimming champion). So, I crashed and was at the point of drowning because I was no longer moving and my body was heavy and, yes, there was clean, clear water in the swimming pool. They pulled me out and gave me CPR. My lungs were full of water. I never swam again (this other person was a swimming champion). The end.

Maybe one of the people traveling with Dulcinea on the Periferico is from the Republic of San Marino. From the Republic of San Marino? From the Republic of San Marino. There are people from the Republic of San Marino and you can find them in Mexico. You're very surprised by this and feel proud to be in Mexico. Because you also have a strange origin and, all of a sudden, you find yourself with someone from San Marino. A Sammarinese. And, furthermore, San Marino is neither far away nor unknown to you. You begin to remember why. Well, you have your reasons. One is the famous album of symbols and flags you put together as a child, and, of course, the ones for San Marino were there. One of the stamps they sold in school or corner stores in little brown paper bags depicted San Marino. Later, in another album, the philatelic one, a stamp from San Marino that someone gave you. And, above all, you associate it with a person. Yes, I know: with Colonel Trucharte. And you can be sure he isn't fictional: Colonel Trucharte existed.[7] Like you and me.

Right, Colonel Trucharte fought in the Spanish Civil War. When Dulcinea was picking strawberries in the forested region of Saratov, Colonel Trucharte was capturing Italian tank operators in the Tremp area. Later, Colonel Trucharte lived in Cuernavaca and Dulcinea would visit him. The Colonel would give her books by James Oliver Curwood, and once he gave her a stamp from San Marino.[8] The Colonel had been in San Marino. The Colonel described the sea and a wall. The Colonel made the best Valencian paella. The Colonel organized the seafood for the paella with military precision. The Colonel liked Spanish tortilla. Dulcinea too.

Who are those passengers in the car and where are they from? From San Marino. From San Marino or the Isle of Man. If the driver is Amadis, he's from the Isle of Man. They say Amadis is from Gaul, but he could very well be from a little farther away, from the Isle of Man. The Isle of Man has Europe's oldest parliament. Its coat of arms is three legs (a kabbalistic number) that if they were to spin, would draw a circle (an alchemic term) representing the yearning for infinite wandering. The University of Liverpool's Marine Biological Station is in Port Erin and Amadis works there.

Amadis is an islander and loves the sea. As a boy he went fishing off the docks, and one day he went onto the high sea with fishermen. There was a storm and it took a while for him to return. The calm, rippling waters, the gray sky and the foamy droplets all returned the tranquility of adolescence to him. Insane wind blowing on his face, asphyxiating him and making his mouth open in search of more air. The loss of reason amid immeasurable ocean swells. A most tribal and brotherly impulse. He pulled on the thick rope as strongly as did the fishermen around him. United with them, like the hand to the arm or the arm to the body. There was no need to think. Or rather, thinking was the effort and tension of every muscle, the perfect attunement of movement and breath, concordant knowledge in unison. Knowing that you are still an individual, but that you are everyone. Communion with man, not God. The ship leaned to one side, water swept the deck, it was difficult to keep legs steady without buckling. But the cable helped. Not caring whether

---

7. Muñiz-Huberman met Coronel Trucharte, one of the officers in the Spanish Civil War, as an exiled compatriot in Mexico.

8. James Oliver Curwood was an early twentieth-century writer and conservationist from the United States. His books were known for their wilderness adventure stories, especially in the Yukon and Alaska.

gripping hands bled. Salty droplets burning lips. Amadis had the urge to lick his lips and taste the salt. It was like hope. If he could still notice the taste, maybe he would make it. And if not, he'd succeeded in working alongside fishermen, on a ship on the high seas, in the eye of a storm. It was enough.

The rhythm eased: shorter waves: calmer winds. Little by little the ship righted itself. Whoever hasn't been marked survives. The boy returns with the fishermen. The boy is now a different person. He's now the Other, a man. He can see himself not only from within, but also from the outside. All of a sudden, he feels independent. He has lost and gained. He returns with proof and signs of his exploits. Others need to be convinced. Others need affirmation. Amadis has procured it.

If Amadis is the one driving, it could very well be that Amadis. Amadis in Mexico. Why not? Didn't Trotsky end up in Mexico? And André Breton? And Pavlova?[9] Amadis in Mexico. Sure.

Because what is living in Mexico? Does it mean something? Does anyone really live in a set place? Or do we live everywhere at the same time? Yes, I'm in this car, on the Periferico, in Mexico. But is it real? Am I not also living in the woods of Pushchino or Saratov, in the house in Cuernavaca, in houses in Mexico City: in Condesa, in Napoles, in Mixcoac, in San Angel?[10]

I live in those houses: I see them, I feel them. I am in them. Each room, each door, each window. Each balcony. Oh, each balcony! For me, each balcony is not empty, but rather, full.[11] A small exit to the air outside. An escape from the house. On the balcony I'm free.[12] Because I shut the door behind me, take a few steps into another frontier and when I want to, I return. It seems as if I've gone away, but the door is close enough to open it. And yet, the faraway world comes to me: breezes, rain drops, shiny sun, birdsongs, a child's scream from I don't know where.

And I don't only live in my houses. I live in other people's houses. And in houses from books. Above all, in those. Any kind of house. Any kind of town, city, or country. In the countryside. In the mountains. By the sea. In several castles and palaces. On those boats, with the same amenities as the houses Conrad describes. Naturally also in mobile homes. And, despite the cold, in some igloo. Without forgetting my greatest dream of all: a little house atop the branches of a sturdy tree.

---

9. After the Mexican Revolution, beginning in the 1920s through the 1940s Mexico City became an intellectual center for exiles and traveling artists such as the ones listed above.

10. The list after the colon are all names of different neighborhoods in Mexico City.

11. This reference to empty and full balconies plays with the idea in the film *En el balcón vacío* (1961; *The Empty Balcony*) about the experiences of Spanish exiles in Mexico. The empty balconies refer to the houses left behind in Spain. See García Ascot.

12. It was on a balcony that Muñiz-Huberman's mother first revealed her Crypto-Jewish identity.

It's true I live in all those places and could describe my daily life in each one.

Do I actually live in Mexico? Am I really in Mexico? On the Periferico? In a car? Not necessarily. Where you are isn't where you are. Where you think you are, yes. Where you imagine you are, of course. In reality, we don't live here. No one lives here. I'm in the car, but I only want to arrive. No matter where I'm going, I only want to arrive. I don't even realize I'm in the car, except for the houses that pass by, the shapes that fade away.

We want to arrive. Unless we don't want to arrive. You understand, right? Of course, we don't want to arrive at the end. The absolute end. Death. The final card. The dance of death.

So you live and live. You ensure and you endure. You persevere and you relapse. You become sick. You get better. And you die. You come and you go. Barely noticing. You throw everything into the trash. And if you're traveling by boat, over the railing.

Like snails, you move slowly. Your trail shines on rocks and grass. You used to collect them. You kept them in the bathroom. Until one day someone turned on the hot water and the snails cooked. They began to froth and foam. The bubbles multiplied and overflowed onto the white porcelain walls.

You had learned to follow their shiny trail and patiently you found them in any little nook and cranny, in leaves or soil. After the accident you stopped collecting them and you no longer felt the suction of removing them from their hiding place. You didn't want them anymore. Even though you always felt a fondness for them.

Yes, I adore snails. Extraordinary snails with their houses on their backs. Fragile shell that crunches frighteningly if you step on it. I only stepped on a snail one time. Also in the bathroom (before the boiling), when I went in with the lights off. A mixture of disgust and pity. Feeling, and regretting, that you've squashed a snail. Slime spilling out. The sharp brown marbled shards of shell. The crushed little body. Why? I had only gathered them to give them lettuce.

A snail is a sign of a slow, dense life. A snail is serene. Unhurried. It retracts so easily. It has four antennae, two short and two long. They're an example of instantaneousness if you try to touch them. Their lullaby goes like this:

Little snail, snail, snail
Where's your little tail, tail, tail?
Your mommy's and your daddy's
Leave a trail, trail, trail.[13]

---

13. Adaption of song mine. The original text in Spanish cites a traditional Spanish children's song that begins: "Caracol, col, col / saca los cuernos al sol. . . ." The song shows that parents teach their children how to live through imitation. Muñiz-Huberman, pers. comm.

A snail is peaceful and prefers to leave its trail without concern or arrogance. I don't think it's oblivious. Its shiny trail must be its way of grounding itself. Of announcing crystals and mysteries of light. Leading the way to a vulnerable body and a fragile soul. It leaves behind the slippery color of the monk's cowl, and the sky must seem so far away. When it contemplates the flight of a butterfly, it thinks that it too knows how to fly another way. It always moves forward: I haven't seen one hesitate. It doesn't get sidetracked and it's unerring. It considers its path with aplomb, it foresees its death. The snail is wise.

Could this car be a snail? I don't think so. I have never felt tenderness for a car. What's a car? The swift memory of horse-drawn carriages.

Horse-drawn carriages that Dulcinea never knew. But that existed at the beginning of the century. Her parents used them. Now, no one knows what they're like. What were they like? According to what Dulcinea's mother used to say, they were spacious, comfortable, padded. With little windows and curtains. With a soft and sleepy rhythm. Drawn by horses or fine mules. With a little folding stool to climb up and down. Painted black and polished to a shine. The coachman wore a tall hat and a cloak and capelet. A whip in one hand. Reins in the other. Horses trotting. It was nice to go in a horse-drawn carriage. Dulcinea's other source is literary. She had read *Black Beauty* by Anna Sewell and one of the episodes was about the life of carriage horses for hire. How they were treated; what they ate, the mixture of oats, bran, and barley; the blankets they were covered in after work; how they were brushed; how their hooves and horseshoes were taken care of. And then another idea she always associated with horse-drawn carriages was Pierre Curie's death by trampling. Which she had seen. Yes, she had seen it in the movie *Madame Curie*, with Greer Garson and Walter Pidgeon, soon after she had arrived in Mexico. Knowledge has many twists and turns. One could say that Dulcinea was, in fact, familiar with horse-drawn carriages.

At least she did see and even ride on wagons once when the country farmers came to deliver vegetables to the International House. The children climbed up on the wagon, drawn by a strong horse with a long mane, a thick tail, and kind black eyes. If it was his last delivery, the farmer took them for a ride around the surrounding areas when he finished unloading. So Dulcinea knew the clickety-clack of riding in a wagon drawn by a strong horse with a long white mane. Feeling the hard wood and the sparse straw to soften the bumps. How peaceful it could be to see the sky that is not sky and the clouds moving.[14]

---

14. "The sky that is not sky" is an intertextual reference to the Golden Age sonnet by Bartolomé de Argensola, "A una mujer que se afeitaba y estaba hermosa" ("To a woman who applied makeup and was beautiful"). In the sonnet, the poet writes, "Porque ese cielo azul que todos vemos, / ni es cielo ni es azul . . ." ("Because this sky that we all see / is neither sky nor blue . . ."), thus suggesting the artifice of perceived reality. See Argensola, "A una mujer."

Those are her personal memories. But Dulcinea is also made of narrated memories, the memories of others. Those that were told by others, for example, her parents. And her parents speak of her grandparents and even her great-grandparents. In such a way that Dulcinea almost reconstructs her history. If her parents are really her parents. But even if they're not: they have a story that they pass down to Dulcinea. It isn't important whether it's true or made up: what matters is to tell the story: reality is in imagining. In alphabetizing and enumerating. This is what stories are for. So that, from the moment Dulcinea hears them, she begins to interpret and transform them into other stories. So everything fits together perfectly. So loose ends are tied together. So mysteries are solved. So incongruities are the law of rationality.

Of all the narrated memories, those concerning her grandparents all include carriages. So, circulating throughout her body are genes that rumbled around in the insides of carriages, stagecoaches, berlins, landaus, buggies, tilburies, cabriolets, tarantasses; and if there are still remnants of some Roman, quadrigas; and of some Hittite, iron chariots; and if their origin is Apollonian, sun chariots. As a last resort, she's left with the first wheel.

Dulcinea rolls along on the Periferico. Her thoughts are spiraling. She looks out the car window. Houses are spreading out. Fragments of fields and sections of landscape begin to appear. Groups of trees. Wildflowers in patches of color. The Ajusco volcano stands out clearly: its profound bluish-black.[15]

Dulcinea returns to the thoughts of her Dulcinea who wanders mountains and valleys. The autumn cold is now palpable and wind howls through the gorges. The last shepherds that Dulcinea and Amadis see warn them not to continue farther. Among the rocks and boulders are hideouts of outlaws who won't hesitate to do anything. There are landslides and savage beasts. Snowstorms can break out unexpectedly and sweep the travelers into a bottomless ravine. No one would know they'd disappeared until the following spring when the ice melted, when their bodies would be revealed in hard blocks of ice.

Dulcinea and Amadis must continue on. The prophecy was that their feet would not stop. Because if they stopped, they would know the end. As in a whirlwind, they continue their ascent, their capes floating above their shoulders. In the distance behind some broken-down walls, something balances in the air. Hanging from the highest branch of a tree without leaves. The body of a hanged man. Amadis wants to cover Dulcinea's eyes. But Dulcinea has seen it.

---

15. The Ajusco is a lava dome volcano located to the south of Mexico City and is a popular destination for residents and tourists to participate in outdoor activities.

The body of a hanged man as if stuffed with sawdust. Dancing around like a rag doll. Softly swinging, unhurried, unceasing. With an airy eternity before him. For him, everything has already ended. With his bruised face and popped-out eyes. The rest of his body swaying to and fro. Unhurried. Unceasing. Swinging softly. Almost a part of the landscape. Wearing a long white nightshirt to his feet. Bare feet. Pale toes. Translucent nails. An incredible rag doll. An imitation of a marionette. The mouth hanging open, a puppet's yawn. An inside-out mime. Ready to fly. His body was raised, but not his soul.

Nonetheless, a tranquil scene. A certain order recovered. It's the peace of death. It is, at long last, the complete lack of knowledge. And partly the return to the darkness of the very origin.

Dulcinea and Amadis continue walking. Who knows what they will encounter. Farther away, wolves. Two or three have appeared on a rock and they raise their howls toward a stormy sky. Then thunder is heard. Which at first, with its slow pace, is not an alarming sign. It suggests a deep rhythm. A constant resounding. It's so brief. It can terrify, but only for a moment. If anything, it's soothing. It announces longed-for rain. A reliable voice in the sky. Thundering. Jupiter thundering. No, thunder isn't scary. It's pleasant. Magical. For Dulcinea and Amadis, it's a warning to look immediately for some opening in a rock or some semi-cavernous place to take refuge.

The cavern is spacious and illuminated by an intense radiance rising from its depths. Like butterflies they move toward the light. The intense rays almost burn their eyes. They begin to discern objects. Thick drapes of the whitest satin with moving patterns and differing hues hang on the walls. Velvet fabric and cushions spill over chair-like rocks. A throne, with a canopy and golden drapery. Gold and white embroidered tapestries. The fine crystal of each chandelier, with blue and rose-colored reflections to interrupt the white. Torches aflame to add even more light. Open semicircle with successive passageways that, in turn, expose halls illumined in red, blue, yellow, green. With drapes in those colors and chandeliers as well. Disparate sensations. Fluctuating emotions. Dissimilar thoughts. Elusive ideas. Haziness.

No one knows from where the music spills forth. Dulcinea and Amadis think they're alone. They can't tell whether the music comes from within themselves or from the transmitting air. Whether someone is playing it or whether it descends from above.

They believe they're alone. But when they look around more carefully, they make out white cloth, white robes. Shapes. Bodies. On the throne a figure moves. Chiffon and lace, veils and edging. It is her. With her golden hair. With a golden diadem. With golden skin. Translucent princess. Fine nails. Neck of a swan. Thin ankles. Delicate feet. Unreal waist. Her only adornment, gold: necklace, bracelet, ring, broach, pectoral. A child, perhaps?

With her hand, she beckons them closer. She has them sit by her side. She orders drinks and delicacies for them. Her beauty seems as if it could easily break. Everything about her is clear. Like cut crystal. Fragmented diamond. Sculpted ivory. Flawless marble. In short, a unicorn's glass.

I know your story. Not only the one you know. I know your story before you and after you. I know the story of your parents. I've been waiting for you. I've brought you here. What the hermit did not tell you, I will tell you.

I am Blizmanah.[16] I live without time. This is the Cave of Transparency. Where all is known and all exists. Where the tunnels are made of light and the insides of crystals. Where a drop of water is a mirror. The moon, clairvoyance. Ice and stalactites. Ice and stalagmites.

Now I'm going back over all stories. Recounting them. Imagining them. Changing them. I weave the threads of some with the threads of others. I melt all colors into one, my prism is white. My inventions never cease. I am the mistress of words and languages. My library fills the air. The pages of my books float without being written. No page is numbered. No syllable comes before any other. No one sees the letters and no one confuses them. The accents and rhythms know how to place themselves. The sentence shapes itself, fleetingly forming and unforming itself. The idea penetrates everything. The image reflects itself. Abstraction is the moment of understanding. It's the encounter with the unpronounceable.

Thus, I know your story. In all its tenses. I conjugate your verbs until the moment of your death. And I can even continue conjugating them after that.

I don't need heirs: they are in me forever. They are in my cipherable and decipherable stories. Congruent and incongruent. Sublime and perverse.

My world isn't laughter or tears. It's the world of pure mental imagery. It's overflowing essence. Tense emotions. Broken equilibrium. Opposites in motion. The fraction of a pendulum. Not the sanctification of words but rather the heretical instinct. Sounds thrown into the air only to begin falling from their own weight.

I know your story. Your story etched on an iceberg. On an invisible stela. On an indivisible expanse.

---

16. This name is a combination of the Hebrew בְּלִי (without) and זְמַן (time) in the feminine form. Therefore, "Blizmanah" means "Without Time."

The Marquise Calderon de la Barca wanted to enter the caves of Cacahua-milpa.[17] Her attendants were hesitant. But not Dulcinea, who moved up to be first in line. Once she was past the opening, the darkness was complete, except for the torches the guides carried. Entering into caves was entering into a parabolic kingdom. Spirals, curves, a cut-off cone. Circular comparison. Interminably high gates. Chambers and chambers of marvelous objects. With stories. Carved-out waterfalls, clouds, and rivers. Formations on the ceiling and formations on the ground. Chiseled stalactites that looked like extraordinary beings: gnomes, fairies, giants, ghosts. Plants and trees, palms, columns, pyramids. The devil, the male goat, the beheaded man. Stalagmite snakes and stalagmite leopards. Terrifying echo, deformed and enlarged. Pillars, obelisks, labyrinths, and nooks. Petrified. Undaunted. Immutable. Frozen moss. Paralyzed leaves. Stone flowers. Tall domes reaching beyond sight. Double galleries. Spacious passageways. More vast chambers. A perfect, empty amphitheater, waiting. A silent organ. Silent pipes. Air that does not vibrate. Spectators that don't appear and if they do, it doesn't matter. Nothing is being performed. Immobility. Theater of the motionless. Instruments abandoned in a world yet to be created. A rehearsal of forms.

The great natural workshop, says the Marquise, while they walk and walk, and when they don't find an exit, they decide to go back. Dulcinea has seen shapes of angels and has felt their frozen movement. Amadis is there. It is his reflection on the ice lake. It's him. Dulcinea walks away to be at his side. They don't have to speak. They only look at each other. Their hands intertwine. Their bodies are mutually attracted. Their heads come together. Their lips part slightly and their tongues seek each other.

They find Dulcinea leaning against a pillar, faint. When she comes to, she smiles, but she doesn't know why. Barely moving her lips, she says: Amadis? No one hears anything. Is that the echo of his steps? No one hears anything.

When the party leaves the caverns toward the light, it's like being born. They don't want to remember what they saw in the last chamber. A powdery skeleton among the rough stones. Fingers still clawing the crevices, legs crawling, the head leaning to one side. Already a part of the immutable shapes, in a decaying, colorless coffin, perhaps with the beating of bat wings.

The sun was a relief. It exposes all. There are no mistakes. Duplicity and hypocrisy are impossible. A flat world. Without texture. Without imagination, for sure. Warm and peaceful. In the light of the sun, the Marquise's party looks old and pale. Only Dulcinea comes out flushed, eyes shining.

---

17. Located near Cuernavaca, the Grutas de Cacahuamilpa National Park houses these caverns, one of the largest cave systems in the world.

It's clear that what is difficult to describe are internal caves. The grotesque caves. This is what Dulcinea probably thinks about on the Periferico.

Dulcinea probably thinks that internal caves are darkness and this suffocates her. Yes, she does think that. Sometimes she ventures into them. Sometimes it's very hard. Sometimes she sinks. She's been able to go in deeply, but she stumbles into a dense haze that impedes her movement. From then on, even if she were to extend her arms and try to grope her way forward, she would get nowhere. She feels as if she isn't even moving. There are shrouds and shrouds of mist and her eyes are completely blind. She's certain that if she could take that step she can't take, she would discover it. What would she discover? She doesn't know. But she would discover it. The secret? Yes, the secret. What we don't want to know. The beginning? Yes, the beginning. Or the end. The end? Extremes touch. There, in that dark place of the soul, beginning and end blend together. Dulcinea keeps asking herself about her origins and who her parents were. She feels as if she emerged from nothingness. She has no memory of her beginning. You have to believe the parents who say that's who they are. It's possible they have some sort of evidence, but Dulcinea doesn't have it. It's an act of faith. When there is no faith. Her parents say it's true. Dulcinea isn't convinced. Her parents don't even need to affirm it because they're sure. Dulcinea is not. She has no proof. She doubts. Furthermore, she doesn't want them to be her parents. She doesn't want anyone to be. She doesn't like debts. Or resemblances. Or similarities. Much less, analogies.

But she insists that dark place could be the key. The key itself, therefore, the answer. She can't go farther than that. It's the beginning. It's genesis. It's chaos. Impossible to put in order. Thus, there's fear. Blindness. Groping. Dulcinea is going to have to accept the impassable barrier. But since it's obvious she's not going to accept it, she will continue stumbling into the haze.

The downside is that she fleetingly gathers hope. She glimpses a divined clarity. Which is immediately extinguished. She isn't able to see it, but the intuited gap could be reached next time. That would be enough. From there, she would penetrate it without anything stopping her. It would be like finally finding the beginning of the yarn. So much knitting (because Dulcinea has knit a lot) and not being able to untangle the skein. At this moment, Dulcinea remembers having heard that Bach was a good knitter. Of course, Dulcinea's work is the opposite: unraveling to arrive at the beginning, at zero. Zero roundness, zero infinity.

That divined clarity could open itself completely in an instant, and it would happen, first the revelation and then communion. But, in that case, it wouldn't be a concrete discovery (her parents) but rather the loss of self in absolute knowledge. It would be her integration into the encompassing light. The loss of herself and immersion. From which she couldn't leave. Where questions would have only one untransmissible answer. Where there wouldn't be any more questions.

Dulcinea has felt that her body is rising. Her body is nothing and is floating. The intermeshed union of functions and inner workings has suspended its movement. Yes, the body can stop being a body. And if the body stops being a body, gravity stops working and the soul escapes as it pleases. Overflowing water runs everywhere. Only when it disappears is it forgotten. But since it's a loss that isn't recognized as a loss, you never recover it again. The soul-water-vapor rises toward the sky.

Yes, you can float. If the law is voided. If the flow is calmed. If the cascade of images fills all the cracks.

The cracks are the most important. That's where things and rivers end up. Everything comes to rest there. Such a wide space that forgotten things build up. Dust from ancient mud. Essences behind doors.

Cracks. Tibetan singing bowls of other memories, in order, one on top of another. Stacked in a row.

Anfractuosities.

Folds.

Nooks and crannies.

Sheds.

Hiding places.

Corners.

Curves.

Drawers.

Pockets.

Hems.

All of them, clandestine places.

If they could be examined, light would spring forth.

The sun keeps rising, thinks Dulcinea.

What broken rhythms do you carry in your mind, Dulcinea? The rhythms of memory. But memory made into words. Words that don't come out. That bang against my skull. Would you like your head to explode? Yes, I would like that. I would like to end this. To end this trip on the Periferico. I don't even know where I'm going. Do you? No, neither you nor I know. Would they know? Amadis? And the other people? They should know. Only you and I don't know. But since we don't speak. We won't find out. Why are you in this car on the Periferico? I don't even remember getting in. Me neither. We're in Mexico, right? Yes. It's not the forested area of Saratov. Or the boat going to Odessa. Or the train that went from the United States to the Mexican border. Or the highway. Or the stagecoach. Or the plane. Or the Horses of the Apocalypse, clearly. Clearly?

Love springs from broken rhythms. Which Amadis has Dulcinea made love with? What she remembers are images. The images she sees while making love. The repetition of the dream she has had. Colors and crystal shards. Taut, smooth skin. While she was sleeping. At sunrise. With the sun's rays penetrating through the space where the curtain didn't close tightly. With open eyes and closed eyes. Feeling her body. But feeling her soul overflowing. Where everything is harmony. The ultimate perfection of death. A breakdown of the predictable mathematical knot theory. No daily life or sounds from the streets. It happens in the middle of a flower garden with a fountain with four spouts, tree branches, two cups, one of water and one of wine, and a dove that topples them.[18]

Yes, but with which Amadis? Dulcinea doesn't know. Maybe only with the first one: who is the first? Every one of the three.

Dulcinea had a little notebook in Russia in which she wrote down important things. Or rather, dates. Really, specific dates. The dates of battles won by the Russians. She had started with the battle of Poltava and had gotten up to the battle of Kursk.[19] She wrote them all down with carefully traced numbers with a pencil whose point she sharpened before each use. The little notebook fit comfortably inside her dress pocket. Nobody knew about this notebook except for Leninito. After all the teachers had gathered the children to hear the news on the radio, and after they had explained the reports about the war, Dulcinea would slip away to her room without anyone noticing. There, she would take out her little notebook to write down the concise facts. Leninito had followed her once and rubbed his hands together excitedly and jumped up and down when he saw the letters and numbers. Dulcinea brought her index finger to her lips to urge him to be quiet. Years later, when Dulcinea was ready to leave for Mexico and Leninito looked at her with terrified eyes, she took the little notebook out of her pocket and put it in one of his hands and covered it with the other, asking him to take care of it forever.

---

18. This image comes from a Gnostic, mystical poem entitled, "Razón de amor" ("The reason for love"; Lupus de Moros (?)). In part of the poem, a lover arrives at a fountain to find two glasses of water, one of holy water and one of wine (the blood of Christ). See London, "The 'Razón," 28–47.

19. The Battle of Poltava concluded in 1709 and established Peter the Great as the decisive victor over the Swedes in a conflict over land in northeastern Europe, leading to the decline of Swedish power as Peter built the Russian Empire. The Battle of Kursk occurred in 1943 on the Eastern Front of World War II. Known as the biggest tank battle in history, it was also the first time Hitler began to withdraw his troops from the Eastern Front and marked the beginning of more failed German offensives, allowing Soviet troops to advance westward toward Germany. See "Battle of Kursk."

Today, Dulcinea tries to remember the dates. But the dates are no longer important. The faces of the children have grown blurry, they're all the same. They have eyes, noses, mouths, ears, foreheads, chins, hair, no one distinct from another. She only remembers a few of the teachers. Milagros, from Valladolid, who taught her how to make Spanish tortilla. Events don't count. Their order has become confused. If only she had the little notebook. Now everything is either before or after.

Why do I long for the little notebook so much? Why do I want to cry when I think of it? Why do I need that lost order? If I had children, I could tell them: that battle was on that date. And we would feel stable and safe in the world. No one could tell us: no, it was on this other date. I would take out my little notebook and say: you're wrong—here it says when it was. And my children and I would have no doubts and we would smile roundly. This is what my little notebook would be for.

Was it useful to Leninito? Did it help him learn dates? Would he have learned something in the end? The dates of some battles. No. He must have known that the little notebook was an object of love. And he wouldn't have lost it. But this story ended with him. Because Leninito died and they might have buried the little notebook with him.

In the little notebook I had painted some Spanish Republican flags. Red, yellow, and purple. I had written: Long live the Spanish Republic. I had drawn a map of Spain, with all its provinces, regions, rivers, mountains. The little notebook was my secret.

It's good that I don't have the little notebook. Nothing should remain on paper. Paper is fragile and easily lost. That's why I write only in my mind. That way nothing will ever slip away or get lost. The space is infinite and unending. I don't feel limited by the size of a page or a pencil or a pen. I don't tire or cross out or erase. Perfect sentences form in the moment. I don't get caught up in words. Thoughts are faster. Feelings convey what cannot be expressed in words. This is my great revolution: silence is the only language. Here within, no one knows what I think. There are no mistakes, no misunderstandings. Correction is instantaneous. I don't compromise or risk myself. I reach the highest peaks. I can think about the most sublime and the most abject. And no one finds out. What a comfortable and perfectly hermetic room is the mind.

Here I include, because they are in me, those who made silence a fountain of knowledge. Harpocrates reigns with a finger over his lips.[20] Hermes

---

20. The Greek god of silence, Harpocrates is often depicted as a child with his finger over his lips. Ironically, the Greeks misinterpreted this Egyptian gesture meaning "child" as a sign of silence. See Greenberg. The Mexican poet Sor Juana included Harpocrates as a symbol of the silence of night

Trismegistus guards his wisdom.[21] Giordano Bruno, their heir, develops the art of memory so the veil of the unpronounceable won't reveal secrets:

The most profound and divine theologians say, that God is more honoured and loved by silence than by words; as one sees more by shutting the eyes to the species represented, than by opening them . . .[22]

What is missing is darkness. In darkness I see everything. I don't know if my eyes are open or shut. I'm surprised if I think they were open and they're shut. I can't tell the difference. Things are where I think they are. But if I begin to walk, I run into things. I've lost my perspective. Everything is farther away. I try to orient myself with my arms extended. They show me where things are. My hands feel along the walls. My fingers, the cracks. I keep my eyes open out of habit. Thinking they'll help me to see more in the dark. Silence in darkness. Secrets in darkness. Hidden things in darkness. As I girl, I couldn't sleep in a completely dark room. It was like a coffin. I needed the curtains open a crack. It's still the same. Sometimes I've awakened and, without seeing the faint light, felt dead. If my heart hadn't been beating erratically, I would have screamed out from underground. That's why I don't like tunnels, or subways, labyrinths, ditches, trenches, drains, submerged cities, tanks, or submarines. If I'd had to go to war, I would have flown a plane. Death from high above. Falling disintegrated. Fragments of stars accompanying me. Tumbling brilliance. Wings aflame. Fire and light. No closed eyes in the dark night. No extended arms groping about.

Yes, the silence of the night. Which terrifies more by not being silent. The more noise it makes, the more it quiets the silence. Miniscule sounds, from the inner ear and the imprisoned soul. The constant screeching that you only hear in darkness. The voices of all of nature. Jumbled sensations. Thoughts that are enveloped in cocoons and chrysalises. The silken thread that weaves itself in all colors and in none, for lack of light.

I can't bear all these sounds that surround me. They burst my eardrums. The purulent viscosity runs not from words but from concepts.

I don't want to hear anymore.

I wish I were deaf.

---

in her famous mystical poem, "El primero sueño" (1692; "First Dream"). See Juana, *A Sor Juana Anthology*, 166–98.

21. Often associated with the Egyptian god of wisdom, Thoth, Hermes Trismegistus was celebrated as a Greek philosopher, mystic, magician, alchemist, and founder of hermeticism.

22. Bruno, *The Heroic Enthusiasts*. Bruno was a sixteenth-century Italian philosopher, mathematician, poet, and hermetic occultist.

~

THE SIXTH SEAL

Dulcinea, you have successfully stopped speaking. Now you need to stop hearing. You're on the way. It's hard for you to understand what others are saying. Most of the time you only hear one word, you guess the rest and come to your own conclusions. It's not important if it coincides or not with what the other person wanted to say to you. In the end, the other person was only trying to reach you by babbling from a force that emerged from within. People don't know clearly what they want to tell you and struggle to utter the syllables. Often they implore you to figure it out, to complete their words or, even better, their thoughts. You tend to do it in silence and this makes them think you agree. Even if your distraction had carried you on another path and you were thinking about your own ideas, they would not realize it. It's enough for you to agree, nodding your head, and everyone's happy.

Sometimes your heart skips a beat. What are the others saying? You weren't listening to a single word. You don't understand anything. Maybe you shouldn't nod, but rather shake your head. How do you know? And even though you try, you've lost interest. You keep looking in the eyes of the other person, but your mind is elsewhere, in other places at other heights. You've successfully stopped listening. If you ever thought you were living in prison, you've been able to escape. You fly away without anyone reaching you. You continue looking into the eyes of the other, but nothing happens, there is no sympathetic visual current flowing between you. It's an unchanging image that no one notices. It's seeing without seeing. It's having your eyes open so as not to see anything. It's denying reciprocity. Also denying mirrors and clear water, polished glass and reflections in cold metal. It's being exclusively yourself, having cut ties with the world.

Having cut ties with the world, starting over again.

Who enchanted you, Dulcinea? Who froze you like an ivory statue? The other little girls with whom you played freeze tag, do you remember? One of them would tag the others and they would stay frozen in place. That's how you ended up, Dulcinea, and the enchanter forgot the formula to break the spell. Do you remember how Don Quixote suffered when he found out Dulcinea was enchanted? There was no way to pull him out of his sadness and little by little he lost himself to melancholy. Until one day he just lay down in his bed to die.[1]

Your eyes don't welcome the gaze of other eyes. You eyes only rest on landscapes and objects. Nor can you sustain the gaze of animals. They want to ask you something and you don't understand. You're thinking about other things, other tasks.

---

1. See note 80 from the "Introduction."

You aren't here, Dulcinea. Where are you?
In my house. In my own house.
Far inside my own house.
A precious house with white walls.
With lots of light.
Comfortable chairs.
Interior gardens.
Enclosed gardens.[2]
Windows to the clouds.
First tree branches, then sky.
I live in me.

Dulcinea knows. Her parents will never forgive her for having been the survivor. Her brother remained in Russia, buried far away. But was she her brother's keeper? He was the firstborn, the one to offer God the pleasing gift of firstfruits, the heir, the carrier of the seed. The promise. She, the second-born, a mere receptacle. If only she had also died in Russia, she heard them say one night. Better to have no child. They hated her. They would lock her up. They would do the impossible to make her life a living hell. It's so easy to destroy a little human being. Simply by using words that pierce the tough cranium to trample the soft gray matter. A clean operation, without scars or blood clots. In this case, no one bleeds out. If Dulcinea wanted to, she could destroy her brother's image. By saying he fled and they shot him in the back. Like what really happened, which her parents don't know. Or like what didn't really happen, which her parents also don't know. She could make them doubt. She could get the words rolling, set them in motion. But she doesn't speak. That's why.

She writes. Inside herself. She resumes the story of Blizmanah, the timeless princess. Blizmanah, the blond princess who tells Dulcinea and Amadis stories. Who says she knows Dulcinea and Amadis's story. The story of all times and tenses. Not only grammatical tenses, but also musical tempos.[3] To the beat of the flute, the lute, or the rabel. Slower or faster. Also dance tempos. The carole. The tarantella. The basse danse. The ronde. The saltarello. The galliard. The pavane.

---

2. Here the enclosed garden is part of Dulcinea's ideal dwelling place. In addition, *Enclosed Garden* is the title of Muñiz-Huberman's collection of short stories, *Huerto cerrado, huerto sellado* (1985). The intertext in this part of the novel alludes to the verse in Song of Songs, "A garden inclosed is my sister, my spouse; a spring shut up, a fountain sealed." Song of Songs 4:12 (KJV).

3. Muñiz-Huberman plays with the Spanish word "tiempo," which can mean time, tense, and (musical) tempo.

Then the music begins to play. Chirimias. Harps. Viola da gamba. Drums. The voices of the chorus. And then the dances. Dancers come from all four corners. They all come bowing in procession. On the first beat they bend their knees and slide their right foot. On the second beat they extend their left leg in front of their right. Then they alternate the movements. A semi-circle to change places: the gentleman and the lady. Hands intertwined high in the air. A bow. And they begin again.

As in the song of a troubadour, a couple starts to dance: the gentleman is a falcon and the lady a swallow. He attacks, she dodges. They barely brush up against each other, then they quickly separate. He pulls her toward him passionately and she escapes from his arms. And no one who sees them would doubt they were made for love, for dance, for land and air.

Dulcinea and Amadis forget their condemnation and their suffering. They look and listen. They enjoy themselves and slide into another world. Later, they are ushered into the great dining hall, where a banquet of exquisite delicacies and dainty sweets is beyond what mind and taste buds could imagine. Dish after dish. Drinks. Desserts. Liqueurs. Lace tablecloths. Linen napkins. Cut crystal. Silver tableware. Embossed cutlery. Pleasure and delight of the senses. Fleeting happiness. A captured moment.

The honeymoon chamber has been prepared for Dulcinea and Amadis. A mahogany canopy bed and gossamer curtains. White Dutch linen. A thick quilt of white down. Silk trim. Burgundy velvet. Satin. Muslin. Damask. A basin and rose water. In the bed, arms that strip and legs that intertwine. Locked lips, tongues dancing. Bodies thoroughly united through sex, no free space, no unfilled opening, crucible that overflows. Soft scent of semen, with a touch of apple or quince. Vibration and rhythm. The guiding rhythm of the world. Compass. Magnet.

At sunrise, awake. Love that is reborn with the first ray of light. Like a dance, beginning again. Familiar moves. New moves. Improvised. Slow and fast. Enveloping embrace. The song of a finch or a nightingale?

But I can't continue thinking about that story. I'm worried about mine. Why can't I understand or resolve mine? My thoughts are directed at my story. Without moving forward or untangling confusions. I'm only dedicated to this task and to unraveling myself. In the end, are my parents my parents or not? I hope they're not. Then my heart would overflow because of my prodigious birth.[4] I would carry the special mark with me.[5] But I have them here at my side, glued to me. They could even be the people traveling with me on the Periferico. But if I decide they aren't, they aren't. I don't want them to be. So they aren't, and that's that.

I see these people at my side and I don't recognize them. They're so alien, it's like seeing them through the lens of an inverted telescope: far away and very tiny. But making frightening gestures. What ugly faces, bulging eyes, strange noses. They can't be my parents. They're frightening, so frightening. Mostly her, the one who could be the mother: with heavy makeup, blush, super-red lips, shades of various colors on her eyelids. And worst of all: eyebrows that were previously plucked out and then painted on. What would her face look like without makeup? How would a face without eyebrows look? Abnormal. Very abnormal. What an untouchable mask of colors and thick pastes. I don't remember her. I don't think she's my mother. I only see colors and creams. During the war, she didn't wear makeup. It's not her.

And him. Who is he? Sitting and silent. Silent. An expressionless face. Where did he lose his life? How sad and faint are his hands on his thighs. So many age spots, almost joined together. The lackluster corners of his mouth. His half-open lips with an occasional trickle of saliva. Dull eyes, with little flakes of dried-up pus in the corners.

Two such unfortunate and strange beings. Could it be them? The ones who made her suffer so much. Now, she would almost cry for them. But the barrier could no longer be crossed. Even if Dulcinea were to retain an emotional tie, she wouldn't be moved by it. Her desire to remain hardened was greater. Without words, there's nothing to say. Now, when it was her turn to take care of them, it was too late and she couldn't do a thing. Sometimes she thought, I should soften but it was just a thought, nothing else. She couldn't stand the thought of brushing her skin against theirs. She carefully avoided contact. She could never kiss them. Or hold their hands. Or help them. Or even be helped by them. The two of them had turned into a single sensation of repugnance.

Could this be proof they aren't my parents? What does it mean, flesh of my flesh? I don't feel like the flesh of anyone. For that matter, I really dislike the word "flesh." So I don't eat it. Our destructive teeth and molars, made to tear and grind up meat. I prefer vegetables. Vegetables don't have blood. You can't say, blood of my blood. They're clean. Pure. Transparent. Juicy. I

---

4. Prodigious births are typical of religious and epic heroes, like Moses, Samson, Jesus, Buddha, King Arthur, or even Quetzalcoatl (Aztec mythology).
5. Reference to the mark or curse of Cain in the Biblical story of Cain and Abel.

feel closer to a vegetable. Maybe for that reason I shouldn't eat them either. Teeth are truly terrifying. Would I prefer only drinking? Yes, I think so.

Chronos devouring his children. It was Goya's painting that showed me the truth.[6] They'd ripped out my insides. They took away my speech, my soul, my spirit. They skinned me. I became empty, with an echo resounding in my insides. A ceaseless drum, like the drums of Calanda.[7] Gunshots in the sierra and the sound of armored vehicles on the pontoons of the Ebro.[8] The razed countryside.

They leveled everything. They covered the fields in salt. And they were their own fields. They removed stone after stone. And they were their own walls. They poisoned the wells. And it was their own water. They blew up rocks. And it was their own land. That's how I was left.

They did all the damage inside me. The war was inside me. The destruction was inside me. The grenades, the bombs, and Guernica were inside me.[9] The destroyed homes, the lifeless bodies, were inside me. The father who walked miles with his son's corpse in his arms, who crossed the border, and whose dog followed him, was inside me. The women in black were inside me. The girl gunned down on the road whose bike was thrown to the side was inside me. The poor old man wanting to run away was inside me. The furniture broken into pieces was inside me. The mutilated horse was inside me. Hunger and rotten cabbage were inside me.

Then they want me to smile, dance, and bow. Like the bear owned by the Romanian gypsy from the Condesa neighborhood.[10] Awkwardly trained. Beaten with a club.

Sometimes I think: it's all lies. Everything was running smoothly. A well oiled machine. I played. I sang. I laughed. Also lies. Nothing went well. Only dreams were perfect. When you would go under the dining room table and

---

6. See note 14 in the "Fourth Seal."

7. There is a tradition in Calanda, Spain, in which thousands of people beat drums nonstop for 24 hours from noon on Good Friday until noon on Easter Saturday.

8. The Battle of the Ebro was the longest battle of the Spanish Civil War from July to November 1938. Republican and Nationalist forces clashed along the border of the river and many Republican lives were lost. The Nationalists were then able to enter Catalonia and eventually take Barcelona. Unable to recover, this battle was a turning point, making it clear that Natonalist forces would prevail. The Spanish Civil War ended on April 1, 1939. See Stewart, "The 1938 Battle."

9. Guernica is a town in northern Spain in the Basque region that was bombed on April 26, 1937 during the Spanish Civil War. Pablo Picasso's famous cubist painting *Guernica* (1937) depicts the tragic aftermath of the bombing, including suffering animals, people screaming, and dismembered bodies.

10. Gypsies (in this case, from Romania) have immigrated to Mexico during different time periods, mainly at the end of the nineteenth and beginning of the twentieth centuries. They settled in various cities throughout Mexico, especially in Southeast Mexico City in neighborhoods such as Condesa and Roma. See Carey, "Romani Heritage."

pretend to be a guerrilla fighter against Franco. When a shortened broomstick served as your gun. When a red handkerchief was a sling for your wounded arm. Yes. Those were the best times. Alone. Playing with myself. My mind, which is from God, always accompanied me. Reason, which is of man, never ruled over me. Imagination, which is from the Devil, was always with me.

I can feel myself exploding. Something in me is about to explode. It's my head. My head that hurts so. It's been filling up so much, I don't know what to do. Can you shake and clear out a head? Clean it, adjust it, and make some space? Polish it, shine it, and begin again?

If only I could penetrate craniums. Open a little window. Peer through to the other side of each skull. Contemplate the moving images. All the movies and pictures in the world together. All of them. I mean all of them. Absolutely all of them. Can you imagine? All the projectors and all the reels playing at the same time. This is what you would find if you were to go through a little window and peer through to the other side of craniums.

I also feel unease in my heart. A pain. A heaviness. Everything is black there. A black abyss in which I cannot see the end. It's darkness and fetal movements. Primal emotions, as in an embryo or in death. But the heart doesn't go insane and it doesn't worry me so much. It's not warm or cozy. Maybe there's a bone in its place. It's not the center of anything. It's unimportant. If you had it in your hand, it would slip away like a fish.

Those are my two true organs. The rest have been invented by biology and microscopes. They don't exist.

And the soul? Better not to talk about what you don't know. Like Wittgenstein.[11]

Okay then, my dear Dulcinea, where were we? Well, in those dark corners of my origins. Which will remain impenetrable. That's how it is. The only thing left to do is to push yourself and force out the memories. Bring to light some other recollection.

---

11. Wittgenstein, *Tractatus Logico-Philosophicus*, 90. Tractatus 7 states, "Whereof one cannot speak, thereof one must be silent."

But you're wearing out, your memories are getting rusty. They don't slide out smoothly like they used to. Your head hurts. When will it explode? Yes, let it hurry up and explode. Please.

Where are we going? Where are we on the Periferico? Have we started all over again? I don't know. I just let myself be carried away. The others don't worry. They know where we're going. Really, it's comfortable to just let them take you around and around on the Periferico. It's not an ideal ride. But it's still something. Were you confined before going on the Periferico? I don't know. Confined where? In a house? In a room? No, not at all. Confined within yourself. Within myself? How would I be confined within myself? I'm free in myself. There's no greater freedom than me. My inner world is the biggest of all. (Like yours, if you so desire.) Absolute freedom only exists inside. Inside me. (Inside you, if you were to want it.) Don't you see that silence is cosmic harmony? That no longer using words is being in union with God? The mystics were wrong: they talked too much. Only the Kabbalists were right: the ineffable is unpronounceable.

And you tell me again that I live confined. I live in freedom.

Is it raining again? I think so. That sound of raindrops on the window glass is what keeps me alive. Or better yet, I know that I'm alive because of the sound of the raindrops on the glass. And then to see them. See how they slide and make rivulets from top to bottom. Placing my finger on this side of the glass and feeling the coldness. But only on the tip of my finger because the rest of my body is warm in the heat of the car. The car is a shell. It most resembles the inside of a snail shell. A moving house.

And so it rains. Inside the car, it doesn't matter. Or outside either. No matter what, it's inevitable. What do you do when you face the inevitable? Unavoid it? Neither the rain nor the car stop. The Periferico continues. Inevitably.

Only a few raindrops are falling. It thunders. Far away. The day is still gray. But it doesn't rain harder. It should be a downpour. To clean the asphalt. To wash off cars. To clean walls. To clean people. Wet them. Drench them. Soak them. Purify them?

The rain lacks decisiveness. Why doesn't it become a flood? There should be another one. It's time. We're bored. It wouldn't be bad for us to wipe the slate clean and start over.

Have you forgotten the Apocalypse? No, no. It's always present. Let's see.

And I will give power unto my two witnesses, and they shall prophesy a thousand two hundred and threescore days, clothed in sackcloth.

These are the two olive trees, and the two candlesticks standing before the God of the earth.

And if any man will hurt them, fire proceedeth out of their mouth, and devoureth their enemies: and if any man will hurt them, he must in this manner be killed.

These have power to shut heaven, that it rain not in the days of their prophecy: and have power over waters to turn them to blood, and to smite the earth with all plagues, as often as they will.

And when they shall have finished their testimony, the beast that ascendeth out of the bottomless pit shall make war against them, and shall overcome them, and kill them.[12]

The truth is you stopped believing in God ever since you were a little girl. Since the day you asked if it was spelled God or Got.[13] And by solving the orthographic problem, you implied a theological one. But like any good disbeliever, today you still look for God, just to confirm that He doesn't exist. And you keep looking for Him. And you don't find Him. And you keep looking for Him. In contrast, those who believe don't look for God. Of course. God is present in atheists, the people who truly fear Him. Don't you think the mystics had their doubts? Undoubtedly.

That's why you like the Book of the Apocalypse so much, so vengeful and cruel. So tormented and desperate. So fantastic and bizarre. So senseless that it doesn't even adhere to its metaphors. Not even the symbols are consistent. Much less the myths. And it defies grammar. It's the language of a raving lunatic. A catastrophe of words. Semiotics turned upside-down. I just roar with laughter. That's why I like it.

Dulcinea, with whom do you speak? With me-you. With God? Does God think? And, therefore, He exists?

But in reality this doesn't matter to you anymore.

No, I prefer to return to my stories. Which one shall I resume? I'm glad I can still choose. I can choose the story I want. Am I really free? That also doesn't matter now. I feel free inside. (Confined from the outside.)

Well, my dear Dulcinea, let's go. Yes, yes. My story. It's Dulcinea's turn, when she's emerging, flushed, from the caves of Cacahuamilpa with the Marquise Calderon de la Barca, pale and aged.

---

12. Rev 11:3–7 (KJV).
13. In Spanish, the narrator questions if God is written as "Dios" or "Dioz," a play with Spanish phonology, especially since unlike in Spain where the letters "s" and "z" are pronounced differently, in Mexico they sound similar. The narrator shows the innocent yet theological questioning of the young Dulcinea who wonders if God is the same with an "s" or a "z".

That is the difference. Dulcinea saw life in the caves. The Marquise, death. Dulcinea soared. The Marquise sank. Dulcinea breathes in fresh air. The Marquise, stale air.

Dulcinea feels her feet lift from the ground. She floats and goes to other places. She lives in other places. Unconfirmed places. Without keys or access. Crossed through. Transparent. Absorbed. Places in which. Either you are. Or you aren't.

Dulcinea accompanied the Marquise when she visited the San Hipolito hospital, where they confine the mentally ill. The old convent is an agreeable place, with courtyards of orange and lemon trees and a refreshing, melodious fountain. Some patients settle under the trees and others gaze at themselves in the waters. They seem peaceful. There's a certain languidness. A certain foreshadowing of postponed suicide. Of praised passions. Of obsessive signs. Of broken gestures. Someone embraces a column and doesn't separate from it. Someone else takes delight in his impeccable clothing, with its excellent quality in the latest fashion, and he greets people over and over, doffing his hat as they pass. If the orderly tells them to go to the dining room, they go to the dining room. If he tells them to go to their cells, they go to their cells. Too much order. White walls. Nothing to do. Sometimes, one person will tell another he's crazy, and the other looks back at him scornfully. An old man doesn't stop asking: when will I leave this place? A child who doesn't talk balances his legs on a tall chair.

The Marquise is satisfied. She's done her good deed for the day. Dulcinea has seen the black room and punishment cells. Miniscule space. Neither a window nor a crack of light. They slide a wooden plate with food through a slot. Until the person locked up calms down and stops screaming and hitting the padded walls. Then, with great precaution, he's taken back into the exterior world, little by little. Moved from one cell to another less-cruel cell, his movements observed. When he has ceased being dangerous (do we ever stop being so?) he goes on to inhabit his permanent cell.

Dulcinea separates herself from the Marquise and looks for the furthermost cells. She's afraid Amadis is in one of them. Melancholic. Isolated. Forgotten. Someone might have given him a concoction and made him crazy. Someone might have accused him of passing through mirrors. Of demonic acts. Of the arts of desperation. Amadis could have done penance and he could have gone mad. He could have sold his soul and languished in confinement. In the depths of a cave. On the top of a mountain. Dulcinea obsessively looks for him. Amadis could be that man in black with a white silk shirt and a lace ruffle. The one who is greeting people left and right. The one in the last cell who tirelessly reads. It could be Amadis. But if she manages to see his face, it's not him. The smile makes her doubt. No, it's not him. He hasn't recognized her. It's not him. Or is it?

Dulcinea doesn't know. She's not sure. Amadis eludes her. He looks like Amadis and he doesn't. He is and he isn't. If he doesn't say it's him and introduce himself as such, she doubts. He has to say: I am Amadis. So she knows. Whoever doesn't say that isn't Amadis.

However, that man in black. With the white silk shirt and lace ruffle. Greeting. Or reading.

As she was leaving the convent, Dulcinea looked one last time at the cell and the man's dark, desperate, and suffering eyes, which expressed the finality of the act: they would never see each other again.

It was death. Death is never seeing someone again. It's the death of the Other and it's your own.

From that day on, Dulcinea decided to dress only in black with a white lace ruffle at her neck and wrists.

Dulcinea's days pass. She doesn't want them to slip by. If they slip by, time flows without knowing where it will arrive. There must be some way to delay the fragility of time. Time doesn't exist. Artificial. Arbitrarily measured. A children's game. We're going to play with time. Once upon a time. Time was born, grew up, and died. What can be done to delay time? Behold, Dulcinea has just discovered it: by writing. Writing stops time. By writing, you sign a pact with the devil. By writing, you turn over your soul. By writing, you intertwine with the Ouroboros.[14]

Dulcinea can begin modestly with a diary. In a notebook with leather covers and gilded edges she can begin writing about her strolls with the Marquise, their familiar places, parties, and soirées. Then, if she wants to complicate things a little more, she can write about Amadis. This way she will be testing her fortitude and persistence. Above all, her resolve. Because writing will be a secret act, without anyone asking or demanding it. A solitary act. An act of recovery.

Will Dulcinea write a diary?

---

14. The Ouroboros is an ancient symbol of a snake or dragon in a circle biting its own tail. Originating in Egypt and later passed on through Greek traditions, the Ouroboros represents ideas such as infinity, eternity, and the perpetual cycles of life.

The car has braked unexpectedly on the rain-soaked pavement. Dulcinea felt her body thrown forward. She resisted the pressure and was able to propel herself back. The shock to her neck was very forceful. It crunched painfully. It interrupted her story. The other people in the car became upset and uttered various exclamations. She doesn't care about that. The complaints and petty weariness of others. She lacks emotions and if she were to have them, they would be like that: a sudden braking. It seems like they're asking how she feels. That doesn't matter either. Now they have something to talk about. They're never lacking a pretext to voice their words. Out loud. Out loud and each one excitedly repeating, sometimes in unison, what happened. The unexpected braking. Why talk? It's just a fact. It just happened that way. Nothing happened. And then beginning again and repeating again. They won't stop for the rest of the trip. They can go on for hours. Talking about it all night. And even the next day.

Dulcinea no longer listens. Others' emotions don't mean anything to her. She's cold. Unmoving. She saw her brother fall right next to her, riddled by bullets. She never cried. What is that transparent secretion? What are those uttered words? The only thing that matters are the empty spaces. The holes that can't be filled. The abyss that no one will descend. That which is unknown. Ignored. Hidden. That lacks a term or meaning. The non-concept and non-knowledge. Another way of understanding things that isn't the usual. So many centuries have already passed—right, Dulcinea?—of using the same method. What a waste and what uselessness. Such little inventiveness. Always spinning in circles. What could be done, Dulcinea, what could be imagined?

Dulcinea doesn't know. Dulcinea doesn't answer. If you were to speak, Dulcinea. If only you could break your spell. What are we going to do with you? With me, nothing. I'm okay. It's the others who aren't okay. I've dared to be myself. I won't leave my spell. No one will break my spell. All of you are the ones who should become enchanted. Find the magic wand that will enchant you. And make you silent. Captured in light.[15]

---

15. The end of this paragraph depends on the phonetic play of words "prendar" (to enchant or to give a piece of clothing) and "prender" (to capture or to light/turn on an appliance). Dulcinea is evoking the childhood game of freeze tag or "juego de los encantados" (game of enchantment) in Spanish. In that game, "enchanted" or frozen players can become unfrozen if they give the caller a personal token or belonging. The last two sentences of this paragraph allude to becoming enchanted ("prendados"), as in the game, and next being captured in light ("prendidos"), from the verb meaning both captured and lighted, hoping to be freed by a token ("prenda"). This play with words and associations is like a game in itself into which Dulcinea invites us to become enchanted.

Through mountains and valleys you will search, Dulcinea, for your beloved.[16] And your beloved, Dulcinea, won't be there. He won't appear. He won't be there. You'll never find him. Through mountains and valleys you won't find him. Your beloved comes from the pages of books. He's shapeless. He's faceless. He's all shapes and faces. Amadis. That's his name. Amadis, he who loves God. Amadeo, he who is loved by God. Amadeus. He loves God. Like Mozart's music. However, it's not possible. Through mountains and valleys you will continue searching, Dulcinea, for your beloved.

However, it is possible. You know about love, Dulcinea. You know what's told in the Song of Songs. You know it so well that when you take the book into your hands, it opens precisely to that part.

By night on my bed I sought him whom my soul loveth: I sought him, but I found him not.[17]

If it was your soul that loved him, how then did you search for him with your body at night in your bed? Or did you need to show your soul that you existed through your body? And where was he? Like a warrior with his sword on his thigh. And if it's his thigh, his thigh is naked, and if it's his sword, his sword is naked. On tepid flesh, the coldness of steel. Putting your hand on his strong thigh and the chaste sword separating you. The edge almost cutting you, announcing the gleam of blood. His warm thigh, root of his smooth member. Even warmer, smoother. With its curly hair, impeding skin from touching skin.

You didn't find him. You sensed him. You sensed him behind the walls. You sensed him wanting to open your garden. Your seal. Closed. But when you went to find him, he wasn't there. He had gone. Even though ointments and myrrh dripped down your naked skin. Again your body was disappointed. Meanwhile, your soul escaped in search of him. Again, you didn't find him. And the soul that was leaving you was your death.

Your body close to his and your soul flying in pleasant favonian breezes, in fragile transparencies, in what is not seen, in forested secrets. A soul that should find its double. Freeing itself from its earthly ties to be elevated to a star or reduced to embers. It should know how, but doesn't. Magical arts won't free it with marvels and miracles. Small soul that likes to be enclosed, refusing the light of the spheres.

---

16. This first sentence and susequent paragraph use the Bible's Song of Songs as an intertext to represent both the love between a man and woman and, at the mystical level, between God and humankind.

17. Song of Songs 3:1–3 (KJV).

A soul that would fuse a faithful image. That from two would make one and from one, two. That would forget the columns, the marble vase, and the alabaster tower.[18] That would return to the lost body. Covered by dense muscles once again. Restless nerves. Resonant bones. And it would be content.

Be content? You think so, Dulcinea? No. I won't be content. I would rather return to what doesn't exist. To desire. To the waters of oblivion.

And the soul? The soul ascends from inert matter to the senses, from the senses to imagination, from imagination to reason, from reason to meditation, and, finally, is crowned as love.

This is why Dulcinea, merely by opening the Song of Songs, knows all about love.

But Dulcinea doesn't see it that way. She thinks she doesn't know anything about love. Only from divine love can one descend to earthly love.

Days pass in Princess Blizmanah's marvelous cave. Dulcinea and Amadis don't seem able to explore its entirety. No matter where they walk, they can't see the end. The tracks twist and turn and the paths keep changing. The landscape is never the same. The same corridor leads to different chambers. And what is different is no longer different, only to become so again. Fountains overflow and splash onto rocks. The cave has been forgotten: light and plants are from the outside world. Wind doesn't blow nor is there any restlessness. There's no way to measure time. Everything is the same age. Nothing erodes. Nothing decomposes. Caves like to guard secrets. Accumulate them. True History is in caves. Birth. A great blanket of protection and preservation. Heat. Fire. A broken pot. An abandoned wolf's pelt. Red paint. Burials. A winter night's dream. The first stories.

Dulcinea and Amadis are delighted to discover the unusual. Antiroutine and wondrous daily life: living inside a kaleidoscope. They know that Princess Blizmanah has promised them a story. Their story. Which they are not in a hurry to know. They have already found the one who knows it and won't keep quiet like the hermit did. However, Blizmanah slips away. Blizmanah dissolves. For days (days?), they don't see her. Nobody stops their activities. The inhabitants of the Cave of Transparency don't have anything to say.

---

18. These symbols all represent sacred spaces, for example, temples and the Holy Grail or the cup of the unicorn. The paragraph uses mystical references aluding to the soul's ascent to sacred space and later descent back to the earthly body. They also refer to symbols Amadis and Dulcinea have seen on their travels.

Then they begin to remember and recite *romances*.[19] Dulcinea and Amadis hear the story of the beautiful Melisande and her unexpected love. The one about Fonte Frida, the little turtledove, and the traitorous nightingale. The one about Gerineldo, Gerineldo, the king's most beloved page. The one about the maiden warrior who asked for a spinning wheel after she had learned to handle weapons and horses. The one about the sad prisoner who didn't know if it was day or night but for a little bird that sang for him at daybreak. The one about the Count Niño who crossed the sea for love and death was what he found. The one about the happy morning of Saint John's Day when men and women prepared to hear the mass of love. The one about Prince Arnaldos and the good fortune he had in the waters of the sea, also on a Saint John's Day morning.

And the time of stories is timeless. And it's a space that jumps to other spaces. It's a life desired. True life of the transposed image. It's spellbinding. It's enchanting. It's the soul's light.

Consequently, loss and oblivion grow larger for Dulcinea and Amadis. They no longer understand why they are there. They know neither what they were seeking nor how to find their destiny. They're unaware that they have a destiny. That they'd been condemned to wander. That they should unravel a secret and a key. That a curse weighs upon them.

In the Cave of Transparency, memories break down. Dulcinea and Amadis don't separate their hands. They're the same in face and body.

You're leaving Dulcinea and Amadis in happiness, right, Dulcinea? You still don't want to tell them of their misfortune. You can prolong their love in shortcuts and oblivion. Let time disintegrate in the Cave of Transparency without them noticing. At least let them discover what you haven't. Let them dwell in delightful fields without knowing what you already know. Let them embrace the marvel of a rocking cloud. Not reaching it, but enjoying it. Let them contemplate the green of leaves bathed in the light, three hours after noon, unaware of time. Only feeling, not thinking. You'll do the thinking, right, Dulcinea?

The thinking. The plotting. The doing and undoing. The inventing. The crossing out. The making things go backward or forward. All in your head

---

19. *Romances* are Spanish folk ballads that took stories and themes from popular lore and epic poetry and set them to music. They were popular beginning in the Middle Ages, when minstrels and jongleurs would travel from town to town singing these stories of heros, love, and adventures. This paragraph contains references to *romances* found in the famous *Romancero general* (1600), one of the largest collection of Spanish *romances*. See Durán, *Romancero*.

and in your time. In your unlimited internal space. Dulcinea, you're enjoying it. No, I don't always enjoy it. I suffer. I have nightmares. I don't remember them and I still feel anxious. My imagination weighs on me and I fear waking up. You don't know if you're imagining or living? No. It's the same. Same difference.

Well then, continue your stories, Dulcinea. You have to keep moving forward. Who could stand traveling on the Periferico if it weren't for your stories? The truth is that the Periferico fades a little. It's faint in the background. Fortunately.

So, your other Dulcinea has posed the question of whether she would write a diary. And she keeps asking herself. Since she's in a country so different from her own. Since she doesn't have anything to cling to. (She can't even grasp at straws.) Since Amadis appears and disappears. Since it isn't fun to go from soirée to soirée and from excursion to excursion. Since she's bored with the Marquise Calderon de la Barca. Since she's already counted all the splendid beams in her room. Since the flames of the fire in the fireplace are beginning to repeat their silhouettes. Since she's already tried new foods and the incalculable varieties of chiles. (Which is to say, she got burned by different levels of spiciness.) Since she's no longer surprised by Popocatepetl or Iztaccihuatl.[20] Since she's already figured out the intrigues, entanglements, ambiguities, hypocrisies, and corruptions. Since only the landscapes console her. (And avocados, which she loves.) Since she would like to board a ship back home right away. So, she decides yes. She will begin to write her diary of life in Mexico. Not to compete with the one the Marquise is writing. Not because she's thinking of publishing it. Not to interrupt her idleness. Not because of a desire for glory or fame. None of that. Simply to put things in order. Dulcinea is a person who likes to impose order. Her drawers in place. Her clothes neatly folded. Her books, from smallest to largest. Her jewelry perfectly separated. Her combs by shades of tortoiseshell, and her shawls by shades of white, ivory, and bone.

So, she will order her days. She will begin with her departure from Spain, her journey by sea, her arrival at the port of Veracruz. Then the most important things she has done with the Marquise. After that, her boredom. Her gigantic boredom. The senselessness of it all and her lack of ubiquity: where is she? So, if she doesn't know where she is, the question that truly matters

---

20. See note 6 in the "First Seal."

is: where is Amadis, her double? Because if he's there, she's there. And not the reverse. (Writing is useful so she can physically feel herself: yes, I am me.)

She begins to write. It's pleasant to fill blank pages with signs. At first it's easy. One simply has to make an effort to remember. One memory beckons another. Leaving her home in Toboso. Her house in Cadiz, in front of the sea. Describing rooms, furniture, carpets, windows and their latticework. The courtyard with orange trees: the thick dark green, the scented balls of sweet fire. The transparent song in the mouth of the well. Familiar sounds. Distant music and couplets. Afternoon jasmine with its strong perfume. The sun sinking into the sea, first slowly, then suddenly. Turning to the dark sky to discover the first star. Calm sensation that life will continue, the promise will be kept, the covenant will be strengthened. All while dinner preparations are heard in the kitchen. For food is also continuity. It's a break from monotony and a renewed cycle.

Dulcinea decides not to rush her diary. Memories can be slow. She's full of them. Composing them becomes delightful. She's flooded with pleasure. From preparing the notebook, admiring the thickness of the pages, sharpening the quill, and placing the ink within reach. Later beginning to write: the learned movements on the one hand, and the surprise of a different stroke on the other. Not abandoning the flourishes or neglecting them. A taste for calligraphy. The art of letters. As beautiful as illustrating. As painting. (Like the monk in the cell with the colored manuscript and gold powder.)

The first thing that moves Dulcinea is the writing itself. Being able to fill pages and pages with shaped and pointed writing. Slanted and even. Each letter in proportion to the others. The complex imagination of the capital letter. The impeccable space after the period. Wetting the quill (brief pause) and the smell of fresh ink. Making sure the point doesn't drip, so as not to smudge the paper. Then after finishing, before turning the page, passing the blotting paper over the writing. Turning this paper over too and seeing the strokes in mirror image. Invariably repeating this process. To the side, the fine sand ready in case there is something to erase. Carefully applying it, rubbing and then blowing lightly so the excess flies away.

Dulcinea will keep trying to capture the world that slips away from her, the world of her life. Imprisoning it. Framing it. Holding it.

In this way, she might be able to brace time and contain it between her fingers. Pleasure would last long and light would extend beyond the afternoon. She would not notice her hand's swollen veins as she writes, nor the darkness that has encroached. She would resume her deep childhood pleasure, when she delighted in copying pages and pages from a book, calmly forming the letters. But without falling back into the impatience she felt at times, now that the book is within her and she is surprised by its many layers.

Having the feeling—right, Dulcinea the scribe?—that the book is already done and that all you have to do is transfer it to paper. Scribe. Going so fast that you might lose track of the words' order. Undoubtedly your hand is slow and, afraid of losing track of the words, you sacrifice beautiful handwriting; you neglect the flourishes and rush the quill, and now neither the upward and downward strokes nor the evenness of the lines matters.

Well, Dulcinea, enjoy your diary because your creator, by not writing anything, has an advantage. She doesn't worry about paper, quills, letters, or speed. She would be worried about not having ideas. Not thinking. That the source of light would end. That sclerosis would seal her. Or that madness would invade her. And whatever else might come along.

But Dulcinea the scribe is happy. She's found her refuge. Where she can continue in greater solitude. She closes the door and no one bothers her. She doesn't even hear when someone knocks at the door. The barrier has been erected. There's no password to cross that border. You're either on one side or the other. Path with no return. Lock without a key. Closed trunk sent to the bottom of the river.

Dulcinea thinks she has taken a vow. That her black dress with the white neck is part of the cloister. That the state of grace elevates her at moments. That she will have to live among others without their knowing she no longer lives among them and that sometimes she will highlight her earthly ties so as not to lessen her purity by having to give explanations. Because who understands Dulcinea the scribe? No one.

Unless it's Amadis. Amadis should also take a vow of writing. For writing is a vow:

The Marquis of Santillana said this:

As it is true that this sky is blue, a divine affection, an insatiable spiritual lure; in which, as material seeks form and imperfection seeks perfection, this science of poetry and troubadour poetry was only found in noble and elevated spirits.[21]

---

21. Translation and modernization mine. Santillana, *Proemio e carta*.

Friar Luis of Leon said this:

One must choose, among the words in use, only those most adequate to the task, we must think about their sound, sometimes we must even count the letters, weigh and measure the words so that they may express clearly what we are trying to say, and also so that they do it in harmony and sweetness.[22]

Saint John of the Cross said this:

For who can describe that which He shows to loving souls in whom He dwells? Who can set forth in words that which He makes them feel? and, lastly, who can explain that for which they long? Assuredly no one can do it; not even they themselves who experience it. That is the reason why they use figures of special comparisons and similitudes; they hide somewhat of that which they feel and in the abundance of the Spirit utter secret mysteries rather than express themselves in clear words.[23]

Wittgenstein said this:

It should limit the thinkable and thereby the unthinkable.
It should limit the unthinkable from within through the thinkable.
It will mean the unspeakable by clearly displaying the speakable.
Everything that can be thought at all can be thought clearly.
Everything that can be said can be said clearly.[24]

22. León, *The Names of Christ*, 267.
23. John of the Cross, *A Spiritual Canticle*, 7.
24. Wittgenstein, *Tractatus Logico-Philosophicus*, 45. From tractatus 4.114–4.116.

THE SEVENTH SEAL

Dulcinea, you're going to write your diary in your room with high ceilings and black beams. You're going to write your diary and it's no big deal. Easy. You're wrong—what I'm going to write is my other diary. About what I don't know and don't understand. What's not true and what doesn't materialize. I'm going to write, for example, about Amadis. Amadis who appears and disappears. Amadis who is my double. Amadis who is my soul mate. (Do we have the same body?) (Having ridden through the forests in search of disenchantment.) Where is Amadis?

Dulcinea, you leave your scribe Dulcinea with the pre-pleasure of sitting down to write. With the preknowledge of starting to think. With the pre-happiness of ordering, at least, a small chaos. You also don't want to tell Dulcinea her destiny. Just like you haven't told it to Dulcinea and Amadis in the Cave of Transparency.

For Dulcinea and Amadis are still in the Cave. Just like the shadows of chess pieces, you cannot bring yourself to move them. As long as there's no movement, there's no remorse. The shadows can grow, but at the same angle. Only the angle of light will change.

Why doesn't the princess Blizmanah speak? Why doesn't she deliver her message? She can no longer put it off. She must summon Dulcinea and Amadis. Her timelessness begins to become defined. Dulcinea and Amadis carry time with them and this is the danger she risks. She should distance herself from them. They can break her continuity. She won't hold back the message anymore.

Here is what she said:

The moment arrives because it must arrive. For you. Not for me, for I am timeless. I warned you that I knew your story. Before I exhaust the dimensions and can no longer turn to the past, before I forget what it is.

I met your parents, announcers and repeaters of your (hi)story.[1] Tormented example of the double of the double. In telling your story, I will finally be able to erase time. Every day will be the true beginning for me. Origin and birth. Everything new at dawn and everything new at dusk. I will no longer remember anything.

---

1. The word "historia" in Spanish has a double meaning, referring both to "history" and "story"; thus, the use of the term "(hi)story" in the translation highlights the polysemic possibilities for interpretation and asks the reader to consider how story and history overlap and interact with our notions of "truth" and "fiction."

So, while I still remember it, I will tell you your (hi)story. Your parents, twin siblings, children of twin siblings, themselves children of twin siblings, children themselves of twin siblings. And so on back to the first children. The first ones, twin children. Twin parents. All of them separated and dispersed. All of them finding their way back to each other. Links in an unbroken chain. An established point of fusion. One hand clasps the next. The cycle is unending. A change of guard. The same seed germinating again.

She said this and then the princess Blizmanah stopped speaking.

Now Dulcinea and Amadis know. Now they know and accept it. They don't have anything to say. They look in each other's eyes, take each other's hands, and leave the Cave of Transparency. It is over.

They resume their journey. This time knowing there will be no end. Each one thinks to him or herself. A strange bubbling overflows in their thoughts. They could reject each other in horror or they could love each other even more tenderly. Each one abandoning him or herself. Orphans, siblings, lovers.

You just moved the pieces, Dulcinea. Now you can rest. The movement will last a while. In the meantime, what's going on with you? With me? Nothing. I'm starting to feel tired: I know this story. I just want to be done. You'll get there, don't worry. The doors will open. Won't it be late when they open? It doesn't matter, so long as they open.

As a child, you would have liked to live in a doll maker's house. The idea came to you after you read the story of Pinocchio. Wooden dolls moved by strings. Hanging from the ceiling. You would walk among them, knocking into them and making their little bodies clack. Some were all done and others needed to be painted and clothed. There were collections of heads, legs, and arms on shelves. You liked to guess which one would be for which doll. You made up stories about them, and sometimes brought one down to move it and make it walk and dance. You took advantage of the different pieces of scenery piled up in the corners. You dusted them off. You put them in the background while you played, absorbed, losing track of time. For days you repeated the same story, from beginning to end, without variation. Later, you began to change it. Things happened that you didn't like. Dangers. Illnesses. Scary things. And later, when everything was going horribly wrong, you would return to the first version, which was a relief to tell all over again.

You had your favorite dolls and then there were the scary ones, the ugly ones or bad guys. The ones you tried not to see, the ones who bumped into you or stared at you perversely. You turned them away from you, but one of them always managed to turn back around and scare you.

You took great care of the ones you liked. You talked to them and they answered you in your pretend voice. Before you left, you dressed them and put them to bed. The others continued hanging in their places, trembling slightly in the air. Shaking. Swaying. Rocking.

It seems as if the doll maker set aside your favorites, since the others disappeared and left empty spaces. You would get so happy when one of the bad ones went away, though not losing the fear that the same could happen to one of yours. So the first thing you would do was to check that they were all there and then that day you could feel at peace. Then, quickly noting the emptiness of the missing one.

That emptiness was death.

You didn't think it had been sold and had started its life elsewhere. That doll had died. For you, it had died. Which is the same as not seeing. (Regardless, you never lived in a doll maker's house.)

All your games, Dulcinea, were singular: for you alone. When your brother died, now you had someone to play with. Yes, then you were two: two who spoke, two who accompanied each other, two who went on adventures. You spoke to him until Amadis arrived. Now Amadis fills your mind. You erased your brother: you don't want to have anything to do with him anymore. What a nightmare. Good thing Amadis's face is smiling. You only see part of his face in the rearview mirror and you're not sure it's him. But it must be him. He erased your brother. At first, you thought it was your brother, that he was alive. Later, your brother ceased to exist. It was Amadis who existed. You began to speak to Amadis in your silence. He was the one who accompanied you and with whom you went on adventures. You only needed to look at him—you didn't need to say a word. And, like a good melancholic, you and Amadis dreamt about those desires to travel, the nostalgia, the yearning. Now he was more real. Amadis was at your side. Within reach. Awake, you saw him. Right here, in the car, you see his neck and you could caress it. Such a straight and fragile neck. You don't know why this brings to mind images of guillotines and hatchets. (Because of the many books you read about the French Revolution: you see a neck and it reminds you of guillotines.) (Why does every little thing evoke history for you? You see a sewer and think of the Romans.) (Why not modern times? Because I don't want to.) (Too many garbage lovers, not enough Llull lovers.)

Dulcinea, you don't have a place in this world. You keep thinking about Ramon Llull. Who does that? Me. Me. Me. I feel like I'm going to burst. How is it that no one else thinks about Ramon Llull? Do you see how it's hopeless?: I don't have anyone to talk to. I only read, read, read. I think, think, think. I burst, burst, burst.

Yes, I feel embedded in words. Having spent so much time without speaking, words are drowning me. Like an ancient galleon filled with gold at the bottom of the sea.

And there could be beautiful things, right Dulcinea? Yes, there could. That rusty galleon at the bottom of the sea, with half-open coffers, coins and jewels spilling over, and little fish swimming back and forth. Like a movie. With little bubbles and all. And a diver, who could be Amadis, Amadis, Amadis. Where are you?

I've lost Amadis. Who's driving the car? Could it be him? Who is he? And the other people? Could they be them? No, no they aren't.

Why do I feel this urge to open the door and throw myself onto the Periferico? What holds me back? Since I no longer recognize anything, since I can no longer distinguish anyone, whether I am one, or I am two, or I am three. If I am a polyphonic mute, what can you expect? Nothing—not even you opening the door and throwing yourself onto the Periferico. It would be a good ending, but you don't dare. Too passive. Your problem is inertia. Inaction. Apathy. The ancients would describe you as an incurable melancholic. Robert Burton, in his *Anatomy of Melancholy*, wrote:

But forasmuch as this malady is caused by precedent imagination, with the appetite, to whom spirits obey, and are subject to those principal parts, the brain must needs primarily be misaffected, as the seat of reason; and then the heart, as the seat of affection.

. . . such as are solitary by nature, great students, given to much contemplation, lead a life out of action, are most subject to melancholy.[2]

Totally applicable to you. Why is it that you cannot decide anything about your life?

I can't decide anything about myself (not even to open the door and throw myself out, as much as I would like to) because I can't see the future. I don't know what there is where there is still nothing. So, how will I imagine what doesn't exist: reality is unimaginable.

But if you imagine the lives of your other Dulcineas, why can't you do the same for yours? Because I can't control my life: those of my Dulcineas

---

2. Democritus Junior, *Anatomy*. This quote comes from the original work in English and varies slightly from the Spanish text. See the First Partition, Section One, Member Three, Subsection Two: "Of the part affected. Affection. Parties Affected."

are easy: I make them up. After that, I have no energy left and I don't want to do anything with myself. It makes me tired, very tired, and I fall asleep. Now I'm going to lay my head back in the seat and I'm going to sleep a little.

Dulcinea dreamt and this is what she dreamt, as she had dreamt so many times before:

She was riding in a car with Amadis on a very long highway that had a high wall on the right. Suddenly something unexpected was happening, and it caused Amadis to draw her close and slowly approach the side of the road. Then they saw how a desert was advancing toward them. More like beautiful sands. Amadis kept hugging Dulcinea, protecting her from danger. Another car was passing them and for a moment Dulcinea thought that was where the danger would come from, but it wasn't. They got out of the car, still embracing each other tightly, and walked very slowly, getting closer to the wall. They felt a shadow cover them, the enormous wings of a gigantic bird. The desert was absorbing them and now the grains of sand were rose-colored, like the reflection of sunlight. It was inexplicable and beautiful: peaceful like the end. Not only the end of Dulcinea and Amadis, but of everything. Loving and serene death. Reconciled. Amadis embracing Dulcinea. Amadis guarding Dulcinea. Amadis drawing in Dulcinea. The end of the world. Ultimate destruction. The beautiful sands of the desert softly enveloping Dulcinea and Amadis. It was, truly, the Revelation.

When Dulcinea awakened, the sun was beginning to set and the sky was an orangey pink, the same colors as in her dream. It was, truly, the Revelation.

The car advances along the Periferico. The exit for Tlalpan will come up soon.[3] There are trees to the right. The orangey pink of the sky keeps intensifying. It seems as if the journey is coming to an end. Dulcinea senses it. She's tired. Exhausted. As if the asphalt were ending and a dirt road were slowing down the roll of the car. As if the space were a prolonged yawn. Tangled tree branches. Thickening dust. Birds crowded along power lines (and raindrops at one end, about to fall).

Those images cradle Dulcinea. Happiness can arise from contemplation. Forces of nature (landscapes and animals) are the only acceptable order (or disorder). Where there can be equilibrium. A certain state of bliss. A tran-

---

3. Tlalpan is one of Mexico City's sixteen boroughs. Located in the southwest region of the City, Tlalpan is mainly composed of forested lands and small communities, with most of its urban population in the north of the borough, where the southernmost part of the circular Periferico begins to turn back northward. On this stretch of the Periferico, travelers see several hospitals, including a psychiatric hospital. Muñiz-Huberman, pers. comm.

quil union. A music that, in singular moments, envelops us in the feeling of complete integration, of happiness through the loss of the individual as we turn ourselves over to the infinite.

Those are the moments that matter. That allow Dulcinea to continue her daily endeavors. That in their fleetingness absorb eternity. That heal memory and impact the core. The rest is emptiness. It's all about finding what surrounds the emptiness. In order to elude it. The scalpel that circles the scalp tries to expose the secret. But it hits the hard cranium and later the soft encephalic mass. Nothing more. Thought is untrappable. Madness reconstructs it.

What can Dulcinea do if she has cut the moorings and heaved the anchors, if she has sailed into spaces from which one never returns? It's undeniable: she can only sink.

Dulcinea has been able to survive because of her internal voices and characters. If they were to be silenced, her life would end. She has not had her own life, she was only a passenger brought or sent: choices she never made. Except for those related to reading. Which, consequently, have led her to greater silence and solitude.

Maybe the problem is the opposite. The only possible life is Dulcinea's. Only those who read, who keep quiet, who remember are the ones who live. For others, life is only what has been lived and reality is only what is before them.

True wisdom shouldn't be pushed aside. It's a mixture of experiences. A mixture of time. A mixture of anticipated pain. And the discipline of precise language.

Dulcinea has no doubts. Dulcinea is sure of herself. The moorings and anchors don't matter: they're meant to be severed. She awaits her end: sailing into those seas of God.[4]

---

4. Machado, "Parábolas." The line "Those seas of God" comes from the poem "Parables" "(Parábolas") in *Fields of Castile* (*Campos de Castilla*) (1907–1917) by the Spanish poet Antonio Machado (1875–1939). In the stanza, a sailor makes a garden next to the ocean and then travels "those seas of God." Later, in 1969, inspired by Machado, the Spanish musician Joan Manuel Serrat would put the poem to music in "Parábola." There is also a similar theme in the medieval *romance* of the Infante Arnaldos about the ineffable call of the sea. For the English translation, see "Count Arnaldos." Also, see Spitzer, "The Folkloristic," 173, 183–84.

Those seas of God or those unreachable heights, which turn out to be the same. It's like the Infante Arnaldos, embarking to hear the song no one knows how to hear. But which Dulcinea hears from within.

Dulcinea possesses an internal treasure. No one else knows it. Dulcinea is her whole world. It encompasses her and everyone else. She is so silent, and yet she loves so much. She loves like no other and without anyone knowing. She dies from so much love. Without ever showing it. Proof of love destroys love. Actions pulverize it. Gestures, caresses, words: the biggest catastrophe ever invented. Signs: ineffective language. Great, great love is that which is not expressed. Everywhere, hermetic silence.

Reinvent the world. So much repetition isn't possible. Who can believe in something? Man? God? Blasphemous guffaws. A new love and a new science must be created: how is it that two and two are still four?

If the world must be invented, make it explode first. Long live the bombs. So that the same errors don't return from the void. The same inventions and the same bombs. Man is indestructible: his monstrous blueprint is endless. Weeds never die. Rotten genetics. Abortive chromosomes. Fetal bile. Fecal blood. Vomitous material. Discarded bodily fluids.

Dulcinea, you struggle between abject hopelessness and pure hope.
　　Like every other human.
　　No more, no less.

Well, since you're addressing me, I should tell you that you're wrong. I will never be like every other human. No more, no less. I have ways of escaping norms and statistics. Fortunately I live in another world. I elude any measure or classification. I live where I want and when I want. Similarly, I will decide my fate. The day I turn the last page of the last book I read. Ça y est.[5]

I, Dulcinea, enclosed in all directions by this body, can fly. I extend my arms, begin to ascend and fly. I, Dulcinea.
　　In the air, I see and contemplate everything. The wonderful adventures of Nils Hölgersson are my adventures.[6] It's my journey and yet, it's no small

---

5. French for "That's it."
6. See Lagerlöf, Wonderful. The Wonderful Adventures of Nils (1906/1907) is a Swedish book written by Selma Lagerlöf (1858–1940), the first woman to receive the Nobel Prize in literature. The

feat because I can travel and fly even more. Nils Hölgersson didn't leave the ground much. I reach higher and higher.

All of those wonderful fairy tales I didn't read as a child are what made me fly. Those limitless fairy tales, with castles, elves, princes and princesses, spells, magical powers, crystals, vials, potions and ointments, seals and rings, clues and tests. With curses and horrors. Missteps and mix-ups. Storms. Snow. And flowers in the month of May. Injustices. Punishments. And deaths. So that everything would apparently end well. Everyone happy. And what was beautiful and good would gild the countryside.

Now that I have read fairy tales, I've mixed them all up and they're all one long and complicated story to me. Tips of colorful strands stand out from skeins of yarn and if I pull on one, it turns into another color and I can't follow it back to its beginning. I mix up the characters and the adventures, and I can't remember any one complete story. Vivid scenes stand out to me, but as in dreams, isolated and disconnected, terrifying and seductive. I struggle to repeat one complete story and it's impossible to grasp the ambiguity or push through the fog. There's no beginning, middle or end. Order doesn't exist. Logic hasn't been invented. Instincts stir and bubble as in a witch's cauldron. Trees stop whispering. Rivers stop flowing. Beasts don't attack. Birds are frozen in wisps of air. Raindrops on the ascending scale. I can't find harmony. Always stretching and stretching without being able to reach the tip of memory.

Just as I have not recovered a single fairy tale, I haven't recovered my childhood. What was most important to me: knowing whether these parents are my parents. I haven't been able to figure it out. In other words, I still haven't found myself. I affirm myself through my name (Dulcinea, Dulcinea) and I'm my own progenitor. I feel like the first one or the source. Without anyone preceding me. Without anyone following me. However, these parents are parents, and whose are they if not mine? They're beside me. They accompany me. They're still with me. But why, then, don't I recognize them? Why don't I remember them? Neither the blood, nor the placenta, nor the cord.

If you can't remember something, does that mean it didn't exist? Probably. Not for me. But, what if it really did exist and I don't remember it? It didn't exist. The only thing that exists is what you remember. Wonderful memory.

Because I get lost in my memories, I prefer to leave them alone. Not touch them anymore. It's better to remember my Dulcineas. What will happen to

---

main character, Nils Holgersson, a mischievous young boy, flies across Sweden by hanging from a goose's neck. The book taught its young readers about the geography and history of Sweden.

them? I can't end their stories. If I end them, it would be the end of me. I'll never end them. They'll always be with me. Spinning around and around in me. They're my fairy tales. The ones I tell myself.

Dulcinea the scribe, what has she written in her diary? She closes it and puts it away. No one will know.

After having listened to Blizmanah's words and returning to their journey, Dulcinea and Amadis haven't fallen into fear or despair. Their love is wiser. It's complete and it's round. Like round wind and round color and round sound. Perfect. A machine of wheels and bird's wings. Sky that reveals all. Transparent abysm. Blinding darkness. Neither mystery nor secret. Knowledge in clarity. A rainbow in your hand.

The only love possible is that of Dulcinea and Amadis.

For them, walking the world is an act of love. Nothing can touch them. Not even tragedy. Not even death. Not even life. They can't stop. One foot after the other. A step forward. A footprint. As if the path had already been marked. Rocks that part and trees that leave openings. No worries about finding a shortcut: it's not necessary. Any path is good when there's no clear destination.

There's no arrival: they are the true pilgrims carrying all the guilt of men. And, yet, they are light: they have no despair. Nor do they seek amends. Their love is now divine love. They are redeemers and safeguards. They could climb a pillar and spend the rest of their days there in loving contemplation.[7]

They have been chosen for the work of revealing the deceptions of convention. Of unraveling laws. Two on the road, in solitude. Perfectly accompanied. Worlds and worlds with them. All of History and all stories. Summaries and examples. Truth and fiction. Stories that are forgotten and stories that are repeated. Stories that are dying. That are reborn, conceived from the first stories. Without memory. Without recollections. With all memory and

---

7. The allusion to climbing a pillar is a reference to the ascetic saint, Simeon Stylites, who spent thirty-seven years on a small platform atop a pillar in what is modern-day Syria. Trying to escape the intrusive interruptions of the world, Simeon climbed the pillar to find solace and inward contemplation. In 1965, Luis Buñuel made a film called *Simon of the Desert* (*Simón del desierto*) based on this fifth-century saint and his unique form of devotion. See Buñuel, *Simón*.

recollections hidden. The things that have to be shaken up and brought to light. The archaeology of every life. The fragments and the shards.

After leaving the Cave of Transparency, Dulcinea and Amadis, who don't know whether they dreamt it or it is real, face that other world that appears to be concrete and real (and which still might be a dream). A world in which rocks are rocks, wood is wood, and the weight of a sparrow in the air is the weight of a sparrow in the air.

So they keep ascending that mountain they have never stopped ascending and they continue penetrating through paths and mountain passes. At these heights, snow falls silently and its transparency thickens into whiteness. A cold breeze on their faces and the feeling of filling their lungs deeply. Warm capes and carved branches made into walking sticks in case they need them. Clear stretches where the snow doesn't fall and the earth retains its dark tones. A true restoration of landscape. The book of nature as a white page. The cold punch of ice writing stories that few read. For the first time, Dulcinea and Amadis are part of the nature that surrounds them. That mountain and that snow wouldn't make sense without them. Dulcinea and Amadis are there so that mountain and snow might exist. Dulcinea and Amadis are there so the creative spark might exist. Dulcinea and Amadis are consciousness. They extend their arms and a curtain of crystalline snowflakes drops as in the final scene on stage.

Lo and behold, when Dulcinea opens the cover of her diary, the great theater of the world springs forth.[8] She does not contemplate the words, not what she wrote yesterday, not the calligraphy brushstrokes. It's the great theater of the world that appears before her eyes. Figures that stir and move about. It's the set, the costumes, the swords, the bonnets. Costumes heaped in a pile that come to life when worn. Bodies that dazzle. Black eyes and red lips. Dusted wigs and high-heeled shoes with buckles. Everything moves among the pages. Everything flutters and slithers. In the lively shapes they have assumed, the words rush and trample and one by one, their features eventu-

---

8. See Calderón de la Barca, "The Great Theater." Reference to Pedro Calderón de la Barca's Golden Age play, *El gran teatro del mundo* (*The Great Theater of the World*, c. 1634). The play is in the genre of the *auto sacramental*, a kind of morality play that used allegory and was popular to teach Church doctrine. Following a long history of philosophical thought that life is like a play, in this work, the Author (God) creates the world as a theatrical performance in which each person has a predetermined role (e.g., king, laborer, rich man, poor man, etc.). Whoever plays his or her role well is rewarded while those who don't are punished. In this citation, the title itself evokes the concept that if life is like a play in which we all have roles, we are merely characters in a work of literature; likewise, as Dulcinea creates stories, she also creates the world we inhabit as characters.

ally disappear and they become a heap of worn-out skeletons. Dulcinea gets frightened and closes the cover quickly, and the diary keeps calm: not one figure has spilled out from the edges. If Dulcinea slowly begins to open the cover, the great theater rushes out again. There's no space to write: the stage, props, curtain, and lighting are already there. The characters know their roles and start to act. Dulcinea walks onto the stage, bows, and the performance begins. If the diary is not shut, the show will go on.

Well, I need a break, I can't keep making up more stories. I'm exhausted and the boundaries of every thing, every object, every idea are becoming blurry. I'm beginning to dissolve, like Dalí's melting clock. To fly, like Remedios Varo's apples. To drift, like Magritte's clouds.[9]

Dulcinea, return to your childhood, return to your calm place. You've never recalled anything about your friend, the one who gave you peace of mind before leaving Russia for Mexico. Her name was Aliana, she gave me peace of mind. Aliana wasn't my friend, with her long blond hair, the bangs on her forehead, her bluish-gray eyes. But for me, she was my friend. If I could have picked only one friend, it would have been her. I used to walk through fields with her and we would be the last ones to get back, after it was already dark and dinner had been served. We would hug each other and laugh. We would hold hands and run until we threw ourselves to the ground, the tall wheat covering us. I dreamt it. I dreamt about Aliana. She was and wasn't at my side. Sometimes I saw her and sometimes I didn't. I didn't dream it. She walked with me. She didn't walk with me. Yes, I was dreaming. She kissed me. She caressed me. No. Yes. Aliana.

One night, coming back late like we used to, we saw the house in flames. But it wasn't the house. It was an ancient gray stone palace. Tongues of fires were lapping at the façade and cleansing the real walls behind it. The house was not being destroyed; rather, the palace was being born: the gate, the picture windows, the towers, the galleries. Then the fire wasn't fire, it was water that dampened the gray stones of the palace and made them glisten. There was a fountain at the entrance and ponds on either side. Solid green thickets. Clusters of flowers on trellises. The children were safe and were still carrying some of their belongings. The teachers walked through the transformed pal-

---

9. References to three surrealist painters and famous symbols from their works. Salvador Dalí (1904–1989) was from Spain and the melting clock is a reference to his painting, *The Persistence of Memory* (1931). See Dalí, *Persistence*. Remedios Varo (1908–1963) was Spanish-Mexican and her painting, *Still Life Reviving* (1963) shows apples and pears circling above a table. See Kaplan, "Remedios," 48. Finally, the Belgian René Magritte (1898–1967) is famous for many paintings featuring clouds with objects or people framing the clouds or floating in them.

ace's new rooms, looking for places to settle the children. Suddenly, Aliana wandered away and signaled me to follow. She knew where to find the best room for us. She brought me through the long corridors, dusty and dark, until we reached a closed door she knew how to open. Maybe the two of us were hoping to find a magical place: chests, wardrobes, high-backed chairs, old tapestries, thick carpets, a canopy bed. Nothing. There was nothing: bare rocks, moss hanging from the walls, moisture, shadows, a rough gray. One door faced a large terrace where lush greenery and weeds had grown between the uneven tiles beneath the cool shadows. From the terrace, the view reached a wide avenue of light-colored packed earth, lined by birch trees, trunk close to illuminated trunk. Images already foreseen or dreamt or desired.

We settled into that room, far from everyone, without anyone able to find us. The next day, the house went back to the way it was, without any signs of fire or flood. The same everyday faces. Without surprise. Without questions. The same food. The same plates. The same embroidery on the napkins. The same checkered tablecloths. The same stains on the walls.

One day later, Aliana was leaving: she was in the first group to reunite with her parents. When she said goodbye to me, she told she me wouldn't be writing to me and I shouldn't write to her either. I suppose this way we keep our memories intact.

Some afternoons, without Aliana, as the last to return, I would see the palace, the fire or the flood, the children being rescued and, sometimes, I would find the hidden room again.

Other afternoons, it wasn't like that.

The children were leaving. Little by little, they were reclaimed. But now they weren't children. I don't know what we were. But we weren't children. The years weren't counted, but the years had counted. The separation was strange. Meeting my parents again would be like meeting strangers. Like when we got new teachers. Adult beings who took care of us. Who didn't know us. Whose faces were unexpected. Whose tone of voice was different. They came and went: we always stayed. Their faces were empty holes.

I wasn't in a hurry to leave. This had been my life. I was free in my imagination. Now living with two other people would restrict me. Two people who were saying they were my parents. I couldn't deal with normalcy: not having to flee or protect myself from bombs or snipers. Losing those woods in which I immersed myself as if I would never leave. I had my own fairy tale and I felt they were going to snatch it from me.

During those months when the children were dispersed, I only thought about how to bring my story with me. If it wouldn't be too much to ask, I would pray that my parents wouldn't find me.

In the end, Leninito and I were the only ones left, and this would have been for the best. The letter arrived: I could have lost it on purpose, but they just would have sent another and another and another.

I knew that, like my brother, I had died in those woods and my story would get lost. Leninito had also died there. On those last days, I showed him my secret places in the woods and brought him to the door of the room Aliana had opened for me.

After that came destruction and silence.

And I heard a great voice out of the temple saying to the seven angels, Go your ways, and pour out the vials of the wrath of God upon the earth.[10]

That wrath was what touched me and split apart all the layers that formed me. The veils came off, thinly, transparently. And the anger was there, and the fury and the howling. I had been torn apart by the rage of others and now it was my turn to rebuild myself.

Which was not easy, because all the pieces of me had literally been scattered to the four winds. And I couldn't remember the maker. And I didn't have the master plan. In other words, I hadn't created myself. But, now, in pieces, I had to re-create myself.

When I got to this point, I was asking myself whether I should or should not do it. If it was worth it. If so, why? Or, if so, for what?

Or worse: even if I wanted to: how would I start? Because the fact is that we find ourselves all of a sudden. We don't know when: suddenly we're ourselves.

We don't know from where we emerge or what the transition means.

That's why, alone with myself, I don't know what to do. If God had made me from clay, I would have had an explanation. (One time in Spain, before they sent me to Russia, my father called me on the phone and I thought he was God. I never recognized his voice again.) Of course, I was made from clay, thus my cracking.

Can an archaeologist reconstruct things? No, I don't think so. He glues things together. The cracks remain. Water could still leak out. But I can't even find the pieces. I can't even give the appearance of being mended. I'm

10. Rev 16:1 (KJV).

broken into pieces. My head has escaped into the heights. I've lost my heart. One foot is on the ground and the other hovers in the air. Disharmonious arms. Eyes spinning. In slow motion but at different speeds. I can't find unity: only silence consoles me. My fingernails detach and my eyelashes fall out.

What I would like is complete emptiness. For my brain to be a black hole that gives off light to no avail. No, not that. I would prefer not to talk to myself anymore. Not that either? No, Dulcinea, you like to talk to yourself. You make everything up. Even your own brokenness. You decided that comedy doesn't work: long live tragedy. You enjoy it so much. A lot. More.

Dulcinea, you're neither a potter nor an archaeologist: you cannot reconstruct your childhood: you can't know what your brother's death was like: you can't recognize your parents. Dulcinea, you haven't resolved anything.

You also haven't been able to amuse yourself. Your stories of the other Dulcineas don't interest you. You've left them incomplete. Dulcinea, what are you doing?

Nothing. I've never done anything. I've always been quiet, alone, in a corner. Like a rag doll. Discarded. Without a face.

I've gathered scattered images in order to guard them jealously in their disorder. I've collected every kind of disposable object. I possess a piece of polished metal from some place in my house in Madrid. A dry leaf from I don't know which tree in Valencia. And a shell too. A piece of birchbark from Pushchino or Saratov. Sand from Chachalacas.[11] A small stone from Tzintzuntzan.[12] A sheet with the names of transfer stations from New York to Balbuena. A bullet casing I can't remember where I found. The first words my mother said to me on the way from the Balbuena station to the Cuauhtemoc borough after I had just arrived from Russia: as a child, you had plump wrists.[13]

I move these objects around and around, putting them in place and then moving them again. They leave the drawer of my memory and sift through my fingers. I delight in them and I don't dare throw them away. They have no form and they are disintegrating. Some are more than forty years old.

True treasures.

A coffer of riches I discovered.

---

11. Chachalacas is both a famous beach in Veracruz and the name of a bird found along the Caribbean coast of Mexico and Central America.

12. Now a town in the Mexican state of Michoacan, Tzintzuntzan was the pre-Hispanic capital of the Purepecha people. In its archaeological site, among the stone structures, the "yácata" pyramids of Tzintzuntzan stand out for their uniquely circular form.

13. Named after the last Aztec emperor, the Cuauhtemoc borough, located in the north of Mexico City, is a cultural hub, encompassing the historic center, including the main square, or Zócalo, and the ruins of the main pyramids of the Aztec Templo Mayor.

(No one knows anything.)
(A secret is a secret.)
My head is not emptying.
It weighs on me more and more.
It has filled up and I don't have any blank space.

I saw the deer on the white snow get closer to the house when the tree bark wasn't enough to satisfy their hunger. But they got scared and fled back into the darkness.

In the boat, on the ocean, a seagull perched on the mainmast.
    A dolphin jumping and showing his smooth head.

I heard these words: the height of the mountain or the depth of the valley?[14]

Sunrise. Sunset.
Warm placenta.
Welcoming amniotic fluid.
The no longer hard wooden coffin.
Dead soldiers. Mud packed on their boots.
The hydrocephalic child.
The developmentally delayed child.
The beautiful doe-eyed child with long, thick eyelashes.
Lost fetus. Decomposed fetus.
Traces of abortions among gauze and cotton, in the trash.[15]
The blue eyes of a Siamese cat.

The whole world in my hand. Which is the hand of God. Which is the mind of the cosmos. Microcosm. Macrocosm. When will I give up?
    Emptiness will be its shape.
    I will love the television screen and kiss shiny plastic.
    You, Dulcinea? Come on. You dance to another tune. You can't be an ascetic because you won't surrender yourself to ritual. You've shredded your

---

14. See note 3 from "The Fourth Seal."
15. The word *aborto* in Spanish can mean both "abortion" or "miscarriage," so either meaning can be understood in this line.

story, you've fragmented your moment, you've dissected your soul. Forget it, why don't you just look through the car window?

Dulcinea looks through the car window. At that moment, Dulcinea knows they will crash. Or Dulcinea desires it. It would be a way to come to an end. But Dulcinea also doesn't want that. She has always envisioned her death in a crash and the violence of iron and fire. But it's not like that. The Periferico keeps thinning out. There are fewer cars. Few. Very few. Scarcely a one. The path is clear. Only them. The strangers. Dulcinea and Amadis. One lone car. The strangers aren't there when Dulcinea wants to look at them. Amadis continues to be there and she does too.

The two of them, nothing else. Maybe they have crashed and the bodies of the strangers have fallen onto the highway. Dulcinea and Amadis. Like in the beginning. Like with the clay and the breath.

The car glides like a sleigh on snow or a boat on the ocean. Clouds are spreading apart. The light becomes intense, before disappearing.

Dulcinea should remember where they are going. She only remembers the desert sands invading the highway. Intense colors and a headache that splits her head in half. And if it does split and her head falls off? No. She wouldn't like it to roll on the ground. It seems as if a knife is opening her cranium. She has felt it. The cold. The sharpness. And the cutting.

Tranquility. A delayed sunset. Without effort. Without contrast.

The Periferico ends. The car enters a side road. The asphalt is left behind, a dirt road.

There are trees: birds settling themselves and singing their last song. Sagging branches weighed down by fruit. Pleasant silence. Chiaroscuro.

I like this place, thinks Dulcinea.

In the background, a castle. Steep rocks leading up. Light in the clouds. The almond-shaped eye of God.

The doors (to heaven) open.

Mixcoac
September 12, 1983–July 25, 1984

Bibliography

Afzal, Cameron C. "Wheels of Time in the Apocalypse of Jesus Christ." In *Paradise Now: Essays on Early Jewish and Christian Mysticism*, 195–210. Edited by April D. DeConick. Atlanta: Society of Biblical Literature, 2006.

Alemán, Matheo. *Guzmán de Alfarache*. Retamar, Spain: Ediciones Perdidas, 2003. http://www.librosdearena.es/Biblioteca_pdf/GuzmandeAlfarache.pdf.

Arbel, Vita Daphna. *Beholders of Divine Secrets: Mysticism and Myth in the Hekhalot and Merkavah Literature*. Albany: State University of New York Press, 2003.

Argensola, Bartolomé Leonardo de. "A una mujer que se afeitaba y estaba hermosa." *Poemas del alma*. Accessed May 25, 2021. https://www.poemas-del-alma.com/bartolome-leonardo-de-argensol-a-una-mujer-que-se-afeitaba-y-estaba-hermosa.htm.

Auerbach, Erich. "The Enchanted Dulcinea." In *Cervantes' "Don Quixote": A Casebook*, 35–61. Edited by Roberto Gonzáles Echevarría. New York: Oxford University Press, 2005.

"The Battle of Kursk: The Largest Tank Battle in History." *Sky History*, accessed May 25, 2021. https://www.history.co.uk/article/the-battle-of-kursk-the-largest-tank-battle-in-history#main-content.

Berceo, Gonzalo de. *Miracles of Our Lady*. In *History of Spanish Literature*. Vol. 1, edited by George Ticknor. New York: Harper and Brothers, 1849. Project Gutenberg, released June 17, 2017. https://www.gutenberg.org/files/54928/54928-h/54928-h.htm.

Bergman, Ingmar, dir. *The Seventh Seal*, 1998; Irvington, New York: Criterion Collection, DVD.

Book of Alexander (Libro de Alexandre). Translated, Introduction and Notes by Peter Such and Richard Rabone. Liverpool: Liverpool University Press, 2009.

Bruno, Giordano. *The Heroic Enthusiasts, Part Two [Gli Eroici Furori]: An Ethical Poem.* Translated by L Williams. London: G. Norman and Son, 1889. Project Gutenberg, released November 16, 2006. www.gutenberg.org/dirs/1/9/8/3/19833/19833.txt.

Buñuel, Bruno, dir. *Simón del desierto (Simon of the Desert)*, 1965. Mexico: Gustavo Alatrise.

Calderón de la Barca, Fanny. *Life in Mexico: The letters of Fanny Calderón de la Barca.* Edited and annotated by Howard T. Fisher and Maron Hall Fisher. Garden City, NY: Doubleday and Company, 1966.

Calderón de la Barca, Pedro. "The Great Theater of the World." Translated by Rick Davis. *Theater* 34, no. 1 (2004): 128–51.

Carey, Lydia. "Romani Heritage: A Glimpse Into Mexico's Misunderstood Gypsy Community." *Culture Trip*, February 21, 2018. https://theculturetrip.com/north -america/mexico/articles/romani-heritage-a-glimpse-into-mexicos-misunderstood -gypsy-community/.

Castilleja, Diana. "Angelina Muñiz-Huberman: construcción de un "yo" fragmentado." *Anales de Literatura Hispanoamericana* 44 (2015): 21–33.

Caufield, Catherine. *Shmiot Fugue: Neomysticism in the Voices of Three Jewish-Mexican Women Writers.* Beau Bassin, Mauritius: Hadassah Word Press, 2017.

Cervantes de Saavedra, Miguel. *Don Quixote.* Translated by John Ormsby. N.p., n.d.; Project Gutenberg, last updated August 26, 2019. https://www.gutenberg.org /files/996/996-h/996-h.htm#ch22b.

Costeloe, Michael. "Prescott's *History of the Conquest* and Calderón de la Barca's *Life in Mexico:* Mexican Reaction, 1843–1844." *The Americas* 47, no. 3 (January 1991): 337–48. https://www.jstor.org/stable/1006804.

"Count Arnaldos." In *Ancient Spanish Ballads: Historical and Romantic*, 136–37. Translated by John Gibson Lockhart. Charleston: BiblioLife, 2009. First published in 1886 by C. S. Francis and Company.

Dalí, Salvador. *Persistence of Memory.* 1931. Oil on canvas, 24.1 x 33 cm, Museum of Modern Art, New York, https://www.moma.org/collection/works/79018

De Amicis, Edmondo. *Cuore (Heart): An Italian Schoolboy's Journal.* Translated by Isabel F. Hapgood. New York: Thomas Y. Cromwell Company, 1915. Project Gutenberg, released May 24, 2009. https://www.gutenberg.org/files /28961/28961-h/28961-h.htm.

DeConick, April D. "What is Early Jewish and Christian Mysticism?" In *Paradise Now: Essays on Early Jewish and Christian Mysticism*, 1–24. Edited by April D. DeConick. Atlanta: Society of Biblical Literature, 2006.

———. *Paradise Now: Essays on Early Jewish and Christian Mysticism.* Atlanta: Society of Biblical Literature, 2006.

Democritus Junior (Robert Burton). *Anatomy of Melancholy.* London, 1652. Project Gutenberg, updated February 27, 2021. https://www.gutenberg.org/files /10800/10800-h/10800-h.htm.

Durán, Agustín, ed. *Romancero General: Ó, Colección De Romances Castellanos Anteriores Al Siglo Xviii*. Madrid: M. Rivadeneyra, 1877. https://bibliotecadigital.jcyl.es /es/consulta/registro.do?id=2272.

Filer, Malva. "The Integration of a Fragmented Self in the Works of Angelina Muñiz-Huberman." *Studies in 20th Century Literature* 27, no. 2 (2003): 263–78. https://doi .org/10.4148/2334-4415.1556.

García Ascot, Jomí, dir. *En el balcón vacío (On the Empty Balcony)*, 1961. Mexico: Ascot/Torre.

Goya, Francisco. *Saturn Devouring One of His Sons*. 1819–1823. Oil on canvas, 83 x 146 cm, El Prado Museum, Madrid, https://www.wikiart.org/en/francisco-goya /saturn-devouring-his-son-1823-1.

Green, Otis. *Spain and the Western Tradition: The Castilian Mind in Literature from "El Cid" to Calderón*, vol. 1. Madison: The University of Wisconsin Press, 1963.

Greenberg, Mike. "Harpocrates: The God of Silence." *Mythology Source*, April 19, 2021. https://mythologysource.com/harpocrates-god-of-silence/.

Hadzelek, Aleksandra. "Places of Exile: The Transculturation of Spanish Exiles in Mexico." *Journal of the Australasian Universities Languages and Literature Association*, 113 (2010): 69–85. doi: 10.1179/000127910804775595.

John of the Cross. *A Spiritual Canticle of the Soul and The Bridegroom of Christ*. Translation by David Lewis. Corrections and Introduction by Benedict Zimmerman. Wincanton, England, 1909. Electronic Edition with Modernization of English by Harry Plantiga, 1995. https://www.documentacatholicaomnia.eu/03d/1542-1591 ,_Ioannes_a_Cruce,_A_Spiritual_Canticle_Of_The_Soul,_EN.pdf.

Juana Inés de la Cruz, Sor. *A Sor Juana Anthology*. Translated by Alan S. Trueblood and foreword by Octavio Paz, 166–98. Cambridge, MA: Harvard University Press, 1988.

Kaplan, Janet A. "Remedios Varo." *Feminist Studies* 13, no. 1 (1987): 38–48. doi:10 .2307/3177834.

Klee, Paul. *The Diaries of Paul Klee, 1898–1918*. Edited and Introduction by Felix Klee. Berkeley: University of California Press, 1968.

Lagerlöf, Selma. *The Wonderful Adventures of of Nils*. Translated by Velma Swanston Howard. Garden City, New York:Doubleday, Page and Company, 1922. A Celebration of Women Writers, https://digital.library.upenn.edu/women/lagerlof/nils /nils.html.

León, Luis de. *The Names of Christ*. Translation and Introduction by Manuel Durán and William Kluback. New York: Paulist Press, 1984.

Lindstrom, Naomi. "Las narrativas visionarias en la producción de Angelina Muñiz-Huberman." *Transmodernity* 6, no. 1 (Spring 2016): 1–15.

Llull, Ramón. *Liber de ascensu et descensu intellectus*. Valencia, 1512.

———. *Libro del orden de caballeria*. Alicante: Biblioteca Virtual Miguel de Cervantes, 2002. www.cervantesvirtual.com/obra/libro-del-orden-de-caballeria-principes-y -juglares--0/.

London, G. H. "The 'Razón de amor' and the 'Denuestos del agua y el vino': New Readings and Interpretations." *Romance Philology* 19, no. 1 (August 1965): 28–47.

Machado, Antonio. "Parábolas." *Campos de Castilla*. Trianarts. https://trianarts.com/antonio-machado-parabolas/#sthash.k2HJkohX.kUKClKJg.dpbs.

Mancing, Howard. "Dulcinea del Toboso—On the Occasion of Her Four-Hundredth Birthday." *Hispania* 88, no. 1 (March 2005): 53–63.

Mark, Joshua J. "Cathars." *World History Encyclopedia*. Last modified April 02, 2019. https://www.ancient.eu/Cathars/.

Marquis, Rebecca. "Riding the Chariot: *Dulcinea encantada*, Merkabah, and the Trope of Return." Paper presented at the 17th International Research Conference of the Latin American Jewish Studies Association, Miami, Florida International University. June 2015.

Matt, Daniel, trans. and comp. *The Essential Kabbalah: The Heart of Jewish Mysticism*. New York: HarperSanFrancisco, 1995.

McGaha, Michael. "Is There a Hidden Jewish Meaning in *Don Quixote?*" *Cervantes: Bulletin of the Cervantes Society of America* 24, no. 1 (2004): 173–88.

Montalvo, Garci R. *Amadis of Gaul: Books I and II*. New foreword by John E. Keller. Translated by Edwin B. Place and Herbert C. Behm. Lexington, KY: University Press of Kentucky, 2003. https://core.ac.uk/download/pdf/232564128.pdf.

Muñiz-Huberman, Angelina. *El canto del peregrino: Hacia una poética del exilio*. Barcelona: Associació d'Idees-GEXEL; Universidad Nacional Autónoma de México, 1999.

———. *Las confidentes*. Mexico City: Tusquets Editores, 1997.

———. *The Confidantes*. Translated by Andrea Labinger. Santa Fe, New Mexico: Gaon Books, 2009.

———. *De cuerpo entero*. Mexico City: Ediciones Corunda; Universidad Nacional Autónoma de México, 1991.

———. *Dulcinea encantada*. Mexico City: Editorial Joaquín Mortiz, 1992.

———. *En el jardín de la Cábala*. Mexico City.: Consejo Nacional Para La Cultura y Las Artes, 2008.

———. *Enclosed Garden*. Translated by Lois Parkinson Zamora. Pittsburgh: Latin American Literary Review Press, 1988.

———. "Exile and Memory in Latin American Jewish Literature." *Yiddish* 12.4 (2001): 84–97.

———. *La guerra del unicornio*. Mexico City: Artifice Ediciones, 1983.

———. *Huerto cerrado, huerto sellado*. Mexico City: Editorial Oasis, 1985.

———. *La lengua florida: Antología sefardí*. Mexico City: Universidad Nacional Autónoma de México; Fondo de Cultura Económica, 1989.

———. *El mercader de Tudela*. Mexico City: Fondo de Cultura Económica, 1998.

———. *Morada interior*. Mexico City: Joaquín Mortiz, 1972.

———. *Las raíces y las ramas: Fuentes y derivaciones de la Cábala hispanohebrea*. Mexico City: Fondo de Cultura Económica, 2002.

———. *El sefardí romántico: la azarosa vida de Mateo Alemán II.* Mexico City: Penguin Random House, 2014.

———. *Tierra adentro.* Mexico City: Joaquín Mortiz, 1977.

Muñiz-Huberman, Angelina, and Miriam Huberman Muñiz. *El atanor encendido: Antología de Cábala, alquimia, gnosticismo.*Mexico City: Universidad Nacional Autónoma de México, 2019.

Nehunia ben haKana. *The Bahir.* Translated, Introduction, and Commentary by Aryeh Kaplan. York Beach, Maine: Samuel Weiser, Inc., 1979.

Orozco, Chela. "The Legend of Popocatepetl and Iztaccíhuatl: A Love Story." *Inside Mexico,* January 2021. https://www.inside-mexico.com/the-legend-of-popocate petl-iztaccihuatl/.

Pardo Bazán, Emilia. *The House of Ulloa.* Translated and Introduction by Paul O'Prey and Lucia Graves. London: Penguin Classics, 2013.

Payne, Judith. "A World of Her Own: Exilic Metafiction in Angelina Muñiz-Huberman's *Morada interior* and *Dulcinea encantada.*" *Revista Canadiense de Estudios Hispánicos* 22, no. 1 (Fall 1997): 45–63.

———. "Writing and Reconciling Exile: The Novels of Angelina Muñiz-Huberman." *Bulletin of Hispanic Studies* 74 (1997): 431–59.

Payno, Manuel. *The Bandits From Río Frío.* Translated by Alan Fluckey. San Francisco: Heliographica, 2005.

Picasso, Pablo. *Guernica.* 1937. Oil on canvas, 349.3 x 776.6 cm, Museo Nacional Centro de Arte Reina Sofía, Madrid, https://www.museoreinasofia.es/en/collection /artwork/guernica.

Place, Edwin B. "Preface." *Amadis of Gaul: Books I and II*, 9–15. New foreword by John E. Keller. Translated by Edwin B. Place and Herbert C. Behm. Lexington, KY: University Press of Kentucky, 2003. https://core.ac.uk/download/pdf /232564128.pdf.

Propp, Vladimir. "The Functions of Dramatis Personae." *Morphology of the Folk Tale.* Translated by Laurence Scott. 2nd ed., 1968. Austin: University of Texas Press, 2009.

Proust, Marcel. *Swann's Way: Remembrance of Things Past, Volume One.* Translated by C. K. Scott Moncrieff. (New York: Henry Holt and Company, 1922), Project Gutenberg, last updated February 7, 2013. https://www.gutenberg.org /files/7178/7178-h/7178-h.htm.

Qualls, Karl D. "From Niños to Soviets? Raising Spanish Refugee Children in House No. 1, 1937–1951." *Dickinson College Faculty Publications.* Paper 43, 2014. http:// scholar.dickinson.edu/faculty_publications/43.

———. *Stalin's Niños: Educating Spanish Civil War Refugee Children in the Soviet Union, 1937–1951.* Toronto: University of Toronto Press, 2020.

Rangel, Dolores. "Creación y locura en la visión apocalíptica de *Dulcinea encantada,*" 123–33. In *Homenaje a Angelina Muñiz-Huberman,* edited by Lillian von der Walde Moheno and Marel Reinoso Ingliso. Mexico City: Editorial Grupo Destiempos, 2014.

Rojas, Fernando de. *Celestina: Or The Tragicke-comedy of Calisto and Melibea*. Translated by James Mabbe. Introduction by James Fitzmaurice-Kelly. London: David Nutt, 1894. https://books.google.com/books?id=r2U7AQAAMAAJ&pg=PR3 &lpg=PR3&dq=celestina+david+nutt&source=bl&ots=aOgn_q96Je&sig=ACfU 3U1E22PLLWVs90AYT_0xMT0YVNkh4g&hl=en&sa=X&ved=2ahUKEwio6 qaI-_TwAhWWtp4KHcNjBUEQ6AEwEnoECBUQAw#v=onepage&q&f=false.

Rossi, Paolo, Stephen Clucas, and Ramon Llull. *Logic and the Art of Memory: The Quest for a Universal Language*. Chicago: University of Chicago Press, 2000.

Ruiz, Juan (The Archpriest of Hita), *The Book of Good Love*. Translated by Elizabeth Drayson Macdonald. London: Dent, 1999.

Santillana, Íñigo López de Mendoza, Marqués de. *Proemio e carta al condestable don Pedro de Portugal*. Biblioteca Virtual Miguel de Cervantes. Accessed May 25, 2021. http://www.cervantesvirtual.com/obra-visor/proemio-y-carta--0/html/001fd8e2 -82b2-11df-acc7-002185ce6064_2.html.

Serrat, Joan Muanuel. "Parábola." *Cancioneros.com*. Accessed June 15, 2021. https:// www.cancioneros.com/nc/2062/0/parabola-antonio-machado-joan-manuel-serrat.

Spitzer, Leo. "The Folkloristic Pre-Stage of the Spanish Romance "Conde Arnaldos." *Hispanic Review* 23, no. 3 (1955): 173–87. doi:10.2307/470575.

Stewart, Words Jules. "The 1938 Battle of the Ebro Was the Largest Clash of the Spanish Civil War." *History of War*, March 19, 2020. https://www.pressreader.com /uk/history-of-war/20200319/281616717433920.

Teresa of Avila. *Obras completas*. Preliminary study and notes by Luis Santullano and essay by Ramón Menéndez Pidal, 11th ed. Madrid: Editorial Aguilar, 1970.

Van Der Heide, "PARDES: Methodological Reflections on the Theory of the Four Senses." *Journal of Jewish Studies* 35, no. 2 (Autumn 1983): 147–60.

Weber, Nicholas. "Albigenses." The Catholic Encyclopedia. Vol. 1. New York: Robert Appleton Company, 1907. Accessed March 7, 2021. http://www.newadvent.org /cathen/01267e.htm.

Wittgenstein, Ludwig. *Tractatus Logico-Philosophicus*. Introduction by Bertrand Russell. Translated by C. R. Ogden. London: Kegan Paul, Trench, Trubner and Company, 1922. Project Gutenberg, released October 22. 2010. https://www.gutenberg .org/files/5740/5740-pdf.pdf.

Yates, Frances. *The Art of Memory*. London: Pimlico, 2007. First published in 1966 by Routledge and Kegan Paul.

———. *The Occult Philosophy in the Elizabethan Age*. New York: Routledge Classics, 2001. First published in 1979 by Routledge and Kegan Paul.

Zamora, Lois Parkinson. *The Usable Past: The Imagination of History in Recent Fiction of the Americas*. New York: Cambridge University Press, 1997.

———. *Writing the Apocalypse: Historical Vision in Contemporary U.S. and Latin American Fiction*. New York: Cambridge University Press, 1989.

Zamudio, Luz Elena. *El exilio de Dulcinea encantada: Angelina Muñiz-Huberman, escritora de dos mundos*. Mexico City: Casa Juan Pablos; Universidad Autónoma Metropolitana, 2003.

~

About the Authors

Angelina Muñiz-Huberman (PhD, National Autonomous University of Mexico) has lived in México since 1942. She completed her postdoctoral studies at the University of Philadelphia and City University of New York. She is currently retired after having taught at the National Autonomous University of Mexico for fifty-four years. She travels as a guest lecturer to international universities in the Americas and Europe. She has published fifty books of fiction, poetry, and essays. She introduced the new historical novel, as well as Jewish mysticism and *converso* themes, in Mexican literature. Exile is one of her primary interests. She has been awarded major prizes, such as the Woman of Valor Award (Hispanic Federation, American Sephardi Federation, Consulate General of Israel, New York), the Xavier Villaurrutia, and the Sor Juana Inés de la Cruz (Guadalajara International Book Fair). In 2018 she received the prestigious National Award of Science and Arts and is Emeritus National Writer. In 2021 she became a member of the Mexican Academy of Language.

Her works have been translated into various languages, and she has received considerable attention from leading scholars internationally. Some of her titles are *Enclosed Garden, The Confidantes, A Mystical Journey, Dreaming of Safed, Dulcinea encantada, El mercader deTudela, De magias y prodigios,* and *La burladora de Toledo.* Her books on Sephardic and Kabbalistic literature are *La lengua florida, Las raíces y las ramas, En el jardín de la Cábala,* and *El sefardí romántico.* A new genre, pseudomemories, is developed in *Castillos en la tierra, Molinos sin viento,* and *Hacia Malinalco.* She is included in *The Oxford Book of*

Jewish Stories, The Schocken Book of Modern Sephardic Literature, King David's Harp, Tropical Synagogues, Oy, Caramba!, The Scroll and The Cross, Passioni e scrittura, Dernières Échos de L`Exil, among other anthologies. Her most recent publications are *Rompeolas* (collected poetry), *Los esperandos. Piratas judeo-portugueses . . . y yo,* and *El último faro.* Her books published in English are: *Enclosed Garden* (LLRP), *A Mystical Journey* (Gaon Books), *Dreaming of Safed* (Gaon Books), and *The Confidantes* (Gaon Books).

Rebecca Marquis (PhD, Indiana University) is associate professor of Spanish at Gonzaga University. Her research focuses on Latin American women's writing, particularly the intersection of female subjectivity, identity, and mysticism. Her work has explored confessional discourse in articles such as "(De)Constructing Confession: Transgressing Borders in Yanitzia Canetti's *Al otro lado*" or "Confessing Diaspora from Within: Transgression and Afro-Brazilian Identity in Helena Parente Cunha's *Mulher no Espelho*," and "From the Convent to the Back Room: Confessional Writing in Carmen Martín Gaite's *El cuarto de atrás*." She has translated poetry by Gilberto Mendoça Telles for the journal *Sirena.* Recently she has turned her attention to the representation of Judaism and Jewish mysticism in Latin American literature. Her work with *Enchanted Dulcinea* considers the ways in which imagery from Merkavah literature and Kabbalah enrich our understanding of identity formation and experiences of exile.